IT HAPPENED HERE

ISBN 978-1-62806-416-2 (print | paperback)

Library of Congress Conotrol Number 2024916259

Published by Salt Water Media
29 Broad Street, Suite 104
Berlin, MD 21811
www.saltwatermedia.com

Cover art by Derek Lingle

It Happened Here

Where what is real may not be what you've been told.

Lawrence C. Slater

Acknowledgments

I doubt if I would have ever sought to publish this book without the help and encouragement of my wife Linda and my daughter Carrin Elwell. Many thanks to them both for urging me onward! I am also much indebted to Mary Lib Morgan. Her expertise as an editor and her scrupulous attention to details gave me great confidence that my manuscript was in good hands. Her pleasant demeanor made working with her a joy!

INTRODUCTION

Strange and inexplicable things are happening in Foylestown, New York. The seen and unseen join in collaboration. The power of the natural and supernatural working in tandem through temptation, lies, and deception... People's lives subject to ruination, often with little or no understanding of what is happening... Little by little, truth begins to emerge like the sun through a heavy fog. The unseen becomes seen.

A clash of powers! Who will win?

Take a journey with Bret and Laura Crossman along with their friends as they discover what they think is reality is not always so. You, the reader, are a witness to the incessant spiritual conflict.

CHAPTER ONE

Foylestown, New York was named after Arthur Foyle, who first settled there in 1795. It was a small, nondescript, rural town thirty miles from any population centers, making it an isolated and close-knit community of about 700 people. Everyone knew everyone. Stores on Main Street had remained unchanged throughout the years. Attendance at the three churches continued to decline as the younger generations slowly drifted into secularism. Still, there was hope for a revival among the faithful.

People lived, died, and were buried in Foylestown. Loyal staff at Fields' Funeral Home remained busy witnessing the passing of an aging population. Johnson Whitley was a third-generation caretaker of the Anastasia Cemetery, succeeding his father and grandfather in providing pristine grounds for the final resting places of Foylestown's finest and its ordinary citizens.

The latest funeral was scheduled for a Saturday in late June. A good portion of the townspeople were expected to attend the service for Wilbur Templeton, a young man who had suffered an untimely death; he drowned in a nearby pond. Rescue workers from Foylestown Fire Department had pulled his body from Anastasia Pond, and Wilbur Templeton was pronounced dead by the medical examiner summoned to the scene.

Forrest Fields, owner and funeral director at Fields Funeral Home, greeted members of the community as they entered the funeral home chapel. No one chatted much, and faces were drawn in somber expressions of grief for the young man every-one seemed to love and admire. People lingered near the open casket to get a final glimpse of Wilbur and pay their last respects.

At precisely 11 a.m., Pastor Bret Crossman approached the podium to begin the service. His tall, lanky frame and dark tou-sled hair seemed to bring confirmation to the somber mood. All eyes were focused on him. The organist had just finished *The Old Rugged Cross* and not a sound could be heard.

He scanned the crowded chapel, paying keen attention to those who were weeping silently. After taking a deep breath, he asked attendees to join him in prayer, then bowed his head and led it. He then opened his tablet and began reading some com-forting Scriptures.

Wilbur's cousin delivered a heartfelt eulogy, and others shared heartwarming memories of the deceased. A friend of Wilbur's with minimal talent but a lot of heart sang *I'll Fly Away*, one of Wilbur's family's favorites.

After sharing a brief and comforting homily, Bret was ready to close the service. He again opened his tablet and read: "I am the resurrection, and the life: he that believeth in me, though he were dead, yet shall he live" (John 11:25 KJV).

Everyone was quiet—except for Wilbur Templeton.

There was a stirring in the casket behind Bret Crossman. A gasp arose from the people. A few people fainted; some cried out; others pointed toward Wilbur.

Bret felt his heart race as he looked at the people in bewil-derment. He turned slowly to see what had caused the noise behind him, and there was Wilbur Templeton, sitting upright in the casket, his eyes blinking rapidly.

Bret felt his knees nearly buckle. "Oh my God!" he cried out. "This can't be happening!"

"What's going on?"

"What in the name of ...?!"

"Who? How?"

People shouted in and out of sync with one another. "What kind of prank is this—and during a funeral?!" One lady in the crowd called out, especially indignant.

Wilbur, appearing dazed, jumped from the casket and ran through a side door into the foyer, then quickly disappeared.

Two of the startled pall bearers immediately rushed outside to track Wilbur. Others joined in the search still in shock over what had happened, but after a diligent hunt, there was no sign of Wilbur.

INSIDE THE CHAPEL THERE WAS total confusion. Wilbur's mother sat in a catatonic state while Russell Templeton, Wilbur's father, pushed people aside and approached Forrest Fields, accusing him of a scheme. Whether genuine or feigned, he was furious regarding his son's missing body. A heated exchange ensued. Forrest accused Russell of stealing Wilbur's body so he could sue the funeral home. Rev. Crossman was dumbfounded, but he hadn't ruled out Wilbur rising from the dead. The townspeople were chattering with all manner of speculation, especially those who were witnesses of the event.

"YOUR BOY IS DEAD, RUSSELL," Forrest said, trying to calm the man who was verbally assaulting him. "You identified him after they recovered his body—remember?"

"I know he's dead, but where is he now?" Russell demanded, poking his finger in Forrest's face.

"I'm asking you the same question!" Forrest said. "Did you remove his body and plant a substitute, Russell? ...wanting to blame me so you can sue me? Is that it, Russell?"

"You fool; why would I steal my own son's body? And supposing I did, where were you at the time? Aren't you responsible for the corpse?"

"You could have slipped in, removed him, and planted a look-alike in the casket without me noticing."

"You're insane! How on earth could I have done that?"

"I wasn't with him 24/7—and besides, the back door to the funeral home might not have been locked."

Russell rocked back on his feet, both hands tightening into fists. "Then who was that in the casket? You're sick if you think I put someone else in there."

"All I know, Russell," Forrest said, backing away from the fists, "is that it wasn't Wilbur in that casket. I ought to know that an embalmed corpse doesn't run away on foot. And right now, neither of us seems to know what happened, so maybe you should calm down."

"Let me tell you something, Fields; if you don't figure out where my son's body is, I'll shut you down for good. Is that clear?"

"But you can't just—"

"See if I can't; I'll hire a lawyer and sue you to the moon; you can bank on it!"

"Get out! Get out of my funeral home or I'll have you arrested for assault!" Forrest shouted.

"I'm out, Fields, but your worst nightmare has just begun."

Forrest stood, trembling—his face ashen, his breathing short and labored. It could have been a minute or maybe ten. Then someone put their hand on his shoulder, breaking Forrest's stupor. It was Bret Crossman.

"I heard most of that, Forrest; just let it go—you know Russell's crazy."

14

"But you didn't see the look in his eyes; he's dangerous, Bret. I don't know what he's capable of, but he could've killed me if we'd been alone."

"Maybe you should report him to the police. I agree; he is dangerous."

"Well, I need to call then anyway; there's a body missing, and that could mean a crime's been committed."

"There's got to be a reasonable explanation for what happened," Bret said.

"Reasonable? What's reasonable about it?" Forrest's voice was still weak from his encounter with Russell.

"Hmm...doesn't add up, does it?"

"Nothing adds up right now. You saw it happen; I didn't. I was in the foyer when all the screaming started."

Bret nodded slowly. "I saw the people's faces, and I turned just in time to see whoever it was leap from the casket and run out the side door."

"And did you think it was Wilbur?"

"Forrest," Bret said calmly, "you and I both know it was Wilbur in that casket. There wasn't any look-alike substituted at the last minute. You would have known it, and everyone who passed by the casket could have easily known if it wasn't him."

"Well, his features weren't normal, Bret. He'd been in the water quite a while, and I suppose it's possible—"

"You don't really believe that, do you Forrest?"

"Well, what other 'reasonable' explanation is there, as you said?"

———— ◌ ————

THE CROWD IN THE FUNERAL HOME was thinning out, but still pressing for answers, making it impossible for them to carry on their conversation.

"Let's go to your office," Bret suggested. "There's something I want to share with you."

Forrest pushed his way past people who were demanding answers. "I don't have answers right now," he said, addressing the crowd. "Please, please go home until we find out what happened."

"But where's Wilbur?" they demanded.

"We don't know yet. There is an explanation; please don't spread rumors. I'm closing the funeral home in a few minutes, so please just leave peacefully."

Forrest opened the door to his office. He and Bret sat opposite one another, mirroring the other's furrowed brow.

"You go first," Forrest said. "You wanted to share something with me."

Bret took a deep breath and leaned forward, placing his hands on the table between them. "I want you to think logically with me, Forrest."

"None of this is logical if you ask me."

"Well, maybe it is if we consider what we know to be true. Let's review the facts. First, it had to be Wilbur in the casket, right?"

Forrest tapped his head with the palm of his hand as if to call forth logical thought. "But there's no way it could have been Wilbur who leaped out."

"There wasn't a substitute though, wouldn't you agree?"

"But—"

"Wilbur was dead, right?"

"Again, I affirmed that. Besides, so did the medical examiner, the fire chief, and several witnesses at the scene. Plus, Russell Templeton. I don't know how much more evidence you can get than that. He was in cold storage for twenty-four hours."

"So, follow me: A dead man in a casket rises and flees on

foot, probably scared to death of the panicking crowd, excuse the pun. Where does that leave us?"

"Surely you're not suggesting that—"

"What's the logical explanation, Forrest?"

Forrest hesitated and drew a deep breath. "But it's not possible that he—"

"Rose from the dead?"

"I don't believe it."

"There's no other explanation, Forrest. You've agreed with what you don't believe."

"My God!" Forrest exclaimed. "What if it really did happen right here in Foylestown? Can you even begin to imagine the implications?"

"All I know, Forrest, is that there's no other explanation—and yes, the implications are going to be staggering."

Church bells in the distance competed with small town traffic noises up close. Forrest finally spoke. "Bret, I just can't wrap my mind around Wilbur rising from the dead; I've got a long way to go before I believe that. I guess if I could see the body, I would believe." Another pause. "And why on earth would he run away?"

CHAPTER TWO

"Where's the body?" Chief of Police Sam Stone asked bluntly.

Forrest motioned the chief to a chair. "We don't know," he replied.

"Let me get this straight, Forrest; you're saying that someone got out of the casket and ran away. But it couldn't have been Wilbur because he was dead. So—you don't know for sure who was in the casket, and you don't have any idea where Wilbur's body is; is that right?"

Forrest groaned. "None of this makes sense to me, Sam, but that sums it up."

"You can't just lose a body, Forrest; you must know that. We're going to have to open an investigation if it's not found."

"Maybe you should start with Russell Templeton; he threatened me a short while ago. The man isn't mentally stable."

"I've had some run-ins with him," Sam nodded and continued, "but you're responsible for the deceased's body."

"I know, I know—but my theory is that Russell removed the body and replaced it with someone he hired as a look-alike. He threatened to sue me. Bret Crossman has another theory which I can't buy into."

"We don't need theories, Forrest. We need a body, and we need to find out who was in that casket, assuming it wasn't Wilbur. Unless we can produce a body, this has to be treated as a crime."

"The body will turn up; it has to. We just need to get some people looking for it and—"

"And what?"

"As I said, start with Russell."

"Okay, I'll question him, but I can't just get a warrant to search his house for a corpse without probable cause. I think we need to organize a search party as soon as possible. Do you think there were any witnesses who may have seen Wilbur—or whoever—run out of the funeral home?"

"None have come forward, but it's only been an hour or so since this all happened," Forrest said.

Sam stroked his unshaven chin and paused for a moment. "By the way, Forrest; ...mind if I look around the funeral home? You know—just to see if the body is still here somewhere. Maybe you can give me a tour. I always was a little curious about what goes on in these places."

"Feel free to look wherever you want, but I'll guarantee you that you won't find him here."

THE SEARCH TURNED UP NOTHING and left both men mentally unsettled. Neither had an explanation that seemed plausible, and Sam began to wonder whether there was an evil scheme yet to be uncovered. He wasn't thrilled with the idea of having to hunt down a missing corpse and would have to contact the county sheriff's office to pull them in on the search if the body didn't turn up soon. *A look-alike? Russell Templeton was a little psycho, but was he capable of stealing his son's corpse?*

"...gotta go, Forrest. I think we'd better keep the whole thing low-key for now. If people approach you, just tell 'em you're aware of it and it's under investigation. But, please let me know if any eyewitnesses turn up. We need to know if anyone saw someone who looked like Wilbur running out of the funeral home...and tell me if they found the real corpse. Get as many details as you can because whoever ran away will likely be charged with impersonating a corpse."

"I need pills," Forrest said. "My head is pounding; it's about ready to explode."

"Oh, and by the way," Sam said, ignoring Forrest, "what was the pastor's theory?"

"...you really wanna know, Sam?"

"Of course; anything more bizarre than what we've considered?" Sam grinned.

"Bret thinks Wilbur might have risen from the dead."

WHAT IF THAT STORY GETS out to the media? Wilbur Templeton rising from the dead. Yeah, that happens frequently here in Foylestown. Just routine, you know. Sam shook his head in disbelief. Sure, he went to church every Easter and guessed it was probable that Christ rose from the dead. Beyond that, he had little regard for church. But now he had a mess on his hands, and he might have to charge people he knew well with crimes. No problem charging Russell if he tampered with the corpse, but Forrest was a friend, and the thought of arresting him troubled Sam. And the pastor? He guessed he'd have to meet with him and interview him since he was an eyewitness to the...what was it anyway?

HIS FEARS WERE CONFIRMED WHEN he arrived at his office and was met by Sara Jacobs, a reporter from the local weekly newspaper, the *Town Herald*.

"Chief, what can you tell us about the events at Fields' Funeral Home? Has Wilbur's body been found—and did someone actually jump from the casket?"

"It sure doesn't take you guys long to want to break a story, does it?" Sam said, eyeing the young reporter. "I can't comment on anything at this point; it's under investigation."

"But it is true that the Templeton boy's body is missing, right?" Sara Jacobs pressed further.

"I'll make a formal statement as soon as I find out the details."

"But—"

"I said when I find out the details." Sam entered the police station and left the reporter still prying for answers he wasn't about to give.

Ten minutes later, he called Bret Crossman—mostly out of curiosity.

Bret answered the phone: "Hello, Crossmans."

"Pastor Crossman?"

"Yes."

"This is Sam Stone, chief of police."

"I've been expecting your call," Bret said.

"Well, yes, I suppose you have. It's obviously about the Templeton kid. You conducted the funeral service and saw what happened. What can you tell me?"

"Have you spoken with Forrest yet?" Bret asked.

"I just got back from speaking with him, and—"

"And he filled you in on the bizarre events, right?"

"Bizarre is the word, for sure. But I'm concerned that unless Wilbur's body turns up, we're going to have to investigate. ...just wanted your take on what happened."

"I doubt if I can add anything more than what Forrest said."

"Well...he said you had another theory."

"And did he say that I thought Wilbur may have risen from the dead?" Bret asked.

Sam paused, then said, "He did mention...that you thought, maybe...but he didn't believe it himself."

"He didn't accept the logic even though he agreed with it."

"Huh? I guess I don't follow you," Sam said, feeling more and more uncomfortable.

"There's no doubt that Wilbur was dead."

"Can't argue with that."

"Follow me; this isn't hard: A dead man in a casket suddenly sits up, gets scared when he hears the crowd screaming, jumps out, and runs away."

"But wait a minute," Sam regained his voice. "Who's to say that was Wilbur and not somebody else in the casket?"

"Well, Forrest put him in there, and scores of people saw him, including me. It wasn't a look-alike, even though Forrest suggested that. I'm sure he told you."

"Look, Pastor—"

"Call me Bret."

"Okay, Bret; I'm no religious man as you probably know, but neither am I a fool. People don't just rise from the dead; there's got to be another explanation."

"Then start your investigation."

"Hey, I need as many allies as I can get on this. Just bear with me on this resurrection stuff. If we find him alive, I'll believe it. If we find his corpse, we'll know it was a hoax. Is that fair?"

"No offense, Chief, but would you really believe if we find him alive, or would you just think he never really died?"

"If I see him alive, I'll believe. You've got my word."

CHAPTER THREE

It didn't take long before the entire town was aware of the events that had taken place at the funeral home. It took even less time for the wild speculation to begin. Russell Templeton's wife was no longer catatonic, but was barely able to stumble to their car while Russell cursed under his breath. What a fool Forrest Fields was. Russell had never liked him; anyone who handled corpses wasn't all there anyway.

Russell didn't need this in his life. It seemed he'd been destined for bad luck since he was relentlessly bullied as a child. He was pushing fifty and had health issues which forced him into long periods of unemployment. The funeral was costing him most of his savings. And for what? He nurtured the anger rising up in his heart. Someone would have to pay. And the thought of a hoax perpetrated by Forrest inflamed his anger, but also fed his imagination.

He thought for a moment: It had to be Forrest who removed Wilbur's body and replaced it with a look-alike; he just wanted publicity—by promoting...*what?* What would he have been promoting if he exchanged the bodies? He knew Wilbur was dead, so the only explanation would have to be that Wilbur came back to life—a total absurdity. But that would draw media attention and put Forrest in the spotlight. The man was sick. Too much embalming had done something to his brain. Delusional—that was it. Forrest was delusional. But now Russell had leverage.

Someone had tampered with his son's body, and Forrest was ultimately responsible. Russell had grounds for a lawsuit, regardless of whether the body turned up or not. It was his son's body that was missing, and Alice, Russell's wife, was on the verge of a nervous breakdown—not that he much cared.

———⊷ ○ ⊶———

"I'LL MAKE HIM PAY," RUSSELL said as they left the doctor's office with a script for Alice. "I'll make him pay alright. I'll sue his sorry butt, and we'll get what's due us. You hear me?" He slammed his car door shut and revved the engine. Alice was barely in the car before he accelerated carelessly.

Alice nodded but didn't speak.

"I said, 'Are you hearing me?'" Russell grabbed her arm and pinched tightly.

"Ouch! I hear you Russell, and I don't like your tone of voice. If there's one thing we don't need right now, it's you going off. You've gotta stay out of trouble!"

"Don't you think we've got trouble right now? What do you want me to do—sing a lullaby? Forrest's got Wilbur somewhere. By God, I'll find out where—and when I do, it won't be pretty."

Alice covered her face with both hands as the tears streamed down her cheeks. "Please don't do this, Russell—please."

"And don't you go slobbering all over either. I can't stand it when you do that."

Russell pushed the gas pedal further to the floor. His speeding habit had nearly cost him his license and had stressed their budget with fines and increased insurance costs.

"You're going to get us killed if you don't slow down, Russell!"

Russell shot a glance at his wife. "Who's driving anyway? It's me, isn't it?"

"Look out!" Alice screamed.

Russell yanked the wheel sharply and hit the brakes, sending the car into a sideways skid, nearly hitting an oncoming pickup truck. The driver of the truck blew his horn and made an obscene hand gesture. Russell regained control and brought the vehicle to a stop on the side of the road.

He cursed and pounded the dashboard. "You see what happens, Alice, when you challenge me while I'm driving? We're lucky we didn't just get killed—all because you opened your mouth about my driving."

"It wasn't what I said that—"

"Don't go there, Alice!"

———— ◖◗ ————

Alice had been considering leaving Russell for some time, and given the recent events, the urge was now stronger. The constant financial pressures, the angry outbursts, and now this. Her heart was shattered at the news of Wilbur's death, but now the grief was unbearable, given the incomprehensible events at the funeral home. Was it possible that Wilbur was alive somewhere? And, if so—where? She and Wilbur had been a part of Bret Crossman's church, Foylestown Community Church, for several years; she had heard the pastor preach on the resurrection of Christ many times. The final words that Bret had read from his tablet at the funeral suddenly struck her: "I am the resurrection, and the life: he that believeth in me, though he were dead, yet shall he live" (John 11:25 KJV). She trembled at the thought but quickly dismissed it. No, that couldn't be true, and she wouldn't let her mind focus on it.

———— ◖◗ ————

THEY ARRIVED HOME FROM THE doctor's appointment and entered wearily. The thought still haunted her that Wilbur might be somewhere in the house. But how could that be? He was pronounced dead, his corpse seen by several people, embalmed, and placed in a casket for others to see. And it certainly did look just like Wilbur. No one could have made someone up to look exactly like him—or could they? For a moment, she thought she was going insane.

"We're home," Russell said. "And quit looking like you're half dead. We've got to make some plans. I'm hiring a lawyer as soon as I can get some money together. You just can't tamper with a corpse."

"...you think it's possible Wilbur might be in the house?" Alice's voice quavered at the thought.

"Are you nuts, woman? No, I don't think it's possible. What don't you understand about being dead? You think Wilbur might be a zombie or something?"

"I'm his mother, Russell. Do you understand what's going on in my brain right now?"

"Apparently not much, Alice. I never thought there was a whole lot of activity in your brain anyway."

That sealed it for her. She would file for divorce when things settled down. She refused to live with a belligerent man who had no regard for her feelings. Alice wondered if it was possible for her to feel more wretched than she felt now. *No,* she decided. *It isn't possible.*

CHAPTER FOUR

Chief Stone knew he was responsible for organizing the search for Wilbur Templeton, but he wasn't keen on running interference between Russell and Forrest. Whatever this hoax was, he disliked it; he hoped it would resolve itself in a day or so.

"Any sign of the Templeton kid or the impostor?" Sam asked Forrest Fields as they met in the town square.

"None," Forrest said, scratching his head. "I've asked everyone I see if they'd seen Wilbur or someone looking like him in town, and I always get the same response: 'He's dead, isn't he? What do you mean, have I seen him?'"

"Look, Forrest, I want you to square with me," Sam said, looking him straight in the eyes. "Are you in on a hoax, trying to get some attention, a little notoriety? Because if you are, I suggest you can it right now. It's not going to settle well with people, and who knows what Russell might do? He's unpredictable. You heard him back at the funeral home. You can be sure he's going to sue you and whoever else might be involved."

Forrest shook his head and shifted nervously. "Sam, do you think I'd be out here searching my butt off for...for whoever...if I was part of a hoax?"

"Well, maybe that's a part of it...pretending to search."

"I've got better things to do than be a part of something that's not going to end well. I can just hear Russell now, bragging about stiffing me for as much as he can. We've got to produce Wilbur's body before he sues."

"Okay then, convince me again it was Wilbur you put in the casket," Sam said. "And what was the time between when you embalmed him and when he was brought into the funeral chapel?"

Forrest took a deep breath, held it for a short time, then exhaled forcefully. "I was briefly distracted when I received a body from the hospital. There may have been time enough for someone to switch bodies while I was tending to that."

"Do you have an attendant? Someone who could have made the switch?"

"No."

"So, it's possible that someone else could have sneaked in and made the exchange, right?"

"...stolen Wilbur's body and replaced him with a counterfeit made to look like him?"

"That's what I'm saying."

"I can't imagine it, Sam—and for what reason?"

"You didn't answer my question: Is it possible?"

"Remotely but yes."

"Oh, man, I hope that's not the case! Then I've got to investigate another crime."

"Well, right now we don't know where Wilbur's body is, and we don't know who the impostor is, assuming there was one. And if this gets into the hands of the media, we're in for trouble."

"Rest assured, Forrest; it already has."

Forrest drew a handkerchief from his pocket and wiped his forehead. "What am I going to do if Russell sues the funeral home? I mean, I've got liability insurance, but he could still bankrupt me. I don't know if the insurance would cover missing corpses, anyway."

"It's not a 'what if' Forrest; it's a 'when'...so you'd better retain a good lawyer. And even if we find Wilbur's body, Russell will still sue for mishandling a corpse."

Just as they both turned to go, Jenna Baxter, a reporter from the *Plainview Daily*, approached them. "Chief!" Jenna shouted and nearly ran over the two who tried unsuccessfully to avoid her. "Can I have an update on the Templeton kid?"

The chief attempted to wave her away, but she stepped in front of him and repeated her request. "Just a brief report, sir. Is it true he ran off from the funeral home?"

"...can't say," the chief answered. "I wasn't there at the time."

"And you?" Jenna shifted in Forrest's direction. "Were you there when the kid supposedly jumped from the casket?"

"...didn't see it either; I wasn't in the chapel at the time."

"So, neither of you were eyewitnesses?"

"...doesn't seem that way, now does it?" the chief answered and grinned.

"But there were witnesses, right? I mean, the chapel was full at the time, wasn't it, Mr. Fields?"

"There were witnesses, of course; but it's best you ask them."

"And what about Pastor Crossman; was he a witness?"

"He was."

"And where is he now?"

"No one knows where he is; he just seemed to disappear," Forrest said.

"Sort of like the Templeton kid, huh?" Jenna responded without looking at Forrest.

"Look," the chief interrupted, "I have to go—and by the way, I told the other reporter it's under investigation."

"And who was that?" Jenna inquired, fearing someone else had the scoop on the story.

"I didn't catch her name," Sam said. "Really, I don't mean to be unkind, but we don't have much to report at the present time. As soon as we find out more, we'll make a formal statement to the public. Please be patient until then." He turned abruptly and headed for his office.

CHAPTER FIVE

Bret Crossman had made his way to the church office without anyone noticing. He looked at himself in a mirror and decided he'd aged ten years. His normally relaxed features were fraught with tension, and his dark eyes appeared to have sunk deeper into their sockets.

What has happened to me? I feel like I've been under a devilish assault. My whole body is drained...and my face! What is wrong with my face?

He rested his head in his hands and rubbed his eyes, thinking maybe something had temporarily affected his vision. No; there was no vision change, but his appearance had changed significantly. The mirror didn't lie.

He slumped into a nearby chair and tried to make sense of the events that transpired at the funeral home. Just hearing the noise behind him and seeing Wilbur leap from the casket made his body shake. He tried mentally going through the entire ceremony, recalling key details. Then he remembered he hadn't seen Wilbur prior to the funeral and had only gazed for a moment at his corpse. *But there was no doubt Wilbur was dead.* And the fire chief and coroner had both declared him dead. And Forrest. He'd prepared the body and embalmed it. There was absolutely no question that Wilbur Templeton was dead.

He'd conducted numerous funeral services without incident. Always well-controlled and methodical. He was sick of the methodical part, and he recalled having fantasies about seeing a dead body rise from the casket while he was preaching.

But they were just fantasies...

Then it struck him. He remembered praying specifically that God would do something unusual at Wilbur's funeral. Something that wasn't routine or methodical. It sickened him to think of the young man's senseless death: a life cut short by a freak drowning. Why was he alone in a canoe anyway? And people said that Wilbur couldn't swim ten feet. Yeah, it sickened Bret Crossman alright. And what sickened him more was the helpless feeling he had knowing there was nothing he could have done about it.

Why, God? It seems like I say it at every funeral no matter what the cause of death is. You are sovereign, aren't you? You could have prevented Wilbur's death. You could have resurrected—

Bret called out to God from his office: "Of course! I prayed and asked for something unusual to happen, but I never expected you would actually raise him from the dead!"

But there was no other explanation. There was no hoax, no impostor, no conspiracy. What happened was what he had prayed for. But, he reasoned, he didn't have that kind of faith in prayer. He'd heard of so-called modern-day resurrections by the Pentecostals in primitive cultures, but he never believed the reports. And didn't resurrections cease with the end of the Apostolic era?

Bret rose from the chair and started pacing nervously around his office. If all this was true, what were the implications for Wilbur's family? The community? And who would believe it? Very few Foylestown folks, if any. And the conspiracy stories would certainly prevail. What if they went beyond the cozy confines of Foylestown?

Did he believe it himself? He shook his head, wondering. *It just doesn't happen these days...it just doesn't happen.*

One thing was certain: he had to tell his wife. Laura would understand him, though not necessarily believe what had happened to Wilbur. A last-minute congregational need had kept her from attending the funeral, so she wasn't an eyewitness.

Bret thought about the others who were there. He had to address this with the church membership—had to explain it the best he could, but if he said he believed that Wilbur had risen from the dead, he might lose half of the congregation. Attendance was already flagging—and this could destroy the whole church.

What about Forrest? It would be in his best interest to believe something supernatural had happened, which might give him coverage for not producing Wilbur's body. But Forrest was a skeptic at best. He never gave any evidence of possessing a personal faith.

And then there was Russell—the embodiment of spite and hatred. *Always* wanting to get even. And he *would* get even—even if it cost him his life.

Bret couldn't settle his mind. He tried praying but couldn't focus. He sat down with his Bible in his lap, but verses seemed hollow and lifeless. Here he was a believer in God, and certainly a believer in Christ's resurrection, but who was he to experience what appeared to be a miracle?

His phone chirped. "Where have you been?" Laura's voice was solicitous; it snapped Bret out of his daze. "I was worried about you not coming home. And what is all the fuss about Wilbur Templeton? I've had people calling and knocking on the door for the last hour wanting answers."

Bret sighed. "Oh God, Laura, you won't believe what's happened. I can't explain it over the phone, but the gist of it is that Wilbur is missing."

"Missing as in not at his own funeral?" Laura asked with incredulity.

Bret smiled weakly at that thought. "No, he was there alright. At least until the end when—"

"When what, Bret?"

"When he sat up in the casket, then leaped out, and ran away."

Laura was silent for several seconds, then asked, "Was it a hoax? I mean, who would do something that stupid and insensitive?"

"That's what I need to talk to you about when I get home. I'm not sure it was a hoax."

She paused for a moment. "Well, are you thinking what I am, Bret?"

"It eliminates all other explanations, doesn't it?"

"Good Lord, how is it possible? A resurrection?"

"Laura, I know Wilbur was dead. Forrest Fields has the death certificate. The coroner had pronounced him dead."

"But he wasn't...," Laura said, her voice trembling.

"As sure as we're talking, he wasn't."

"Oh Bret! What's this going to mean? The town will go crazy."

"And no one's going to believe it anyway—except for maybe a few."

"Well, they're going to have to believe it when they see Wilbur walking around."

"But that's the problem, Laura; he ran away and hasn't been found."

"But they'll find him, won't they Bret? I mean, surely, they'll find him...,"

"They're looking for him now. The chief of police called me, and I told him what I thought happened. Neither he nor Forrest believes it. This is the most bizarre thing I've ever seen. I don't know if I believe it, Laura. I feel like a fool to even suggest it."

Laura sighed heavily. "You're no fool believing it could happen, but there's not a shred of proof since no one's seen Wilbur."

"And what happens if he never shows up?" Bret said, almost to himself.

"Then it was most likely an elaborate hoax."

"Well, I'm on record with what I thought happened. It's incredible how easily we want to believe something supernatural actually happened, only to find out there was another explanation."

CHAPTER SIX

Russell Templeton was no fan of Bret Crossman; he was no fan of religion either. He painfully recalled being molested by a church leader when he was about seven years old. He carried the memory for years and never told anyone. That's when he had decided not to let any notion of God invade his conscience. It infuriated him that Alice had decided to go to Crossman's church despite his protests.

"Look Alice," he had said to her, "if your little pea brain needs that stuff, then go—but don't think you're taking Wilbur. I'm not having my kid indoctrinated with that nonsense."

Over several years, Russell had grown increasingly hostile as he predicted the end of his unemployment benefits—and as his alcohol consumption had increased. He would frequently taunt and demean Wilbur after a bout of drunkenness. Alice would intervene to protect her son, but would suffer a double dose of Russell's vituperation as a result. The only reason she stayed in the marriage was to get adequate evidence to serve him divorce papers.

Despite Russell's efforts to crush Wilbur's spirit, his abuse had the opposite effect. Bret became a father figure to Wilbur and would often have him help at church with menial tasks for which Wilbur earned a small stipend. And the more time he spent with Bret, the more Russell despised them both.

Two weeks before the drowning, an incident occurred that

made Alice question whether the drowning was an accident or not.

"Get him out of my sight before I kill him," Russell had screamed at Alice as he grabbed Wilbur and pushed him against the wall. Though Wilbur was only fifteen, he was strong. He tried mightily to defend himself—but he was no match for Russell.

"Russell, don't!" Alice shouted. "He hasn't done anything wrong!"

"He stole money from me; I had a bunch of cash on the counter a short while ago, and it's gone!"

"You know he wouldn't steal from you, Russell," Alice shot back, not sure of what had happened to the money, but certain Wilbur hadn't stolen it.

"I'll have his hide if it doesn't show up!"

"How much was it?" Alice asked, pushing Russell away from Wilbur.

"It doesn't matter how much, Alice; the boy's a thief."

Russell went for Wilbur again, but Alice stepped between them. "Oh, no you don't; you're gonna have to go through me first!"

"No problem there," Russell shot back and lunged for Wilbur, knocking Alice to the floor.

Alice grabbed Russell's leg and tripped him, sending him crashing against the wall.

"Get out of the house, Russell!" she screamed, "or, so help me, I'll call the police!"

Russell regained his balance, slightly dazed from his surprise encounter with the wall. "You're one lucky woman, Alice," he said, staring at her. His face was contorted with anger but constrained by Alice's threat. "Is that what you want, Alice? You want me to leave so you and the boy can have the pastor over? Maybe you've got a thing for the holy man, huh? Is that it? Real convenient, right? I go, and he comes over."

40

"For heaven's sake, Russell," Alice said after Wilbur helped her to her feet. "You know he's married and, no, he's never set foot in this house, and I doubt he ever will. Maybe he's afraid you'd kill him, too."

"I just might if I was drunk enough. But for now, Alice, you get your wish; I'm outta here and won't be back until—"

"Until what?"

"Until I damn well feel like coming back; is that clear enough?"

And Russell left.

For two weeks, Alice wasn't sure where her husband was, but she had her suspicions; she wondered if his accusations against her and Bret might have come from a guilty conscience. She had, after all, seen another woman flirting with Russell at various times. Why, she wondered, would any woman lower herself to flirt with him?

Two nights before Wilbur's drowning, Russell had returned home, not the least bit contrite. Alice had changed the door locks, but decided to let him in.

"I've found a place to stay, Alice, and I'm moving out. The house is yours—for now."

"Who is she, Russell? The loser I saw hanging off you that day in town?"

"Oh God, Alice, if I don't break your neck, it'll be a miracle."

"So now you invoke his name and believe in miracles?"

"I'm sober, okay? And you're one lucky woman."

"Am I, Russell? Am I a lucky woman? No income; you threatening me and Wilbur; hurling accusations against me, and running off for another woman? What part of 'lucky' don't I understand?"

"She's got more than you've got, Alice," Russell smirked.

"Nicer body, Russell? And money, no doubt."

"Right on both counts, sweetie; how'd you guess?"

"Because I've lived with you for twenty-five years, Russell, and I pretty well know who you are."

"I don't think you really know what I'm capable of, Alice, and right now, it's best you don't. I'm getting some things together, then I'm leaving. I'll take the pickup, and you can have the beater."

"Don't bother coming back, Russell; I've been to a lawyer, and I'll be serving papers on you for divorce—adultery, to be clear."

Russell stood still; his face twisted in confusion.

"That's a baseless accusation, Alice; you have no proof of that!"

"Oh, but I do; I have some sources who know exactly what you've been up to. Wilbur and I will be just fine alone—isn't that right, Wilbur? So don't give it another thought, Russell."

"Yes, mom," Wilbur agreed. "He's never been a father to me anyway."

Two days later, Wilbur was dead.

CHAPTER SEVEN

Forrest called Sam's office to discuss the rumors he'd been hearing. "Sam, are you aware of what some people are saying about the Templeton kid?"

"And what's that, Forrest?" Sam straightened in his chair and removed his feet from his desk.

"Some are saying they don't think it was an accident and that maybe Wilbur took his own life."

"...doesn't surprise me any; people come up with all kinds of theories when these things happen."

"Were you aware that Russell left Alice and Wilbur and was living with another woman two days before the drowning? At least that's what's going around...,"

"Nope, I hadn't heard that; but what do you expect from Russell?"

"People are saying that the kid was so distraught that he took the canoe out, capsizing it on purpose."

"And that's a rumor, right, Forrest?"

"But it might make sense."

"Okay, suppose it's true; we still don't know where he is, and there's no way of proving that anyway."

"...you sittin' down, Sam?"

"Yeah, why?"

"Well, here's another little theory. Most folks know that Russell abused the kid and had no use for him. So, the theory goes that Russell took him out in the canoe under the pretext of wanting to make good with him, then pushed him overboard, knowing he couldn't swim. Of course, Russell then swam ashore, making it look like an accident."

"Who's feedin' you all this stuff?" Sam asked, cocking the phone between his shoulder and ear.

"A couple of people from Bret Crossman's church who claim to have inside information."

"Not provable, of course."

"Well, yeah; but it does sort of give one pause for thought. There might be more to the story than we know."

"Like I said, Forrest; none of it is provable—and it doesn't change a thing, does it?"

"From my perspective, it might. If it turns out Russell pushed him overboard, that means any lawsuit he might file against me is dead in the waters—forgive the pun."

"So now you have a motive for pursuing that theory, right?"

"It needs to be investigated, Sam."

The police chief sighed and said, "Look Forrest, this is all so speculative, and I wouldn't know where to begin with an investigation. You must realize you'll be the first one questioned since you lost track of the body."

"As I said before, you might start by callin' Russell in for questioning."

"Okay, so I say to Russell: 'Did you drown the boy because you hated him? Be honest with me.'"

"Make him take a lie detector test."

"There's no pretext for that, Forrest; besides that, he'd never consent."

"Not complying could be an indicator of guilt; and, by the way, there was no autopsy to see if there was possible evidence of foul play. Everyone, including me, thought it was an accidental drowning. And I found no evidence of any trauma to the body."

"I guess I could call in an investigator from the sheriff's department to see if it's worth pursuing. But the problem with that is we have no body."

"Precisely. Maybe Russell sneaked in and stole it. The fit he threw at the funeral home could have been a ploy to give himself cover. You know, Forrest, the more I think about this whole mess, the more confused I get; nothing makes sense to me. I mean, what are the motives involved here? The only one with a thing to gain is obviously Russell. And if your theory is true, he faces major jail time."

"The town certainly wouldn't suffer from that, now would it?" Forrest smiled.

"Have you spoken with the pastor?" Sam asked, ignoring Forrest's remarks.

"Haven't yet, but I'll track him down. I want to know his take on all of this. Wilbur and Alice were members of his church, and Russell was a sworn enemy."

"Maybe Russell wanted to exact some revenge on the pastor and humiliate him...you suppose?"

"Everything does seem to focus on Russell, doesn't it? Or are we just wishing that he gets his due?"

Sam shook his head. "Living with another woman before his son's death. Maybe we should find out who the woman is and start asking her some questions."

"I'm sure I can find out who she is by asking around. You can't hide those things in this town."

"Apparently it's been hidden from us, Forrest."

"Yeah, well, we're just not part of the gossip circle."

"Keep your ears open to the conspiracy theories; as you said, there may be more to this than meets the eye. In the meantime, I'll call the sheriff about sending an investigator over. It takes the pressure off me."

CHAPTER EIGHT

"You know, Laura," Bret Crossman said to his wife, "Forrest Fields called me from the funeral home to let me know what he and Sam Stone are thinking."

"Yeah?" Laura said, as she reached behind herself to zip her dress. "And what do they think?"

"Sam is calling in an investigator from the sheriff's department just to ask some questions. It seems that Forrest is thinking Russell might have had something to do with stealing Wilbur's body and hiring a counterfeit to take his place in the casket."

Laura sat on the edge of the bed and beckoned Bret to sit beside her. "Does that change your mind regarding what we think happened, Bret?"

"Maybe a little; it's possible Russell could do something like this."

"He must have hired a make-up artist to work on the supposed look-alike," Laura said, frowning.

"And that doesn't make any sense. How could you make someone look like a corpse and have everyone convinced it was Wilbur in that casket; wouldn't they see him breathing?" Bret stood abruptly and started pacing.

"Only a professional could do that. Corpses never look real anyway, so slight distortions wouldn't matter. As far as breathing is concerned, you can take shallow breaths without them being noticed."

"Always the practical one," Bret smiled and turned to look at Laura.

"Hey, I'm not saying I believe their story, Bret; I'm just trying to follow their logic."

"It would certainly take a lot of imagination to believe such a cockamamie story," Bret said.

"But you know it's highly questionable anyone at church is going to accept that Wilbur rose from the dead."

"There could be some; it's hard to tell. But as you said earlier, if they find Wilbur alive, that'll change some minds."

Laura shook her head. "And some won't believe even if they do find him despite the evidence...just like they do today in not believing Christ rose from the dead."

"I wonder what Wilbur's mother believes?" Bret stopped pacing and looked in the mirror to adjust his collar. "She was beside herself at the funeral home, as you can imagine."

"Maybe you should visit her to see how she's doing; she is a member of the church."

Bret turned to face his wife. "You know I've avoided any visits with the Templetons because of Russell. I didn't want him to take it out on Alice."

"Well, according to the reports I've heard, Russell doesn't live there anymore."

"It's still risky, Laura; I'll just call her to see how she is. I can't imagine what's going through her mind."

Laura slowly inhaled, then exhaled through pursed lips and asked, "Is the investigation going to happen immediately, Bret?"

"It has to; Wilbur's body is missing. It's a crime to tamper with a corpse. I'm sure the worst of it will fall on Forrest as the funeral director. He's undoubtedly the most responsible. The sheriff's department will try to keep it as quiet as they can."

"But you and I both know, Bret, if the media gets involved—

especially if it goes outside of town—the story could easily be blown way out of proportion."

"That's what I'm afraid of."

"Do you think you should share what you think happened with the church?" Laura asked, looking quizzically at Bret.

"When the time is right, Laura; it's all too speculative right now."

"Well, you're sensitive and you understand the people pretty well...they'll be looking to you for answers."

"But you know what I was thinking?" Bret said, ignoring Laura. "Who knows what Alice might be thinking. If I were in her position, I would hold out some hope, however impossible things seem."

"But do you realize the implications of this, Bret? I don't think it's sunk in yet. If Wilbur does show up alive at some point, the world will hear about it."

"Poor Wilbur. In that case, he might just as well have remained in the casket."

"And what I can't figure, Bret—if it really was Wilbur, why would he just run away?"

"Precisely my thought, Laura."

BRET COULDN'T SLEEP THAT NIGHT. His mind whirled with a thousand tormenting thoughts. Where was Wilbur's body? And to believe that he could have been resurrected from the dead...

I've got to be nuts; how could I have even considered that? People don't just rise from the dead. Forrest and Sam had to be right: Russell must've planned the whole thing, faked emotion at the funeral, and hired someone as a look-alike. But that doesn't seem plausible—to make someone look like Wilbur. It would have to fool a lot of people who were at the funeral, including me. But then, the body did have some odd distortions to it from having been in the water for several hours. Yes, I distinctly remember there was something not right about the body. And it makes perfect sense for Russell to fake it and sue the funeral home.

Bret shook his wife awake. "Laura, I have to talk to you."

Laura rolled over, wiped the sleep from her eyes, and glanced at her watch. "What on earth for at this hour, Bret? Can't it wait 'til morning?"

"I've got too much on my mind, Laura; I've been rethinking the scene at the funeral home and—"

"And what?"

"I think Forrest and Sam are right. Russell must have planned the whole thing so he could sue the funeral home."

"You're not thinking clearly, Bret; how would he get rid of Wilbur's body, and who would he get to lay in that casket pretending to be dead? Too many people would have noticed, especially Forrest."

"People don't like looking at a corpse for very long, Laura, and they wouldn't suspect anything. And apparently no one touched the body, or they would have felt that it was warm."

"Bret, can't you just drop it for the night? It's been a long day, and I'm sure tomorrow won't be any easier."

Bret knew she was right; he was exhausted and *wasn't* thinking clearly. He finally fell asleep, but not before kissing Laura and thanking her for helping him readjust his thinking. What if Wilbur did appear sometime soon? Then what? Would they be ready for the onslaught? The media? The skeptics and naysayers? Bret knew one thing: If Wilbur did reappear, Foylestown would never be the same again.

CHAPTER NINE

Officer Charles Cameron, the investigator from the sheriff's department, sat across from Sam Stone and questioned him thoroughly regarding the details of Wilbur's funeral. He stretched his arms back and yawned. "So, basically you want us to investigate a missing corpse, and who might've tampered with the body of Wilbur Templeton. Is that the gist of it?"

"I'd prefer you guys took the lead on this," Sam said, nodding. "I'm too close to some of the people to be objective, and I already have a bias against one of the suspects."

"Well, that's an honest take for a change," Officer Cameron said. "But with prejudice aside, who do you think we should talk to first?"

Sam thought for a moment. "Forrest Fields is the owner of the funeral home and the director; it would make sense to start with him. He can fill you in on details I might've missed."

"Who's next?"

"The pastor, Bret Crossman. He was a chief witness to the events at the close of the funeral service. Then, there are multiple eyewitnesses—probably over a hundred people who were there."

"Does the director have their names?" Cameron asked.

"If they signed the guest book, yes. There were some I'm sure who didn't sign it."

"And then, who's the suspect you've singled out?"

Sam rubbed his chin before drawing out his answer. "Russell Templeton, Wilbur's father."

"Tell me why you dislike the guy; I'm sure there must be a reason other than personality."

"He's nasty—always looking for a fight; he's an agitator who's not well liked around town."

"Any trouble with the law?" Officer Cameron asked, raising an eyebrow.

"More than once, but just minor stuff: drunkenness, disturbing the peace, and—"

"And what?"

"His wife, Alice, often called to report threats against her and Wilbur."

"Anything come of that?" Cameron pressed further.

Sam shook his head. "Nope."

"Well, I guess your prejudice is not unfounded then, is it?"

"The whole town pretty much feels the same way, and there's bad blood between him and Forrest—plus, he hates the pastor."

"Not a churchgoer, I surmise."

"Very vocal against it, although Alice and Wilbur attended Foylestown Community regularly."

"So, you think Russell might have removed his son's body for leverage against Forrest—is that safe to assume? To sue the funeral home?"

"He's broke and needs the money."

"...and is capable of stealing the corpse?"

"Yes," Sam said, nodding. "Russell is capable of most anything if it's self-serving."

"Hmm...," Cameron paused. "And does Forrest think the same?"

"He does, and he harbors some resentment against Russell that goes beyond the funeral events. Something longstanding and personal."

"Not unusual," Cameron said. "Personal grudges, family feuds, and—and missing bodies, but you haven't mentioned what the pastor thinks."

"What's your take on miracles?" Sam asked.

"Huh?"

"On miracles; what's your take?"

"As in do I believe in miracles?" Cameron confirmed the query.

"Yes."

"Well, yes and no; I suppose they're possible, but usually there's a rational explanation about events coined miraculous. I think I know where you're going with this. The pastor thinks a miracle took place; am I right?"

"Right; he thinks Wilbur rose from the dead."

Officer Cameron's eyes widened. "Good Lord, this isn't Jerusalem!"

"No," Sam agreed, "but it happened here, whatever it was."

"And that's what we have to find out. Looks like there's criminal activity involved, assuming there was no miracle." Charles Cameron grinned.

"If and when we find the corpse, that will settle the miracle issue," Sam said.

"Then there's the possibility we won't find the corpse or discover the perpetrator. But this doesn't look too complex given the possible motives you mentioned. I don't think whoever did it is too professional; it shouldn't take us long to flush out the body snatcher."

"Reminds me of a movie," Sam admitted and laughed out loud.

"This could get out if the media hounds are onto it. I'm sure you're aware of that."

"A couple of local reporters have already approached me demanding answers; they're going to need some kind of statement soon."

"I'm not too concerned with the local ones, but it could draw some major media attention, so we need to be prepared. The sooner we find the body, the better."

"How much help can you guys spare right now?" Sam asked.

"Probably two or three other personnel at the most. We're shorthanded as it is."

"I have some part-time staff I can lend you—a woman and a man who fill in for me during my off hours. They're dependable and well trained. Plus half the town will be looking for him," Sam added.

"That'll help, given the number of witnesses who knew the deceased and his family. We need to find out what anyone might know in connection with the events at the funeral home; there could be other people involved." Officer Charles Cameron stood and prepared to leave. "Oh, by the way—if it wasn't Wilbur, who was in the casket?"

Before Sam could answer, a television reporter from out of town appeared along with a cameraman.

CHAPTER TEN

Alice Templeton sat alone in her bedroom weeping, her premature gray hair slicked back into a ponytail, her face showing the years of physical and emotional hurt. The tears never seemed to cease. Her only son dead and his body missing; her husband living with another woman; rumors that maybe Wilbur rose from the dead. She was only forty-six but looked sixty. What hope had she now? She thought of suicide, but ruled it out for fear of the unknown. She believed in an afterlife and had heard Bret Crossman preach on it many times. Now, she wished her days would be shortened by God; she could find no purpose for continuing her life.

What a cruel hoax! Where's my son? Who would dream of taking Wilbur's body? He never meant anyone harm! Fifteen short years, and now he's gone forever! Alice buried her face in her pillow and continued sobbing. In the distance, a faint sound kept piercing the emptiness. The phone—it was the phone ringing. Russell had a cell phone, but he never allowed Alice to use it; he thought she wasn't smart enough to figure it out, so they retained a landline phone in the kitchen.

Alice pulled at the fullness of her dress, wiped away her tears, and sat up on her bed. *Who would be calling me? I'm not in the mood to talk to anyone.* But she recognized the voice on the answering machine. It was Bret Crossman. Of all the people she knew, he was about the only one she would talk to. She'd been careful not to disclose too much about her relationship with Russell, but she also knew that Bret was perceptive and could read the hurt in her eyes when she came to church.

She was too late getting to the phone. The message was a simple one: "Hello Alice, this is Bret Crossman. Just thinking of you and praying for you. I'll call later."

She chided herself for missing the call and hoped he would call again soon. He must have known Russell was not in the house, or he wouldn't have risked calling. She was sure that the news of Russell leaving her and moving in with the other woman had spread rapidly through the village. It was the first time Bret had called, and he had never ventured near her home. Russell had a loaded shotgun by the front door, and Alice was fearful that a visit by the pastor might have set him off. She checked the place where he kept it and noticed it was missing. She had no doubt he could kill someone when he was angry and drunk, or maybe just angry. The thought struck her that she could be in danger if the new lady kicked him out and he wanted to return home. Then she laughed: *Lady? Russell with a lady? I was the closest thing he had to that, and he left me!*

The phone rang again, and she froze for a moment. Had Russell found out about Bret calling her? No, he couldn't have. But who'd be calling now? She waited again for the answering machine to kick in.

"Alice, it's Bret Crossman again; I hope you're alright. I understand that Russell isn't living there, so I thought it safe to call."

Alice hurried to the kitchen to pick up the phone. "Hello, Pastor Crossman; it's Alice."

"Alice! I'm so glad I caught you. How are you?"

"Not well at all; I can't quit crying, and I'm afraid of Russell returning. Pastor, what's happened to Wilbur's body?" Alice fought back tears.

"There's an ongoing investigation; I've heard that the county sheriff has a team assigned to find your son's body."

"And what if they don't? What if Russell hid Wilbur someplace they'll never find him? God, I can't think of that right now; I just can't imagine it."

"I want to help you, Alice. What can I do? What can the church do? Would it help if Laura and I came over to be with you?"

"Thank you, Pastor—"

"Call me Bret."

"Thank you...but I just want to be alone for a time. Just pray that I'll be safe."

"If Russell comes back and threatens you, get a restraining order against him, Alice."

"Do you think for a moment that would stop him from coming back?"

"Well, no; but at least it would be a legal step if he—"

"Shows up and attacks me?"

Bret drew a quick breath and said, "You shouldn't be alone if you feel that way; do you have any friends or relatives close by?"

"A sister in Albany."

"Well, that's too far away. I could call the police and have someone keep an eye on the house if you want."

"I thought they were involved in the search for Wilbur."

"You're right; they wouldn't have enough staff."

There was a lull in the conversation. Then Alice said in a halting voice, "Bret, it's rumored that you think Wilbur may have come back to life. Is...is that true?"

Bret hesitated before answering, not wanting to give her any false hope. "Alice," he said gently, "at first, I seriously entertained that possibility since there was no other reasonable explanation, but I'm becoming increasingly aware that God just doesn't work that way today. Sometimes our hopes and desires can get in the way of our ability to think clearly."

"Oh," Alice said, her voice sinking, "I guess it was selfish to wish such a thing. I'm sure he's in Heaven now."

"Yes," Bret said. "I know that Wilbur was a true believer in the most important resurrection that did take place—that of Jesus Christ, and he also believed in the Gospel as it is clearly presented in the Scriptures. In a way, we all selfishly would want him back, but the Lord wanted him in his eternal home."

"Well," Alice sighed, "it does bring great comfort in knowing that, Pastor Crossman, and I so much appreciate your call; it means a lot to me."

"I'm glad I called, too, Alice. Laura and I will be praying for you, and please don't hesitate to call me if I can be of help."

CHAPTER ELEVEN

For sure Cherie Loman was no lady, but she was exactly what Russell wanted. Ten years younger than Alice and more amenable to his personal preferences. Plus, she was a source of income, which meant Russell could live with her without having to work—at least for a while. They were both cynical and sharp-tongued, but not toward each other; they had already discovered common scapegoats for their anger: Alice, the police, the church, it didn't matter—but a special hatred was reserved for Forrest Fields.

"I've contacted a lawyer," Russell announced to Cherie. "I'm going to sue Fields for every dime he has."

Cherie smiled at Russell's boldness—a trait that had drawn her to him. They sat together on a velvet-like sofa in her living room and spent an hour just chatting and getting to know one another even better. The more they shared, the more they realized how compatible they were. Cherie had never been married, but had had several short-lived, contentious relationships. This one was different and to her liking. "Vengeance should serve you well, Russell; after all, the man's responsible for the disappearance of your son's body."

"And that's a crime, too. He's got more coming to him than he realizes once the law gets involved. His little scheme of planting a dummy in the casket and having him flee so he could blame me—well, it ain't gonna work; my hands are clean."

Cherie frowned. "What motivates his anger toward you?"

"It goes back a long way; family stuff, you know—generational."

"Bad blood, as they say? What's the story behind it?" Cherie asked.

"His father and mine inherited mutual hatred for each other. A land dispute which nearly resulted in bloodshed and ruined my grandfather financially. My family never recovered. It's time I evened the score."

"Hmm...so why did you use his funeral home for your son? Wasn't that giving him somewhat of an edge?"

Russell paused before answering and carefully measured his words: "It's the only funeral home in town, so...so we didn't have much choice. Besides, Wilbur's mother insisted that Fields and I bury the hatchet."

Cherie laughed out loud. "I'll bet you wanted to 'bury the hatchet,' didn't you!"

"Right in the middle of his forehead!" Russell grinned and swung an imaginary hatchet. "But then I couldn't have sued him. This way, it's more fun. I get to watch him squirm."

"I've never met the man, but I can't wait to see that, Russ; I kind of like seeing weaselly men squirm a little."

"You know, Cherie," Russell said as he took her arm and looked her straight in the eyes, "that's one thing I like about you; you're a little ruthless—like me. We'll do just fine together."

"A little, Russ? I don't think you know how ruthless I can be."

———— ⚬ ————

ANOTHER HOUR PASSED AS THEY continued discussing the impending ruination of Forrest Fields.

"But what if they find the body, Russ?" Cherie asked, changing the subject.

"They won't! They won't find it; I'm sure of that, because, well, that would shoot down Forrest's scheme against me. He's done something with the body; maybe had it cremated and paid someone to shut their mouth about it."

"Then it's going to be your word against his, right?"

"Right, and I have the leverage because he's responsible for the corpse, not me."

"Could it come to trial?" Cherie asked.

"It could, and just in case he suddenly comes clean and presents the body, I'll still sue him for the emotional trauma."

"Either way the guy's ruined, Russ."

"And that will finally settle the generational score."

"Sounds like a win-win situation for you. How much are you suing him for?"

"I haven't settled on a figure, but once I consult with a lawyer, I will."

There was a lull in their conversation when Cherie suddenly changed the subject. "Do you believe in the supernatural, Russ, and what do you think about other dimensions and the spiritual realm?"

Russell scowled and shifted awkwardly on the sofa. "Why on earth are you bringing that up?"

"Because I've made contact with an entity from the other side."

"You what?"

"Hear me out, and don't think I'm weird. What I'm about to share with you may give us power—not only against Fields, but also against the pastor guy and his church."

"Go on," Russell said. "I'm listening, but I'm not into anything on the other side."

"I think you will be after you hear what I have to say. You want a drink first?"

Russell nodded. "I think a drink would help me swallow whatever you're going to tell me."

Cherie jumped up from the sofa and headed for a small liquor cabinet. "...you like scotch?"

"Whiskey?" Russell said, raising an eyebrow.

"Yeah, the good stuff—top shelf."

"You got any beer, Cherie? My taste ain't too sophisticated."

"Tonight, you're gonna celebrate with me and scotch it is!"

"Whatever; I'm in need of some comfort."

"Well, I like it straight with a little ice so if that's okay with you, I'll get some glasses."

Russell shrugged his shoulders. "Better start me with three shots, then; I might as well get hammered as quickly as I can while you share your otherworldly stuff. An entity, you said. What the hell is an entity?"

"A spirit being or guide, if you want to call it that—possessing higher intelligence than we do."

"Angel or demon?" Russell asked, laughing.

"I prefer friend." Cherie gave him a critical look that squelched his laughter.

"Are you just putting me on with this stuff? I can take a joke, so level with me."

"He's as real as you are sitting there," Cherie said as she put some ice in the glasses.

"It's he and not it? Does he have male parts and all?"

"He's probably seven feet tall, shining, and with a deep, almost metallic sounding voice."

Russell shook his head. "Bloody hell, give me the scotch before you go any further, and, by the way, does the dude have a name?"

"*Prelude.*"

"*Prelude*—as in an introduction?"

"That's what he calls himself."

"What's he introducing, if I might ask?"

"Another world."

"Now you've lost me, Cherie; there's nothing beyond terra firma."

"Oh, but you're wrong, Russ—very wrong. I think you'll change your mind after you hear what I have to say."

CHAPTER TWELVE

"**A** statement! Can we have a statement? What can you tell us about the Templeton boy? Has the body been found? Do you suspect foul play?" The reporter from the Rochester Democrat and Chronicle edged closer to the investigator as he was leaving Sam's office.

"It's under investigation at the present, and I don't have details to share," Officer Cameron said, moving rapidly toward his car.

"But has the body been found yet?"

"No," Cameron replied, "it hasn't."

"Are you treating this as a crime? Is anyone being charged?"

Cameron swung open the door to the cruiser, got in, and quickly shut it, leaving the reporter frustrated. Sam watched from his office window, hoping the reporter wouldn't approach him. His thoughts shifted back to what Bret Crossman had said. A resurrection? No way! Not in Foylestown. Just the idea of it made him shiver. He was getting too old for drama. The town had been so peaceful, with nothing out of the ordinary happening other than the annual craft fair and Fourth of July parade. He hadn't even issued a traffic ticket in two weeks.

But now this! Whatever this was. He'd managed to avoid the reporter, and thankfully his shift was ending soon. But then, would it be? No, he figured there would be no regular hours since the search for Wilbur Templeton was ongoing.

Just as he was about to sit down, a young couple burst into the office and shouted, "We saw him—Wilbur Templeton! We saw him leaving the funeral home with two other men dressed in black."

Sam jumped to his feet. "What do you mean—you saw him? And why wait until now to come and tell me?"

"We didn't want to be made fun of," the woman said, trying hard to regain her composure. "We wanted to wait to see what everyone else was saying first."

"And, besides that," the man added, "the two men saw us and tried to hide Wilbur from our view, and...and here's the weird thing...they just seemed to disappear."

Sam drew a hand through his thinning hair and shook his head. "Tell me you guys haven't been talking to a reporter."

"No, we haven't," they replied in unison.

"Are you guys sure it wasn't someone else?" Sam asked.

"Yes, we're sure," the woman said. "We saw him—we knew it was Wilbur."

"Uh-huh," Sam said. "I think I need a little more convincing than you just saying you saw him."

"And he saw us, too!" the man said. "I'm sure of it; just before the men blocked our view, he glanced our way."

Sam thought for a moment. "And what about the two guys with him? What did they look like?"

"Professionally dressed," the man said, "...almost like they were on official business."

Sam laughed. "Escorting the dead is pretty 'official' if you ask me. Any additional description of the two?"

"I would guess they were in their mid-thirties, clean cut, could've been twins; nothing else stands out," the woman said.

"Still," Sam said, his face drawn in doubt, "I need a little more evidence that it was Wilbur you saw."

The man looked at his companion. She covered her mouth to squelch her frustration. After a short pause, she said, "We can tell you what he was wearing, if that makes any difference."

Sam sat back in his office chair and tapped his desk with a pen. "Okay then, tell me: What was he wearing?"

"A blue sports coat with a white shirt and a dark green tie," the woman said.

"And sneakers," the man added.

Sam scratched his cheek. "Were either of you at the funeral?"

"No, we weren't," the woman said, shaking her head.

"Neither of you?"

"Neither of us," she confirmed.

"And you were just passing by the funeral home at the precise moment you saw who you claim to be Wilbur, right?"

They both nodded.

"This is very strange," Sam said. "I'll need to ask the funeral director what the deceased was wearing in the casket, and we'll settle this for good. Hold on a minute, and I'll see if I can get him."

As Sam reached for his phone he thought, *What on earth am I doing this for? Do these people just want a little attention? Thank God they didn't talk to any reporters.* Maybe it was just a half-assed story...but first, the call to Forrest.

The couple waited patiently for the call to go through.

"Forrest?" Sam inquired as the funeral director answered the call. "Yeah, it's the chief here. Hey, there's a couple in my office who claim they saw Wilbur after the funeral, along with two unidentified men flanking him. I've got a weird question for you: Can you tell me what Wilbur Templeton was wearing in the casket?"

The couple watched Sam's face as he spoke.

"A blue sport coat. Uh-huh. And can you tell me the color of his shirt? White. Okay, gotcha." Sam glanced at the pair, who had their arms crossed and were smiling slightly. What color tie was he wearing? Green, you said? Was it light or dark green? Dark green; okay that should help." Sam sighed and began slowly shaking his head. "One final question, Forrest, and this may seem odd: What shoes was he wearing?"

The color drained from Sam's face as he listened to Forrest corroborate the description given by the couple standing a few feet away.

"He was wearing sneakers," Sam said weakly as he ended the call. "And I guess you heard the rest. What the hell is going on?"

"We told you we saw him," the woman said bluntly. "And we saw the two men dressed in black. You should have asked the director about them."

"I will," Sam said, "next time I talk with him, but right now I need a little air." He handed the couple a pad of paper and a pen. "Give me your names and how to reach you; you'll be hearing from me soon."

The couple hurriedly scribbled the information on the pad and left without saying a word. Sam stepped outside his office, looked up into the sky, and shook his head. *I need to pray.*

CHAPTER THIRTEEN

"**F**orrest just called me and said the chief interviewed a couple who insisted they saw Wilbur leave the funeral home," Bret Crossman announced to his wife.

"And now the plot thickens," Laura said as she sauntered toward the kitchen counter carrying breakfast dishes with her. "And what was Forrest's response?"

"Just as you might expect—he wrote it off as another ploy, wondering whether Russell was behind it somehow."

The dishes rattled on the counter as Laura shot a frustrated look at Bret. "Those two just won't let it die. Excuse the pun but what's going on?"

"Sit down, Laura, and let's talk."

Laura took a seat at the small kitchen table opposite Bret. "Meaning we're back to the resurrection story?"

"So it would seem, and here's a crazy thought that just came to me: I remember at the funeral seeing two men dressed in black seated together at the back of the chapel. I'd never seen either one of them before, but assumed they must be related to the Templetons. Odd thing is they had kind of a Gothic appearance—like some characters out of a novel."

"Pall bearers?"

"I don't think so, and they arrived late; that's why I noticed them. I'm not sure anyone else saw them."

"Did Forrest mention them in his conversation with the chief?"

"He didn't say anything to me about it, but come to think of it, the two men weren't around after the service ended. All of this is coming back to me now that I've had time to think."

Laura groaned. "Bret, this whole thing is getting on my nerves, and there's so much speculation about what happened—with no answers. And what about Alice Templeton? You said you called her."

"I did, and she's devastated, poor thing. She asked me if I believed Wilbur could still be alive...meaning did I think it was possible that he was resurrected."

"And what did you tell her?"

"I told her I had my doubts, but that it was possible since God can do whatever He wants."

"Do you think that gave her false hope?"

"I downplayed it and tried to be discreet; it's just way too speculative."

"Well," Laura said, "it does seem like you've been back and forth with this.

"Look Laura, don't get on me about it, okay? It's been an emotional few days, and I'm trying to sort it out. You weren't even at the funeral."

"Point taken; no, I wasn't there and shouldn't comment—sorry."

They were both silent for a minute, letting things defuse. Then Bret said, "I need to talk to Sam Stone to make sure I get the story correct regarding the couple he spoke with. Forrest may have screwed it up."

"That's a good idea," Laura agreed. "And that way you can find out if there's any progress on the search for Wilbur."

Bret moved to the other side of the table and gave his wife an awkward kiss. "I'm going to my office to make some calls."

"And I've got a meeting in town with some women from the church; hopefully it won't degenerate into rumors and gossip."

———•◦ ◯ ◦•———

BRET DROVE TO HIS CHURCH office, his mind swirling with negative thoughts; he felt like his faith was on trial, and he struggled with unbelief. *What do I believe? Laura was right, I have been equivocal the last couple of days. But, God, resurrections don't just happen. There must be another answer. And, Alice, clinging to a desperate belief that somehow Wilbur's still alive. Well, if he's in Heaven, then he is certainly alive, and the chances of his still wandering around Planet Earth somewhere are slim to none. But I've already told Forrest there's no other explanation than resurrection, and here I am completely baffled.*

But the thought of the two men in black plagued him. Who were they? He would ask around to see if anyone else knew or saw them. Certainly, Forrest or Alice would know if they were friends or relatives.

I just don't have a good feeling about them. Maybe they were part of Russell's scheme, and they made sure they left the funeral right at the time of the great escape from the casket. Hired men prepared to escort whoever it was to a safe place so he could change clothes and sneak back into town unnoticed. And who was "he"? And would he squeal if found? Not if Russell threatened his life and found some way of compensating him...

———•◦ ◯ ◦•———

WHEN BRET ARRIVED AT THE church, the townspeople were gathered about the parking lot as if they were waiting for him. They immediately approached him asking for more information as he exited his car. He wanted to get back in the car and leave—leave for a week or two and not see anyone. But there was little hope of that since some of the people were from the church congregation. How did they know he was coming? Maybe they called Laura, and she told them to meet Bret there. They would have had time since the drive from his house to the church took about fifteen minutes.

He took a few steps toward the church when a woman he knew from town cornered him. "Pastor Crossman, could we speak with you for a minute? You must know it's about Wilbur; we just want some clarification."

Clarification? Right, that's exactly what I want. Let's see... Wilbur is now at an undetermined location. Heaven? Yeah, probably. Or waiting for his post-resurrection appearance?

"What can you tell us?" the slender, middle-aged woman with the bun and long, floral-print dress asked. "Where is Wilbur?"

Bret stepped back toward his car and attempted to open the door, but the woman read his thoughts and moved to block him.

"Mrs. Renfro," Bret said, gently pushing past her while putting the question back to her: "Where do you think he is?"

She turned to address the crowd as they gathered around her. "He wants to know where we think Wilbur is."

Most of the people ignored her, but several people shouted answers.

"He's gone on to be with the Lord; that's what we think."

"He's in Heaven!"

"Wilbur is at peace now."

Then: "This nonsense about rising from the dead has got the town going nuts."

"But who was that in the casket?" a man in the crowd demanded. "Who the heck jumped out? We were there, my wife and I, and we saw what happened. People in town are already skeptical of the church anyway, and now it looks as if we're a comedy show!"

"It's Russell's doing; we know it is," said another. "We've heard rumors that he wants to sue the funeral home."

"Yeah, but someone said Forrest faked it all to get publicity!" said a young man who raised his hand like a school child eager to answer the teacher's question.

"Are you going to answer us?" Mrs. Renfro pressed, hands on her hips and nasty scowl on her face.

"All you've said to this point is speculation," Bret answered. "The truth is that no one knows where he is unless we assume that he is truly dead and passed into eternity. Then we pretty well know where he is."

A few people grumbled, not satisfied with Bret's answer.

"Not good enough!" a former church member shouted. "You should know; you're the pastor of the church, and you conducted the funeral."

God, get me out of here. I have no answers—or the ones I have, they don't want. What on earth do you want me to say to them?

"God knows where he is; that will have to suffice for now," Bret said. "And if you don't mind, I have office work to do. Just be in church Sunday morning; I may have more information then."

Mrs. Renfro huffed and passed through the crowd, muttering to herself, "I have no intention of going to church Sunday."

Wayne Silver, one of the church elders, had just arrived. Noticing the people gathered, he walked closer to Bret, then stood by his side and calmly began addressing the crowd.

"Look," he said, pointing to Bret, "this man has been through a lot the last couple of days, trying to figure out what happened to Wilbur Templeton. You all have a right to know, but we have no specifics at this point. I would suggest that you all go home, get on your knees, and pray for our town. So much is happening for which we have no answers right now. The answers will come eventually, and we will know exactly what happened."

Slowly, the crowd began to disperse. As Mrs. Renfro deliberately passed by too close to Bret, Wayne shot her a penetratingly stern look as if to say *knock it off.*

When Bret got to his office, he sat at his desk and cupped his face in his hands, thinking about the two strange men he saw at the funeral home. He instinctively knew they had something to do with Wilbur and was certain it wasn't good. But what part they played? He had no idea.

CHAPTER FOURTEEN

"**O**kay," Russell said, after downing his triple shot of scotch, "tell me more about this entity you say you had contact with."

"I've been attending this group learning how to meditate," Cherie said eagerly, "just opening your mind as a channel to connect with the spirit realm."

Russell rolled his eyes, sighed deeply, then said, "I wasn't expecting *this* tonight."

"And that's not all," Cherie continued, ignoring Russell's response. "I'm also studying about how to leave your body, you know, to have an out-of-body experience."

"Scotch! I need more scotch, Cherie; you're freaking me out."

"You enter an astral plane where these entities exist. Isn't that wild?!"

"Beyond wild," Russell said, feeling the effects of the alcohol. "This stuff hits you fast, doesn't it?"

"No, I've been at it awhile; I'm still learning."

"I mean the scotch; it comes on you rather quickly."

"You can't drink it like beer, Russ."

"Why on earth, or wherever, would you want to leave your body. You sound like Alice talking about your soul going to Heaven."

"I can't explain it since I haven't experienced it yet, but from what I understand, your soul does leave your body and enters another realm."

"And what about the spooky guy?" Russell asked. "What's he got to offer?"

"Prelude?"

"Yeah, him—or it."

"He told me that the church is deceiving people; that there's no need for God since we're all part of the universe."

"Sounds like my kind of alien," Russell said, laughing. "Any chance of me meeting him?"

"And here's another thing," Cherie said, again ignoring Russell's remark. "He says he knows things about people in town, especially in the church your wife goes to."

Russell sat up straight. "What sort of stuff?"

"He hasn't said yet, but I'm sure he will the next time I meet him. He's mesmerizing, Russ. There's a power there I can't describe but it's so appealing. It's definitely supernatural."

A thought struck Russell. "Okay, assuming this thing is for real and has this power as you say—do you think he would know what happened to my kid?"

"Possibly," Cherie said, nodding.

"But what if...what if he's lying?"

"Russ, what are you saying? You look like you've seen a ghost. Why would he lie?"

"Oh, God, Cherie; how do I know? I can't wrap my head around this stuff, and I can't believe you've just swallowed it whole."

"Follow me, Russ; what if he knows what happened to your son? Don't you think that would give you the power you need against Forrest?"

Russell was silent for a long moment, then said quietly, "Ask him...and let me know."

Cherie stood and turned her back on Russell, confused by his show of weakness. Not a trait she wanted in a man. Not what she had ever seen in Russell.

He tried to recover quickly, having sensed Cherie's brusque about-face. "...must be the scotch," he said. "It gave me a twinge of paranoia when you mentioned the entity's knowing stuff about people in town."

"What have you got to hide, Russell?" Cherie whirled around and confronted him. "Are you afraid that Prelude has something on you?"

"I'm not afraid of him, Cherie, but what if he takes Forrest's side against me?"

Cherie pulled a cigarette from her purse, lit it, and sat down next to Russell. "If he's my friend, he's not going to pull something like that. We both want to see Forrest cut to pieces and maybe Prelude can help us."

Russell blew a heavy sigh and relaxed. "You say this guy has some kind of supernatural power, huh?"

"He's a beast, Russ, from the spirit realm. Of course he has power; that's what I was after. Power! I want power over people, and Prelude is the one who can provide it."

Cherie's face seemed to change right before Russell's eyes. There was a fierceness about her he hadn't seen before.

"Yeah, well, that intrigues me, Cherie; you intrigue me for that matter. I've never met someone who's so...,"

"Ruthless? Don't you remember when I told you that before?"

"Yeah, I do remember you mentioning that."

"And I'm unpredictable, too. That was always an advantage I held over others—especially some of the men I've known."

"Hmm...," Russell frowned. "That certainly would keep anyone on edge, wouldn't it?"

"But we're in this together, right Russ? Nothing wrong with adding an additional player on our team."

"Prelude, you mean?"

"Of course."

"So, when do you conjure him up again?"

"When the time and conditions are right; I can't just do it at will."

"You mean he has the control, right? He's not at your beck and call?" Russell said, smirking, sensing a vulnerability in Cherie.

"I'm still learning, Russ, but whenever I have contact, there's a power there that's superhuman. There's a penetration of some kind—yes, it is controlling, but it's also empowering."

Russell smiled almost unnoticeably as he gave a quick glance at Cherie. "How is it penetrating and empowering? Mentally, physically? I don't get it."

"Knowledge is power, as someone once said, and he knows things that no one else does."

The smile faded from Russell's face. "Has he shared anything with you about me?"

"No, he hasn't—and like I said, don't worry; we're on the same side."

"Some would call it the evil side, Cherie."

Cherie laughed loudly. "The evil side, Russ? What is evil anyway? And surely you don't care...or do you?"

"I don't give a crap about the good and evil stuff!" Russell scoffed. "Whatever gives me the advantage is what I want."

"I thought for a minute you might be caving in a little," Cherie said, with an affected frown.

Russell stood abruptly, his jaw tightening. "Don't misjudge me, Cherie, just because I don't get this supernatural stuff; it's just creepy is all. I left Alice because she was a weak little whiner. She repulses me—and her faith talk makes me want to vomit. And our sycophant son tagging along with her to that moron's church. Wilbur is dead," he said. "It's a shame I didn't get to know him better."

"And Forrest is going to suffer like he can't even imagine; and maybe the pastor, too," Cherie said as she headed for the liquor cabinet. "More scotch, or have you had enough?"

"I've never had enough alcohol, Cherie. Let's have a toast to Prelude."

"To Prelude!" Cherie shouted. "A toast to Prelude!"

CHAPTER FIFTEEN

Forrest Fields had a feeling something wasn't right. Not that he was given to premonitions, but whatever the feeling was made him shudder. Maybe it was a fear of what Russell might do, especially if there was a lawsuit against the funeral home. Forrest was painfully aware of the history between his family and Russell's, and he had no doubt that Russell wanted to avenge the injury done to his grandfather. The hatred that motivated that man was not natural. A chill ran up Forrest's spine as he sensed his life might be at risk. He needed to talk to Sam Stone—but maybe he was just being paranoid. His conversation with Bret Crossman also troubled him. He couldn't dismiss the logic that Bret kept hammering away at regarding the resurrection of Wilbur. It was Wilbur in the casket...Wilbur rising, fleeing. *Oh, God, that just couldn't happen!*

Drops of sweat formed on his forehead, and he pulled his shirt free from his slacks to wipe his face. The extra hundred pounds he'd gained over the last few years put a strain on his heart, and he'd felt chest pains in the last few days. What if he lost the funeral home and went bankrupt? How ironic that the death of others had been his means of living, and now he wondered if he was going to die. He'd almost rather die than face the humiliation of being sued and possibly charged with a crime if Wilbur's body wasn't found.

Another sharp pang...they were getting worse and more frequent. And the paranoia...he couldn't shake it. He'd lived alone since his wife divorced him ten years ago, but now he was certain that there was a "presence" in his house, as he described it. A heavy, palpable presence which pressed against his head and chest. And when he felt the presence, he had difficulty breathing, like he was having a panic attack. Was he going crazy? He'd entertained the idea of seeing a shrink, but he'd have to travel to Rochester—over an hour away.

Maybe Bret Crossman could help. He was a minister and could at least offer some comfort and maybe counsel. But the conversation he'd had with Bret regarding Wilbur gave him no peace. The logic that the minister had pushed so strongly—that Wilbur rose from the dead: The more he thought of that, the more confused he was. Back and forth, back and forth, like the sea driven by the wind. Logic? What was the logic of it? Corpses don't rise from the dead. Period. There wasn't any logic to that. It had to be Russell. Somehow Russell had stolen into the funeral home and exchanged bodies. Yes, he said to himself. *It was Russell after all*. That was logical—and reasonable. Russell was seeking revenge.

Damn his soul.

"Oh!" Forrest cried as he doubled over in pain, clutching his chest, his breath short and labored. "I need help; somebody's got to help me!"

The presence was there...and so was the fear.

Driving me crazy; driving me crazy! What is going on? Gotta call Bret.

It seemed like an hour had passed before Forrest regained his composure and could place a call to Bret Crossman. He instinctively felt the minister might have some answers to what he was experiencing, but he had no doubt they would revisit the issue regarding Wilbur Templeton.

THE PHONE CALL WAS BRIEF; it produced one result: Bret wanted to meet with him in person. Too much was going on to discuss it all over the phone. Could Forrest meet him in an hour at the church office?

"Yes," Forrest said, "I can be there."

"Good," Bret replied, "and don't let anyone know you're meeting with me; I want it to be totally private. I've got some startling news to share with you."

Startling news? Just what Forrest needed, more shock to his system. He wanted *normal* to return. Dial it all back a week or so when he had peace and was feeling quite content with his life—even planning a vacation for the first time in years. At least the chest pain was gone for now. He could breathe again.

"HAVE A SEAT," BRET SAID, motioning Forrest to a comfortable looking chair in the church office. "Would you like some bottled water or coffee?"

"No coffee," Forrest said, frowning. "My nerves are shot as it is. I'll take the water, though."

"Hmm...," Bret said. "I noticed your voice was tight over the phone."

"Was it that obvious?"

"Quite; but understandable with what little you shared with me. I felt we should meet and discuss things in private."

Forrest sagged in the chair and sighed like he was releasing a week of emotional weight. "I can't fully describe what's been happening to me lately, but I'll try. It's something I've never experienced before so my description might be lacking."

"Well, I'm a good listener."

"I live alone, as you know."

"Go on."

"But lately—I would say in the last week—I feel like I haven't been alone."

"Uh-huh, that does sound a little strange," Bret said, frowning.

"And that's not all, Bret. I've had this pressure in my chest, like I was having a heart attack."

"Well," Bret said, "you aren't getting any younger, Forrest, and to be honest, you could lose some weight. I don't see anything unusual about that. Have you seen your doctor?"

"But it isn't just my heart! I've had a strange tension in my head, and strong feelings of paranoia...like something is...is, well, trying to drive me crazy!"

Bret noticed the odd change in Forrest's countenance. A mixture of fear and dread had seized him, and his hands began to tremble. "Good Lord, what is happening to you, Forrest?" Bret asked, rushing to his guest's side.

"Can you sense it, Bret? Can you sense something? The presence?"

"I don't sense anything, Forrest! You need to calm yourself down." Bret put his hand on Forrest's shoulder to reassure him. "There isn't any *presence* here besides you and me."

"You think I'm crazy don't you, Bret?" Forrest brushed Bret's hand from his shoulder and turned to face him.

"I don't think you're crazy, Forrest, but you are being irrational."

"I thought you said you were a good listener!"

Bret sat back and slowly raked his fingers through his hair. Then he said, "Maybe we need to pray about this, Forrest. You've been under enormous stress since the funeral, and we both know stress is a killer."

Forrest shook his head. "I know what stress is, Bret, but this is something different. I just wish you could understand where I'm coming from. I don't think I'm being irrational when I tell you there's something about this that's not natural."

Bret was silent for a long moment, then a thought hit him. "Okay, if this is not 'natural' as you say, then it must be supernatural. Maybe it all relates to Wilbur somehow. His disappearance...resurrection...whatever. Which brings me to the thing I wanted to share with you."

"The startling news?"

"Yeah, that."

"Is it just natural, Bret?" Forrest asked with a weak smile.

"I don't know, but it strikes me as something sinister at the least."

"Supernatural, sinister. I think you're beginning to sound like me telling you about that *presence*. But go on, tell me what is so startling."

"First, let me ask you this: Did the chief mention anything to you about two men in black?" Bret probed.

"What?"

"Two men in black who came late to the funeral and left early."

"No, he never mentioned them. Why?"

"And you didn't notice them at the funeral either?"

"No—and what's it got to do with anything?"

"I noticed them, Forrest. I thought maybe they were relatives or friends of the Templetons. They were dressed oddly and left at the same time that Wilbur rose from—"

"The dead, Bret? Are we back to that?"

Bret nodded slowly. "We can't seem to get away from it, can we?"

"I can; but you keep bringing it up. So, what if Russell hired them to make sure the impostor was silenced once he fled from the funeral. I don't see anything startling about that; it seems to fit right in with my theory that Russell is behind this whole thing."

"Possibly."

"Most likely, knowing him."

"But what if...what if the men in black have something to do with the presence you're feeling?

"Oh, God, Bret! First you don't seem to believe me, then you dump this on me."

"I'm just thinking as I'm speaking, trying to link things together. Maybe all of this is supernatural, Forrest. But, why?"

"You tell me, Bret," Forrest shook his head. "You're the one with the answers for this stuff, not me. What are you suggesting? That the guys in black are aliens?"

"Not aliens, Forrest. Either angels or demons."

Drops of sweat began to form in the creases of Forrest's face. He reached for his handkerchief and noticed tremoring in his hands.

CHAPTER SIXTEEN

The Templeton house was in a poor section of town and was suffering from years of neglect. Russell had no interest in its upkeep, and Alice had no necessary skills. Situated on a barren hill just at the edge of town, the house seemed much larger than it was and had an eerie presence, like it was alive. Alive—but diseased. People avoided going near it, not only because of Russell, but because it appeared haunted. The rutted driveway was chiseled with scars from thunderstorms and winter ice.

Alice seldom ventured out after Wilbur's death and Russell's departure. Bret worried that her withdrawal would eventually ruin her already fragile health. He wondered whether Russell had deprived her of food, given her gaunt appearance, and he was sure she hadn't eaten much in days. She hadn't been in church for two Sundays—another concern since she seldom missed. The fellowship had been a lifeline for her and for Wilbur—an escape from Russell's abuse.

"I'm going to see Alice," Bret announced to Laura, "and I want you to go with me. I'm concerned that she's going to perish if she doesn't come out of herself."

"People deal with grief in different ways, Bret; you know that," Laura responded. "But, sure, I'll go with you. Do you think Russell's been back since he left her?"

"That's what I want to know. Rumor has it that he's living with Cherie Loman. She has an apartment over the pharmacy.

From what I hear, she's pretty wild, which would make her good company for Russell."

"She's new in town, isn't she?"

"Fairly; I think she moved up from somewhere down south about six months ago."

"No kids or other attachments, I assume?"

"I don't know much about her; only what some people at church have said, but it appears she's living alone—or had been."

"Working?"

"At the bank; she's a teller. I've seen her there a few times. Kind of a tough looking woman, dark hair, probably early thirties, with penetrating eyes that seem to look right through you. I guess you could say she's attractive in an odd way."

"Russell's type, then."

"So it would seem."

"I wonder what she sees in him, Bret; he's not exactly God's gift to women," Laura said mockingly.

"He's a rogue—maybe they're a match. Can you be ready in ten minutes? I feel an urgency to see Alice."

"What if he's there—Russell?"

"The truck will be there if he is, and we'll just drive by."

"He's going to kill somebody someday, Bret. I just feel it." Laura shuddered.

"Well, let's just hope it's not Alice. I'm sure she'd be a likely target if that someday comes. Who knows how many times he may have threatened to kill her anyway?"

"And Forrest, too," Laura said. "He absolutely hates the man!"

"It's that generational stuff that's festered for years. Amazing how that carries over."

"Hmm...," Laura nodded.

"I'll start the car and back it out of the garage; are you about ready?"

"...just need to grab my purse and a light jacket. I'll meet you out front."

———— ◦ ————

RUSSELL'S TRUCK WASN'T THERE; THE old Buick he'd left for Alice was parked in the driveway.

She must be home. "No truck—that's a good sign. I'm gonna turn the car around and leave it at the bottom of the driveway; we can walk up. It looks like it could rain again, and I don't want the car stuck up there in the mud. Grab the umbrella in the back seat."

"Shouldn't we pray first, Bret?"

"My thoughts exactly, Laura; no telling what we might find."

The trek up the driveway was about a hundred yards. Bret wondered how any vehicle could maneuver through the furrows in the hardened soil without wrecking the undercarriage. The house seemed to sigh as they reached the path at the top of the hill that led to the front porch. At the door, Bret rapped loudly and waited. No answer. He rapped again. Still no sound.

"Laura, try looking through the porch window. I'm gonna knock again; she could be sleeping or showering."

Laura moved to the side of the porch and peered inside. "I can't see a thing, Bret; it's too dark inside, and the window's filthy."

"I'll try the door to see if it's locked," Bret said, turning the knob.

"I don't have a good feeling about this, Bret," Laura said, moving to his side and reaching for his arm.

Bret put his arm around her and felt her tremble. "Did you bring your cell phone?"

"It's in my purse, in the car."

"I left mine in the car, too, or we could call her."

"We should have done that first, Bret."

"I thought of that, but I didn't want to give her the chance to refuse a visit. I thought this way would be better."

The wind had picked up, and the clouds were now threatening rain.

"One more try, then we'll leave." Bret knocked a third time. "Alice!" he yelled. "It's me—Bret Crossman! Laura and I would like to talk to you."

Silence...then a faint stirring and shuffling sound.

"Pastor Crossman?" a weak voice responded.

"Yes, Alice, it's Laura and me. We want to talk with you."

"Just a minute."

Just as Alice opened the door, thunder boomed in the distance and large drops of rain pelted the ground.

Slowly, suspiciously, Alice opened the door.

What Bret and Laura saw made them sick. The house was strewn with debris, dirty clothes, and half-eaten food. Alice wore a wrinkled nightgown which drooped on her shoulders; the overall effect matched the miserable look on her face. The house smelled of a pungent uncleanness which made it difficult to breath.

"My God, Alice," Laura said, rushing to her side and gently embracing her. "What on earth..."

Alice didn't speak, but burst into tears and rested her head on Laura's shoulder.

"Bret, we should have been here sooner!" Laura said. "I can't believe this."

Bret shook his head. "...totally my fault; I've been too distracted with all that's going on. Alice, I'm so sorry—I had no idea."

Alice looked up for a moment. "It's not your fault, Pastor."

"But we should have known," Laura interrupted. "We could have had someone from the church come over."

"No, no," Alice insisted. "It wouldn't have worked; I wanted to be alone. Besides, no one could have known what Russell might do. I don't blame anyone."

"Well, we're here to help you now; what can we do? Do you have any food?" Laura asked, approaching the refrigerator.

"I've had no appetite, Mrs. Crossman, not since Russell left. It's been a week now."

"Has he been back at all?" Bret asked.

"No. And I hope he never comes back."

The refrigerator was bare except for some spoiled milk and a few uncovered dishes of dried out food.

"You have to start eating," Laura took Alice's hands in hers. "Will you come to our house for a few days?"

"Oh, no!" Alice said. "I couldn't leave here...I belong here."

"But you need help," Bret interrupted. "You can't just isolate yourself like this; let's sit down and talk."

Laura moved slowly toward the window to open a curtain and let in some light. The rain had stopped, although the clouds were still heavy and threatening. Just as she turned to join Bret and Alice, she noticed a vehicle stop at the bottom of the driveway. "Looks like we've got company," she said.

"What?" Bret said, moving to the window.

"A blue pickup truck," Laura responded.

"Is that anyone you know, Alice?"

Alice gasped and covered her wide-open mouth. "It's him! It's Russell! That's his truck!"

"What the—" Bret said.

"Are you sure it's him, Alice? Maybe you should come and look." Laura motioned to Alice, who slowly approached the window almost as if she didn't want to verify what she suspected to be true.

"There's no doubt it's his truck but what does he want? I don't think he'll come in as long as you folks are here."

"Well," Bret said, "we can't go anywhere as long as he has us blocked in."

"Should you go down, Bret?" Laura asked.

"I'll give it a few more minutes, and if he doesn't leave, I'll go down. We need our cell phones anyway; that gives me an excuse to go to the car."

"Be careful," Alice cautioned. "I'm sure he doesn't like you being here."

Ten minutes passed and Russell hadn't moved his truck. Bret figured that Russell was testing him to see if he would come down and confront him.

I'm going down. He could be there all day.

"What are you thinking, Bret?" Laura asked with a worried look on her face.

"I'm going down; just cover me in prayer."

"He's baiting you, Bret; that's what he wants you to do...don't you agree, Alice?"

Alice nodded. "Who knows what he's thinking; he's so unpredictable."

Bret turned suddenly and addressed Alice: "Do you have binoculars?"

"Binoculars?" Alice asked, puzzled.

"Yeah, I think there's someone in the truck with him, but I can't be sure."

Alice went to a small cabinet in the living room where she kept the binoculars and returned a moment later, handing them to Bret.

"I was right," Bret said. "There's someone in there with him, and guess what?"

"What?" Laura asked.

"It's a woman."

"His girlfriend!" Alice cried. "The nerve of that man to bring her here with him and just sit there! Give me the binoculars."

Bret handed them to Alice as he stepped toward the doorway. "I won't be long, but if he tries anything, don't come down; I don't want you involved."

"If he tries anything, I'll call the police," Laura said.

"Well, you may have to if things escalate," Bret responded.

Alice threw the binoculars on a nearby table as if she was getting rid of a disease. "She deserves him, whoever she is."

"Would you take him back?" Laura asked, wishing she hadn't.

"Let me put it this way," Alice said, frowning. "I would sooner let a rattlesnake in before him."

Bret swung the door open and glanced at the sky. A swift breeze was now blowing, and a mist of rain was falling. He went back in to get the umbrella. "It'll suffice as a weapon if I need one," he said with a tense laugh.

"Bret!" Laura protested. "That's not funny."

———•— ○ —•———

THE DRIVEWAY WAS SLICK WITH mud and shallow pools of rainwater. Bret cautiously made his way down the hill and toward the pickup. When he was about halfway there, Russell emerged from the driver's side of the vehicle and approached Bret. Sensing a confrontation, Bret tightened his grip on the umbrella. Both men stopped with just a few feet separating them. Bret felt his pulse quicken; a twinge of fear seized him. Alice's words *he's so unpredictable* flashed in his mind. He'd never confronted another man face to face whom he considered to be a personal threat.

But now...

Russell crossed his arms and glared at Bret in defiance. "Looks like you're blocked in, doesn't it?"

"Just going to the car to get my cell phone," Bret replied, averting Russell's eyes, and taking a step forward.

"What are you doing visiting my wife?" Russell said threateningly, stepping in front of Bret to block his way.

"She's a member of my church and just lost her son—she's needy."

"She's lost her husband, too; did she tell you that?"

"I was aware of that," Bret said, trying to sidestep Russell.

"About the boy," Russell again blocked Bret's way and moved a step closer. "I want to know about the boy; where's his body?"

Bret gripped the umbrella with both hands and positioned it across his body. "I have no idea where the body is; there's an ongoing search."

"I think you know where he is, along with Forrest. You're in it together." Russell jabbed a finger in Bret's chest.

The gesture startled Bret momentarily, and he drew back a step but sensed a growing anger at the accusation. "You couldn't be more wrong, Russell."

"Wrong, preacher? I couldn't be more wrong? Maybe I know things you don't."

"Such as?"

"I have sources you know nothing of, and I would watch my step if I were you—and your pretty wife."

Bret felt a rush of adrenaline surge through his body as he lunged at Russell, pushing the umbrella against his chest. Russell lurched backward, lost his balance, and fell awkwardly to the ground in time to hear "I have sources, too, and your threats don't intimidate me! Now get out of my way while I go to my car—and get your damned truck out of the way, too!"

No one...no one had ever stood up to Russell, let alone knocked him to the ground. He attempted to get back on his feet, still looking bewildered. The passenger door to the truck opened and a tall, thin woman with raven hair emerged.

"You'll pay for this!" she said angrily as she knelt to help Russell up.

———— ✦ ◦ ✦ ————

"Holy cow, Alice! Bret just knocked your husband to the ground!"

"He what?"

"Knocked him down; come over here and see."

Alice rushed to the window just in time to see Russell's girlfriend help him up. "Serves him right, but your husband should be careful now. Russell won't take kindly to this; mark my words. He will seek revenge. That's what motivates him—hatred and revenge."

CHAPTER SEVENTEEN

S am Stone had Russell called in for questioning per Forrest Fields's request. He dreaded having to face him and was disturbed by his unruly behavior. Russell's life seemed charmed in an evil sense. He always beat the system by the skin of his teeth—going free when he should have been in jail. Sam wondered what kind of encounter this would be.

The desk clerk, Lisa Doran, ushered Russell into Sam's office. "Have a seat," Sam said as sternly as possible.

Russell jerked a wooden chair around and straddled it, facing Sam. "Why am I here?" he said in a threatening tone, putting Sam on the defensive.

Sam didn't answer immediately, giving himself the time he needed to achieve calm. He shuffled some papers on his desk, then wrote a few nonsense words on his pad. "For questioning," he finally said.

"About what?"

"Your son's body."

"What do you mean, my son's body; why haven't you found it?"

"Forrest Fields—"

"Knows where my son's body is!" Russell shouted, jumping to his feet. "Why isn't he here for questioning?"

"Sit down!" Sam shouted. "He's next."

"Well, let me tell you something, Sam. I've got a crime to report, and you'd better be calling in Bret Crossman and charging him with assault! I'm pressing charges against him so be prepared to arrest him."

"What? Bret Crossman...assault?" Sam's face twisted in disbelief.

"You heard correct. He assaulted me with a weapon on my property earlier today—he knocked me down."

"The Bret I know wouldn't assault anyone," Sam said, shaking his head.

"Call him in—and see if the good pastor denies it. He was totally out of control and took me by surprise; the man's nuts. Better yet, go find him—and put him in cuffs. He could've killed me."

Sam was stunned. Never in his life would he have thought Bret Crossman would be capable of assault—and was what Russell was claiming even true? He rocked back in his chair and tapped his pen on his desk, trying to think of what to say.

"Call him in!" Russell demanded. "See if he denies it; I've got a witness."

Sam wanted nothing more than to get rid of the bully sitting before him, but he had to question Bret. "Who's the witness?" he said.

"Cherie Loman."

"Who's she?"

"Why does it matter who she is? She was there at the time and will swear to what I've said."

"Never heard of her," Sam said. "Not familiar with the Loman name."

"She moved here several months ago. She's a teller at the bank."

"Oh," Sam said, "I guess I remember seeing her name card once when I was in the bank. Last name of Loman, you say?"

"Correct."

"Why was she with you when you were *assaulted* by Bret?"

"It's none of your business why she was with me."

"I'll call him in; but I'm also going to interview the witness. Was there anyone else who may have seen what happened?"

"No one else was around; it was raining, and the ground was wet—that's why I slipped—"

"I thought you said you were assaulted with a weapon and knocked down."

"I slipped after I was hit; then I went down," Russell corrected himself.

"What was the weapon, Russell? A baseball bat or a crowbar...something like that?"

Russell hesitated before answering. "It was—an umbrella."

Sam had to restrain himself from laughing. The big bully being "assaulted" with an umbrella by a minister; he would have given anything to have seen the purported assault. "An umbrella?"

"Not just an umbrella—a large umbrella."

"Oh, a large one. Well, that makes all the difference, doesn't it, Russell?"

"You can kill someone with an umbrella, Sam. You should know that!" Russell shot back.

"Did he poke you with the end of it?"

"No, he grabbed both ends with his hands and forced it into my chest." Russell held both ends of an imaginary umbrella and thrust it forward.

"So, he didn't try to jab you with it like a knife, right?"

"Look!" Russell shouted, "what difference does it make? The man assaulted me, and that's a punishable crime!"

"...strange that he wouldn't be using the umbrella to keep the rain off himself."

"It had let up by then."

"Well," Sam said, "you're right. If he pushed you down with it, that would constitute an assault. Did you suffer any injury?"

"I think I wrenched my elbow trying to brace myself when I fell."

"Did you get it checked out?"

"I will; it hurts even now...may have sprained it."

"Right, well, get me a doctor's report on that, and I'll call Bret in."

"And arrest him, right?"

Sam rose quickly from his desk, "That's my decision; not yours." He felt certain if what Russell was saying was true, Bret's actions were not unprovoked.

CHAPTER EIGHTEEN

C herie Loman wasn't sure if she was sleeping or not. Maybe half asleep, half awake, but she felt a presence in her room. She sat up abruptly—scared, trembling.

"Who's there?" she called out.

The voice wasn't that of a human.

"Prelude? Is that you?"

A figure she recognized appeared suddenly, illuminating the room.

"I didn't call for you," Cherie said, still trembling.

"But I am here anyway. I have information for you."

"Information?" Cherie asked. "What kind of information?"

"A plan to destroy the preacher."

"Bret Crossman?"

"Correct."

"How?" The thought intrigued her.

"With false accusations."

"Who are the accusers and what are the accusations?"

"It involves you."

"Me?" Cherie felt herself stiffening. "Why me?"

"You are going to accuse him."

"Of what...he hasn't done anything to me, just Russell."

"You will attempt to seduce him, and I will weaken him and create havoc in his marriage. He won't realize what's happening."

Seduce him? I find him repulsive. "Seduce him? I can't stand being around the man. And what about Russell?"

"Russell is weak and a coward at heart. I can deal with him."

Cherie felt drops of sweat forming on her brow. The trembling grew worse. "Why should I try to seduce him? I don't get it."

"It has to do with Wilbur Templeton. I will explain it later. Bret Crossman and his marriage have to be destroyed."

Cherie sat back on her bed, confused—but, in a strange way, energized. She hated anything religious, and the thought of bringing down Bret Crossman stirred her. And Russell? She'd noticed him whimpering when he was knocked down by Bret. Clearly, Bret had more machismo. Yes, she'd also noticed that he didn't back down when Russell confronted him; she liked that. And when Russell didn't fight back? Well, that disturbed her. A plan to bring down Bret Crossman? She was good at seduction, and more than one man had fallen at her feet wounded and pathetic. She could smell weakness and Russell had begun to smell. "How are you going to deal with Russell?" she asked.

"Leave that to me; you will see later. He is not needed." Prelude's voice echoed ominously and seemed to bounce off the walls of Cherie's bedroom.

"When do I start?" Cherie asked.

"When it is time. Much must be done to set the stage. First, I want you to testify in favor of Crossman when you are called in as a witness regarding the incident at Russell's house. That will be the beginning of the end for Russell."

Cherie thought for a moment about the plan. She liked controlling men, and Bret would be a unique challenge for her. She could look beyond the religious junk if it meant bringing him to his knees. Yes, she could do it—she would do it. "But what about the funeral guy?" she asked.

"Forrest Fields?"

"Yes, him."

"He's a minor player—not worth much time. But I can arrange his demise, too, if he gets in the way."

"Not using me!" Cherie objected. "The thought is disgusting."

"I have other ways of dealing with him if necessary. You would play no part."

"Thank God," Cherie sighed.

"Don't you ever mention that name!" Prelude raged. "You must be clear; that name is vile! Do you hear me? Vile!"

Cherie recoiled at the sound of Prelude's outburst. "Never," she quavered. "Never again will I utter that name."

"We are on the same side; am I right, Cherie?"

"Same side...yes, the same side."

"Good!" Prelude said. "And now I will leave. But I will be back to assess progress in our little plan."

And he was gone as quickly as he had appeared. Cherie sat stupefied for several moments wondering if what she had just witnessed was real. Then she judged it had to be. But seducing Bret Crossman? She fell asleep thinking of ways to get at him. He must have his weaknesses...and she had her ways. Then the accusations would come. This would not only destroy him; it would also destroy his church.

CHAPTER NINETEEN

I *don't need this*, Sam Stone asserted to no one but himself. *I've got to call in Bret Crossman on charges of assault...and the witness—who is Cherie Loman? A teller at the bank. A reliable witness? She could just lie to cover for Russell.* He pushed himself away from his desk and started pacing. He had no choice; he knew he had to call Bret, but how he hated Russell! Nothing good was going to come of this, he was sure. And how would Laura take it? And the church? And the fanatical reporters? They would salivate if they could ruin a small-town church. Still not a single clue of where Wilbur's body was. Not a single clue! It was like he'd just disappeared. Maybe Forrest did have him cremated. Maybe Russell had him buried in his cellar. And...maybe...no, that was impossible. Sam was into hard evidence and facts—not fantasy, notwithstanding what Bret had claimed.

"Call Bret Crossman," he told Lisa. "And tell him I just need to ask him a few questions. Be as vague as possible and don't mention the assault charges." Sam figured if the desk clerk called, there would be less of an opportunity to ask questions—and he didn't want to confront Bret over the phone.

"Right away," Lisa responded.

———◦———

"WHAT'S IT ABOUT?" BRET ASKED, when the clerk called.

"He didn't elaborate; ...just said he wanted to talk to you. When can you come in?"

"I suppose sometime this afternoon—say around three o'clock."

"I'll tell him."

"I'll be there." Bret hung up but had a suspicion that it was about the incident with Russell, and he knew Russell would spin it to his advantage. And the crazy, threatening woman. Who was she? He told Laura he was going to meet with Sam that afternoon and to be prepared if it had to do with Russell.

"I saw what happened, Bret. Do you want me to come with you?"

"Let me meet with Sam first; it may not have to do with the confrontation we had."

"Well, I'm on standby if you need me."

"Thanks, Laura. Hopefully that won't be necessary."

"I HATE TO DO THIS, Bret," Sam said haltingly, "but I have to question you about an alleged assault charge."

Bret drew a quick breath. "Does this have to do with the incident at the Templeton house?"

"Yeah, Russell was here a short time ago, and he brought it up. He said you assaulted him with an umbrella, and he had a witness to prove it. He also said he was injured after you shoved him."

"Yeah, a witness who practically threatened to claw my eyes out! And no, the only thing injured was Russell's pride. It wasn't like I beat him up, for heaven's sake."

"He's filed charges."

"Have you talked to the witness?" Bret asked. "Laura saw it too, if you need her side of the story."

"I will question them both, but first I want to hear your explanation of what happened," Sam said.

"Okay, I'll admit I was ticked off at him because he kept blocking me from going to my car, and he was poking his finger in my chest, egging me on."

"And then what happened?"

"I had an umbrella; I took it by the ends with both hands to push him out of the way. Then he slipped in the mud and went down."

"Good Lord," Sam sighed, "and that was the assault?"

"That was it. I think he lost his balance and went down. I admit, it was kind of satisfying. Laura and I had been at his house to console Alice when he drove up and blocked us in. He had a woman with him—the one I mentioned—and she jumped out of Russell's truck and threatened me."

"I don't suspect any judicial officer is going to uphold the charge, Bret; it seems pretty flimsy to me."

"But what if Russell produces a doctor's report of injury? He's probably already bruised himself on purpose or smashed his elbow on something to make it look like an injury."

"No doubt he's that crazy," Sam said. "I wouldn't put anything past him."

"When are you going to call in the other witness?" Bret asked.

"Cherie Loman? She's supposed to be here in about an hour."

"And she's going to claim I mauled the guy."

"Whatever. I didn't notice any visible marks on Russell when he was in, and he sort of favored the elbow, but hadn't had a doctor look at it."

"So, do I spend the night in jail?" Bret said, crossing his arms and smiling at Sam.

"It doesn't appear to rise to that level," Sam said, grinning. "I want to hear what the Loman woman has to say first, so be prepared if she corroborates what Russell claims happened."

"Any other questions, Sam?" Bret asked. "If not, I'll go let Laura know. She might have to do damage control for the church if Russell or the witness start running their mouths."

"And, Bret," Sam said, standing and putting his hand on Bret's shoulder. "I'm so sorry about this. Between you and me, I wished you'd really decked him if the charges hold. At least it would really warrant an arrest."

———— ✦ ◐ ✦ ————

CHERIE LOMAN WAS ON TIME for her meeting with Sam. She was dressed in stylish jeans with a tight-fitting blouse and ample makeup tastefully applied. She had a presence about her that, not including her appearance, made a person take notice. It wasn't easily described but was uneasily felt. And Sam felt that presence as he withdrew slightly when she was ushered into his office. She approached him and held out her hand.

"I'm Cherie Loman," she said, with an engaging smile.

"Chief Stone," Sam answered. "Please have a seat."

She sat, continuing to smile, though less obviously. Sam had to divert his eyes momentarily, which he was sure she had noticed. Regaining his focus, he began: "I had you called in regarding the incident that occurred recently at the Templeton residence between Russell Templeton and Bret Crossman. Charges for assault have been filed by Mr. Templeton. He alleges that Mr. Crossman assaulted him, pushing him to the ground, and causing an injury to his elbow. Mr. Templeton stated that you were a witness to the incident. I'd like to hear what you have to say regarding what transpired."

"Gladly," Cherie said with an air of self-possession. "I was a witness to what happened, but my observations are entirely contrary to Mr. Templeton's."

Sam sat stunned, expecting a tirade against Bret. "Go on," he said.

"Mr. Templeton, Russell, was the aggressor. If there was an assault, I would say it was on his part—not Mr. Crossman's."

Sam cleared his throat and took a deep breath, still shocked at the strange testimony of the even more bizarre woman sitting before him. "How so?" he asked.

"Mr. Crossman was trying to get to his car to retrieve...I believe it was a cell phone, when Russell blocked his way, not letting him by and verbally threatening him. He had previously blocked the driveway so that Mr. Crossman couldn't move his vehicle. Russell then began jabbing his finger into Mr. Crossman's chest—which is really when the assault began. I think Mr. Crossman was only trying to defend himself at that point."

"But didn't Mr. Crossman knock Russ—Mr. Templeton down?"

Cherie burst into laughter. "Are you kidding? That shove wasn't hard enough to knock over a child. Russell just lost his balance and fell into the mud."

"No injury?" Sam asked.

"Injury? Only to the man's ego. Heck, no, there was no injury to his elbow. He faked it."

Sam sat for a long moment before speaking, still unsure of why Russell's star witness had turned on him. The assault charge would surely be dropped as baseless. But that didn't mean Russell was free from seeking revenge—and maybe revenge against Cherie. "Is there anything else you want to add at this point, Ms. Loman?"

"Not really," Cherie said, "and please call me Cherie."

Sam stood and walked toward her. The presence seemed stronger than ever when he took her hand to thank her for coming. "I'll contact you soon," Sam said.

"Please do, Chief," Cherie said with a smile as she started to walk out of his office. Then she stopped and turned around. "By the way," she said, "do you know how I can get in touch with Mr. Crossman? I owe him an apology."

"I can give you the church's number, but I'm not at liberty to give out his personal number."

"That's fine; I think I'll just wait until Sunday and meet him at the church."

"Right," was all Sam could think to say. He stood and watched as she left his office, then looked out a window facing the parking lot to get a description of her car. But she never entered the parking area, and he never saw if she left with someone or just walked away.

———⊷ ◯ ⊶———

BRET'S CELL PHONE CHIMED. "HELLO," he said, "this is Bret Crossman." He recognized the chief's voice. "What's up, Sam?"

"I've just had the strangest encounter with the woman who threatened you at Russell's house."

"Oh, why was it so strange?"

"She threw Russell under the bus."

"What? I thought she was pretty tight with him."

"Apparently not. And here's the kicker; she said she's coming to your church on Sunday to apologize to you. Can you believe that?"

"Hmm...why the sudden turn around?"

"You got me, but one thing's for certain; the charges against you will be dropped based on her testimony."

"So, I'm free then; is that what you're saying?"

"Free as a bird—but not necessarily safe."

"From her, you mean?"

"No, from Russell. When he finds out she's blown his story open, he's going to erupt. No telling what he might do to her...or to you."

"I think I can handle him, Sam."

"No doubt. Ms. Loman implied that he was the aggressor, and he'd assaulted you—not the other way around. An odd thing, too; she had this unusual manner about her." The chief massaged his scalp at the temporal lobe area and slowly shook his head back and forth before continuing. "She just didn't seem normal."

"Well," Bret said, "I can't wait to meet her, Sam. Maybe she needs the Lord, you suppose?"

"And maybe...well, who knows? But she may be in danger when Russell gets word of her betrayal."

"And Alice, too," Bret added. "He might turn on her if his lady friend kicks him out."

"I'd be surprised if she hasn't already kicked him out."

"Probably, based on what she shared with you. So, he won't have any option but to go back to his own house. Are you gonna keep an eye on him?"

"There's not really much I can do at this point; he hasn't broken any laws."

"Yet..."

"Right, but he likely will, so I'm on standby if something does happen."

CHAPTER TWENTY

When Cherie arrived at her apartment, she gathered Russell's few belongings and put them in a large trash bag. She then placed the bag outside her door, locked herself inside, and went to bed.

On his way to her apartment, Russell lost control of his truck, skidded off the road, and hit a tree head-on. The sheriff's deputy stated that he was likely killed on impact. The accident investigator estimated the truck's speed was not excessive. Russell wasn't wearing a seat belt, and the force of the impact drove his body partially through the windshield.

Prelude appeared to Cherie that night and announced the news of Russell's death. "He needed to be removed. I forced his truck off the road."

Cherie's face turned pale. As much as she was starting to despise Russell for his weakness, she wasn't prepared for that startling news. She looked apprehensively at the creature standing before her, mesmerized by the potential of its power. She wondered what this other-worldly creature would do next. Although she was used to being in control and having a power advantage, she now felt impotent—not just physically, but mentally, emotionally. She tried to speak but couldn't. So, she waited... waited for Prelude.

It seemed to her as if his appearance had grown brighter when he spoke of Russell's death, as though that death had transferred energy to him. And Prelude's eyes fastened on her with an intensity that made her feel naked and unclean. She drew the bed covers over her to protect herself from his gaze.

"And now my plan is to remove Bret Crossman. And you will help me. First, I will attack his marriage, then I will destroy his church."

Cherie felt an increasing intensity of pleasure as Prelude spoke. Was he transferring energy to her that he had drawn while speaking of Russell's death? The energy was intoxicating, beyond the effects of mere alcohol or drugs, but expanding into territory unknown and yet to be explored.

Prelude spoke, "I will enhance your power of seduction...and the preacher will yield to you. He will try to resist, but after I've isolated his wife, he will fall. That will be the end of his church."

"And...and what about me?" Cherie asked, thrilled with anticipation.

"What would you like?" Prelude asked. "More power over men? Success? Wealth?"

"All of those!" she responded.

"A little at a time, Cherie. You have invited me into your life, which can reap endless rewards for you."

Endless? Cherie thought. *What can endless mean?* "And if I continue to yield to you more and more?"

Prelude smiled. "I think that will be inevitable, Cherie; something that will be so natural to you."

So natural...so natural... "And why can't I yield totally to you now?" she inquired, looking directly at the shining creature standing in front of her.

"Because we must first build trust, Cherie, as with any relationship."

Those were his final words. He vanished as quickly as he had appeared. Cherie sat on the edge of her bed sensing a joy

114

she had never known. In two days, she would be attending Bret Crossman's church with Prelude's assignment to seduce him. She couldn't wait. Prelude had promised enhanced seductive powers, whatever that meant. And she did find Bret strangely appealing after the encounter with Russell despite her outburst against him. Her delight was in seducing; it was a game, fun, recreation.

To Prelude, it was something different. Something sinister... deadly...

⎯⎯⊷⎯ ◯ ⎯⊶⎯⎯

CHERIE WOKE AFTER THREE HOURS of sleep. The encounter with Prelude rushed into her mind. She felt violated, unclean. Was it real? She had to listen to the local news to see if there were reports of an accident. She turned on the radio next to her bed and waited for the news at the half hour. *The Foylestown Sheriff's Department is investigating a fatal accident involving a single vehicle and the reported death of Russell Templeton.* And there it was, as clear as the breaking day.

"My God!" Cherie said aloud. "It's true; the man is dead. A shower—I've got to get a shower to rid myself of this awful feeling on my skin."

What had she done? She had taken a gamble, and it now looked like she'd lost control—the one thing she was used to having. Yet she had anything but control when that *thing* was around. She had read about possession and had seen several movies showing the effects of demonic control, but she... she hadn't given herself to Prelude. Or had she? And was he a demon or something else? She shivered despite the hot shower water splashing all over her. Yes, she wanted to bring Bret Crossman to his knees—and the stupid funeral director—but

Prelude seemed bent on utter destruction. Was he responsible for Russell's accident like he said? Did he have that kind of power? If so, what could it mean to her life if she failed to execute his plans? And what about Wilbur Templeton? Prelude intimated that he knew Wilbur's whereabouts. He was dead. And the body was somewhere...yes, but where? And now she was snared in a cosmic, other-worldly web. Thrilling? Yes...and terrifying.

FOYLESTOWN WAS CONSUMED WITH THE news of Russell's death, but there was little remorse. A cancer had been excised, but there was a collective guilt among some of the townspeople who had secretly wished for his demise. The accident scene was grisly. It was odd that there was no sign of elevated blood alcohol content in Russell's body. He hadn't been drinking that night. People who had talked with him said he seemed pensive and subdued, like something was on his mind. They found it out of character for him since he was usually testy, especially if he'd been drinking. The accident investigator denied that speed was a factor.

No alcohol, no speed—but brutal impact.

CHAPTER TWENTY-ONE

F orrest Fields shook his head in disbelief. His old nemesis was dead. There went the lawsuit, there went the vengeance—and where was Wilbur? With Russell gone, his son's body might never be found. Would anyone even care? Hadn't the town suffered enough trauma in the last several weeks? Then there was Alice...poor Alice. *Good Lord, how much more could she take?* And now he would have to do her husband's funeral. He suddenly hated his business. Sure, it paid well, and his was the only funeral home in town, but he had no understudy. Death was wearing on him, even though he'd become indifferent to handling corpses years ago. Just the thought of doing Russell's funeral sickened him. He certainly couldn't fake remorse or comfort Alice—if she even needed it. The funeral would be perfunctory. Russell was no God-fearer, so that meant Forrest would have to conduct the service himself, although Bret Crossman might consent to doing it.

Forrest even thought of attending Bret's church sometime soon. Maybe a little exposure to religion would help settle his fatigued brain. And he wouldn't be the only visitor; someone else was planning on attending the next Sunday morning service.

—◦—

CHERIE LOMAN DECIDED TO ARRIVE early in hopes of seeing Bret for a few minutes before church started.

Seduce him...

That's what Prelude had ordered her to do, but she now had some apprehension following the news of Russell's death. She guessed that was what Prelude wanted to maximize his control over her. If she could seduce the pastor, the church would be in turmoil; Bret's marriage would be ruined.

What to wear, she wondered. *A short skirt with a tight blouse. Just the right amount of makeup with a sensual perfume.* Prelude had said he would give her enhanced seductive powers if she obeyed him. She wondered how that would work since she was already pretty good at it unaided.

The thought of additional power intrigued her, and she felt a sudden rush in her body—something she'd never felt before. She looked at herself in the mirror. There was something different...something about her eyes had changed. There was energy emanating from them. But to destroy a marriage and a church? She was hooked by Prelude and feared for her life if she didn't do his bidding. Would he kill her? She felt her body tremble. What kind of being was he? Though at first she thought of him as a friendly spirit guide, she was now convinced otherwise. She had allowed him to take control of her unwittingly...it had been just an experiment, a game of sorts, but it was now something dreadful and menacing.

She decided she would share about Prelude with the meditation group she attended. She hadn't said a word to anyone except Russell, and with him now gone, she had to make a disclosure. No one else had mentioned a similar experience, so she hoped they would understand her. But what if they thought her crazy? She had no proof of anything.

Yeah, well, I met this alien and he's given me power, but he seems to own me, and I'm afraid, and he wants me to seduce a pastor and ruin a marriage and a church, and other stuff—so what do you all think?

118

Yep, that would fly. Everyone would understand and give her advice. Others undoubtedly had had similar encounters...routine stuff, all part of the cosmic game. The entities had no real power anyway; they were guides or playmates. Good guys.

But that night, Prelude came. He warned her not to share anything with the group—it was just between the two of them. And what was her reward? she had asked. More power, Prelude answered—and wealth through power. No longer just a measly bank teller, but leisure, pleasure, whatever she wanted was within reach. All that was required of her was to carry out his plans.

Tomorrow...tomorrow was Sunday—and she couldn't sleep.

———•—○—•———

LAURA CROSSMAN COULDN'T SLEEP EITHER. Something was wrong; she knew it instinctively, and her mind wouldn't shut down. She had keen intuition which almost always proved right, and it usually concerned Bret or the church. She woke Bret at 3:00 a.m.

"I can't sleep; I feel this pressure against me, Bret. I don't like it."

"Pressure?" Bret groaned.

"Yeah, pressing against my mind and emotions like something awful is going to happen."

Bret rolled over in bed toward her, fighting irritation. "Nothing specific?"

"No, but you know this has happened before. It's like God's warning us."

Bret yawned and stretched. "Laura, it's really late and church is tomorrow; maybe you're just anxious because of Russell's death and how it will impact the church."

"It's not just that, Bret! I know something major is going to happen."

"But you have no idea what, right? It seems like God would be more specific than that."

"You read the reports about Russell's accident. There was no alcohol involved and speed wasn't a factor. Both of those things are odd, especially for Russell."

"Suicide, Laura; it was probably suicide."

"I don't buy that for a minute, Bret! He was suing Forrest, and he stood to gain a fortune."

Laura threw the bed covers aside and reached for the light on her nightstand. "I'm getting up, Bret."

"Oh, Lord, Laura, whatever. I just need to get some sleep. I'll see you in the morning."

"You don't believe me, do you?" Laura shot back.

"Believe you what? What am I supposed to believe?"

"Oh, never mind! I'll sleep downstairs and won't bother you anymore."

"As you like; now I'm getting some sleep." Bret pulled the bed covers up, hoping he wouldn't stay awake too.

Laura went quietly down the stairs, yet her mind was anything but quiet.

CHAPTER TWENTY-TWO

B ret didn't sleep that night after Laura woke him. That put
him in a sour mood. He struggled out of bed and headed
for the shower, hoping to wash away the negative thoughts he
was having toward her. It didn't work.

Something was wrong, she'd said. Yeah, it sure was, and his
mind wasn't focused on church. He had two hours to make a
mood adjustment.

Laura was still asleep on the couch when he went downstairs, so he plotted.

"Something's terribly wrong!" he said loudly, waking her.

"Wha—what's wrong? Laura asked, startled.

"I'm just reminding you of last night; remember what you said?"

"You're nasty, Bret! I thought somebody died."

"Well, at least you went back to sleep; I've been awake all
night thinking about what you said."

"What did I say that kept you awake?" Laura asked, trying to
rub the sleep from her eyes.

"Are you serious, Laura? You don't remember what you said?"

"Give me a minute to wake up—oh yeah, now I remember!
I did say I felt like something awful was going to happen. Pressure. I remember a lot of pressure against me—like something
crushing me. It was hard to breathe."

"Well, guess what?"

"What?"

"Something awful has happened."

"Oh, no Bret! Tell me; what is it?" Laura sat upright on the couch with a worried look in her eyes. "I hope it's nothing too serious."

"Look at me, Laura!"

She did.

"Look at my eyes."

"Okay."

"Do these eyes look rested to you?"

"Well, not particularly. You've got some dark circles under them."

"Right! Because I've been awake since 3:00 a.m."

"You poor dear—and with church only a few hours away."

"And you don't get the connection?" His voice seemingly rose an octave.

"Uh-uh."

"For heaven's sake, Laura; you woke me in a panic telling me the world was about to end, then you came down here and went to sleep while I was waiting for some kind of cataclysm!"

"You're exaggerating."

Bret put both hands on his head and twisted it back and forth like he was trying to shake his thoughts back to reality. "Okay," he sighed. "I assume you no longer feel the impending doom; is that correct?"

Laura thought for a moment, trying to recapture her feelings from last night. They started coming back to her in sharp images. "I recall very clearly now," she said. "My brain was in a fog for a moment, but yes...yes there was that intense pressure and premonition. You know, like I've had before—that something was going to happen. Something bad."

Bret sat down beside her. "It's bad enough that I didn't sleep, but I wish you could be more specific, Laura."

"Me too, but I don't have specifics, Bret. I just think we should be aware. All I know is that since Wilbur's death and funeral, nothing in Foylestown has been normal. Think about it. First his death was a little strange; then the funeral and not knowing what happened to his body; then your encounter with Russell and his disturbed girlfriend; then Russell getting killed in a freak accident—"

"And you waking with a strangling pressure...,"

"Exactly! Don't you think it's all a little weird?"

"No doubt, it's weird," Bret agreed. "...makes you wonder what's next."

"We should be mindful that something could happen."

"Yeah, something; but what?"

———•— ☾ —•———

Two hours passed quickly, and both were silent heading to church. The parking lot was jammed with cars Bret didn't recognize, and he suspected people would want answers—answers he didn't have. He sighed heavily, almost dreading entering the church. People saw their car pull into the driveway, and a couple of people approached Bret and Laura as they exited the car.

The lack of sleep still hung in Bret's brain as he tried to maintain his composure and speak as politely as he could.

"I'll be addressing Russell's death once we start the service," he said, knowing full well he was as dumbfounded as they and just as curious to discover what happened...or why it happened. It certainly wasn't his job to know details that would come from the investigation, but people still looked to him for answers, especially since it was so soon after Wilbur's disappearance. "Everyone, please, just head into the church, sit and take a few deep breaths; try to achieve calm and stillness."

Laura stayed as close to Bret as she could, not wanting to get isolated and questioned. The pressure started to return, and she wondered if the something she suspected might happen would happen during the service. She fought to keep her mind from imagining the worst.

Just as Bret entered the front door of the church, a woman grabbed his arm from behind. For a moment, he was startled. He stopped and turned to see who it was as Laura continued into the foyer.

"Pastor Crossman," the woman said, "I need to talk to you."

Bret didn't recognize the voice or the face, but sensed something unusual about her. Had he seen her somewhere?

"Please," she insisted, "just a moment with you."

"Is something wrong?" Bret asked. "Can it wait? I really need to get to my office."

"It's urgent," she said, inching closer to him.

"Step next to the wall," he said. "We can talk for a minute over there." He motioned toward a less congested area. "Now, what is it you wanted to say?"

"Do you remember me?"

"You look familiar," he said, searching her face while her eyes seemed to penetrate his. He noticed she was quite attractive, but her demeanor made him feel uncomfortable. He took a step backward. "Should I know you?"

"I'm Cherie Loman, Russell Templeton's girlfriend—or at least I was before the tragic accident."

"Oh," Bret said, feigning concern. "What an unfortunate accident. I'm sorry." It finally clicked that the woman standing in front of him was the same woman who threatened him in Russell's driveway. But she looked remarkably different—and more attractive. Maybe it was because she wasn't screaming at him.

"I thought coming to church might help me; his death was

so sudden and unexpected. Besides, I owe you an apology for being rude to you that day at the Templeton's home."

"No hard feelings on my part," Bret said. "Was there something else bothering you?"

Cherie smiled, "No, nothing other than processing his death and apologizing to you. I was angry that day."

"Yes, you were."

"How can I ever make it up to you?"

"No need to make it up; you've already apologized. I assume you're coming to church to hear what I might say about it; is that right?"

"Well, yes, that; plus I need to get my life straightened out. Would you be willing to counsel me?"

Bret paused before answering her. "I have someone on staff you could see; they're very good at counseling. You can schedule an appointment through the church secretary."

Cherie drew a step closer to Bret. "But I would prefer you."

"Why me?"

"Because you're the pastor; I need pastoral counseling."

Bret glanced at his watch. "Start coming to church first, then I'll let you know. I don't generally counsel anyone who's not a member of the church or at least attends consistently."

"I plan on being here every week," Cherie said, smiling. "I want to get to know you better."

Know me better? Why would she want to get to know me at all, let alone better? "You should get to know the Lord first, Ms. Loman."

"Well, could you help me with that? I don't understand much about faith, but I'm willing to learn...if you don't mind teaching me."

"You mean personally tutor you?"

"Yes."

"I don't do that, but I do group Bible studies each week; you could attend those."

"Would you make an exception for me?" Cherie smiled coyly at him, catching him off guard.

Why does this woman who wanted to kill me a few days ago suddenly want me to personally tutor her?

Cherie continued to smile at Bret, and he saw something in her eyes that was more than curious or inquiring. He looked away abruptly. "Look," he said, "I really have to go; church will be starting soon."

"Will you think about it—about personally teaching me? I'd be uncomfortable in a group."

Bret wasn't sure why but he said, "Okay, I'll think about it."

"Oh, thank you!" Cherie said. "I'll give you my number after church, and you can call me with the details."

"Yeah, sure," Bret said nonchalantly, and walked away to avoid any further conversation with her.

CHAPTER TWENTY-THREE

There were several unexpected visitors in church that Sunday besides Cherie Loman: Sam Stone, Forrest Fields, and others from town attended for the first time ever. People were searching for answers regarding Russell's unusual death and the still unanswered questions regarding Wilbur. Bret wondered why the sudden interest in church. It seemed to him that people look to God for answers to the unknown in times of crisis, but soon forget him when things return to normal. At least they were there. Bret felt anxious having not expected so many, especially with him not knowing the answers they were seeking.

Cherie Loman sat in the front row with her eyes riveted on Bret. He tried to avoid contact, but would occasionally look her way. She smiled flirtatiously whenever their eyes met. The congregants were not aware of the encounter they'd had earlier or of the request Cherie had made for Bret's private tutoring. Laura was equally unaware.

Initially, Bret found it difficult to focus on his message, given all the distractions, but he finally settled on giving congregants reassurance that God was sovereign and in control, so people could trust that all would be according to His will. After all, Bret was a pastor who had the authority of the Scriptures on which to make his case. Whether or not people accepted it was up to them; he was just going to relate truth as it was written. Most people responded favorably, although some cast looks of disagreement if not outright unbelief.

Russell's death was odd for sure, Bret shared. And Wilbur's disappearance, unsettling. But at least it drew the community together with a common desire to know the truth. Tragedy had a way of pulling community members together, he stated. That was good.

——— ⊷ ◯ ⊶ ———

WHEN HE LEFT THE PLATFORM after the service was over, Cherie rushed to meet Bret. "Here's my number," she said. "Please call me about what we discussed."

Laura was within earshot and noticed when Cherie slipped the piece of paper to Bret. "What's that all about?" she asked, casting a stern glance at Cherie as she wandered away.

"Oh, nothing," Bret answered. "She wants me to help her."

"Help her what?"

"Apparently she's interested in joining the church."

"Who is she? I didn't recognize her."

"Believe it or not, she's the one who threatened me that day in Russell's driveway."

"Her?!" Laura said incredulously.

"Yeah."

"She doesn't even look like the same woman. Of course, I only saw her from a distance. Did she apologize?"

"Yes, and I didn't recognize her at first either," Bret said, while making his way through the crowd. Others were approaching him, so Laura backed away.

But on the way home, Laura quizzed him further. "I didn't like the way she looked at you. Did you notice she was flirtatious...and she dressed suggestively?"

"I just wanted to keep moving through the crowd to greet others," Bret said. "I guess I was unaware of that."

"Well, I wasn't!" Laura objected, "...and I don't like it."

"She wants me to tutor her—personally," Bret said, ignoring Laura's remarks.

"You're kidding, right?"

"No, I'm not."

"And you told her you wouldn't do that, correct?"

"She gave me her number and wants me to call her."

"Bret!" Laura grabbed his arm and squeezed it tightly.

"I didn't consent to it, Laura; I told her there were Bible studies she could attend."

"Well, good; but she still gave you her number so she must be expecting a call."

"Uh-huh."

"You're not going to call her, right?" Laura turned so she could see Bret's face.

"I'll just call her and tell her I can't tutor her privately; that should end it." Bret smiled and put his hand on Laura's.

"You shouldn't call her, Bret. Why do I feel she's going to persist?"

"You think she's got a thing for me or something, Laura?" Bret asked, frowning.

"After the premonition I had last night, I don't trust her.

"And you think she's the reason? That's a bit of a stretch, isn't it?"

"Bret, everything recently is a bit of a stretch; she's just adding the latest piece that doesn't seem normal. Maybe I'm being paranoid..."

"Maybe, but let's table it for now; it was a difficult service, don't you think?"

"I could sense you struggled at first, not knowing what to expect."

"I did, especially when I saw all the new faces."

"It was encouraging though, wasn't it, Bret? I mean to see Forrest there—and Sam." Laura's voice softened. "Who would've ever thought they would show up?"

"Everyone wants answers. I hope I helped, even though I had no answers."

"You pointed them to God, didn't you? What else can you do? I wonder if any of the newcomers will return next week."

"I suspect Cherie will be there," Bret said.

"Cherie, huh? The flirty girl."

"Well, yeah, that's her name."

"And now you're on a first name basis with her?" Laura scowled.

"Come on, Laura! That's how she introduced herself."

"Does she have a last name?"

"I can't remember it."

"I'm warning you, Bret; you're a little naive. Keep your distance from her. I think my gut is right, and it has something to do with the premonition I had last night."

"Right, Laura; I'll keep my distance from her."

CHAPTER TWENTY-FOUR

Bret felt completely drained after the church service—and the exchange with Laura agitated him. Was she jealous, or was the premonition regarding Cherie true? He couldn't dismiss the possibility given Laura's accuracy when she'd had premonitions in the past. He made up his mind he wasn't going to call Cherie anyway, and that should settle it. If she wanted tutoring, she could get it in a group Bible study with other women. He figured that strategy would address both issues: Laura's concern and Cherie's gaining any foothold with him if her motives were suspect.

Sam Stone called him and thanked him for the service. He said he learned some "new stuff" and would consider coming back. Being seen in church would enhance his public image, which had waned since Wilbur Templeton's disappearance. The search continued for his body, and Sam hoped it would be found soon. Foylestown needed some closure—and so did he.

Forrest Fields was less than impressed with the church service and vowed never to attend another. He didn't like all the "God talk"...all the admonitions to leave things in the Lord's hands. He felt it was a cop-out that gave impetus for the townspeople to think that he, Forrest Fields, owner of Fields Funeral Home, upstanding member of the community, was to blame for Wilbur's disappearance. How could they?

There was much heated discussion following the close of the service as people lingered for over an hour exchanging opinions.

———•◦ ◌ ◦•———

PRELUDE MATERIALIZED AND WAS WAITING for Cherie when she returned to her apartment. She stiffened when she saw him, surprised by his presence. She felt increasingly uneasy around him, notwithstanding her desire for power and his willingness to impart it. What had seemed to her to be a harmless adventure into the spirit world was now something deeper, something sinister. She was part of an otherworldly undertaking to affect others' lives.

"You did well, Cherie," Prelude said.

"I hated being in church," she said, measuring her words.

"You had an impact. I am pleased...so far."

His words had a subtle encouraging tone to them, and she began to relax.

"I expect you to pressure him into meeting with you alone. That's when the power I will give you will be most effective."

"How will I do that?" she asked. "I gave him my phone number, but what if he doesn't call me?"

"You are to go to him when he's alone in his office; insist on seeing him. You will have power to overcome him."

"How will I know if he's alone in his office?" Cherie asked.

"I will tell you—and when I do, you must go immediately."

Cherie's mind was whirling with strange thoughts as Prelude continued speaking. She sensed herself falling more and more under his control and, for a moment, considered renouncing her involvement with him. "What if I reconsider my part in your plan? You could always find someone else," she said.

"Cherie, you are the chosen one; there is no one else, and there is no reconsideration. Do you understand?" Prelude announced this with an air of finality.

"Yes," Cherie said. "It was just a passing thought; after all, I'm new to all this."

"You must banish all thoughts that interfere with our plan, Cherie. It takes a total relinquishing of independent thought. It takes surrendering your will to mine. And you do love the thought of seducing the fool pastor, don't you?"

"Yes—yes, of course," Cherie replied. "Not that I have the slightest interest in either, but I've asked him to tutor me privately about the Bible and Jesus—.

"Don't mention that name!" Prelude screamed.

Cherie recoiled at the sound of his voice.

"That is a cursed name; the name of my enemy!" Prelude continued ranting.

"I—I meant nothing by it, Prelude—really," Cherie stammered.

"Don't ever mention that name again! Do you understand?" Prelude's appearance grew darker; his eyes—orbs of fire. His voice froze her. She tried to speak but couldn't. She sat trembling, feeling a strange coldness surrounding her. "You must set in your heart that whatever the fool pastor tries to teach you is a lie. It must be settled in your mind or you will waver. Is that understood?"

"I understand," Cherie said.

"And yes, Cherie," Prelude continued, "I forced your impotent boyfriend off the road into the tree. He had no chance, no chance at all. Seconds before the crash, he was seized with fear."

Cherie covered her eyes to mask what she imagined seeing. "You—you forced him off the road?"

"He had to be eliminated since he was aware of me. I couldn't risk him exposing me."

Prelude abruptly vanished, and Cherie sat stupefied for several minutes. She needed to talk with someone, but who would believe her? Maybe someone in the meditation group. No one in the group had ever mentioned being controlled by an entity, although some said they had contacted spirit guides. A picture of Russell flashed in her mind. She could see him trying to keep the vehicle under control and not knowing that a supernatural being was causing the crash. She could see Russell's face paralyzed with horror as he braced for a head-on collision with a tree. She never really felt attached to Russell anyway, but used him for a time, so to her...his death was no loss.

But what would happen if she failed to complete her assignment?

BRET ADDED CHERIE'S PHONE NUMBER to his cell phone contact list, although he had no intention of calling her. He would soon find out it made no difference to Cherie; she had a mandate and feared the consequences if she didn't visit him in his office as Prelude had demanded.

CHAPTER TWENTY-FIVE

Alice Templeton was so overwhelmed with the disappearance of Wilbur and the death of Russell that she locked herself away in her house, refusing to come out. Bret and Laura had tried to reach her by phone to no avail after their first visit. Upon reflection, she was mortified at what they'd found when she'd opened the door. She wouldn't dare open it again if they returned.

Sam Stone kept coming to church and found that he not only enhanced his public persona, but he looked forward to the sermons and coffee fellowship afterward. His curiosity led to a growing friendship with Bret Crossman.

"...you still believe Wilbur rose from the dead?" he asked Bret after church one Sunday. "We still don't have a live body, so there's no proof to that theory. And why would he not present himself as 'alive from the dead'?"

"Do I still believe it's possible? Yes, but do I believe Wilbur's alive somewhere on Planet Earth? All I know is that if he is, he's in hiding someplace for reasons I don't understand."

"...puzzles me too," Sam responded. "Too creepy to think he's still alive. I knew he was dead when they pulled him from the water—cold as a mackerel."

"And now that Russell's dead, we have no idea if he was involved in purloining the corpse, do we?" Bret wandered over to the coffee stand and helped himself to a second cup. "What are people around town saying?"

"The public sentiment is now focusing on Forrest. A lot of people believe he had something to do with Wilbur's disappearance."

"Gotta blame somebody, right?" Bret said, smiling, then asked, "Is there still a search going on?"

"It's crazy, Bret," Sam replied. "It's still underway but I just don't have the personnel, and we've about exhausted every possibility in town. Besides, the sheriff has pulled his men from the search. I may have to call in the FBI if his body isn't found soon."

"And the media? Are they still hounding you for updates?"

"That's died down; I guess they got bored with me telling them the same thing every day," Sam said.

"You know anything about Cherie Loman?" Bret asked abruptly.

"All I know is that she backed away quickly from wanting your hide," Sam laughed.

"Yeah, that did seem a bit strange—and to turn on Russell so quickly."

"And then his fatal accident with no evidence of alcohol or speed as a factor. Seems to me there's got to be a connection there, wouldn't you say?"

"What are you suggesting?" Bret asked, thinking about Laura's premonition.

"Oh, I don't know; ...just seems odd to me."

"Did you get any strange vibes from the Loman woman when she was in your office?" Bret asked cautiously.

"As in psychic or something?"

"Yeah, maybe that, but I don't feel comfortable around her." Bret glanced beyond Sam and saw Cherie staring at him, smiling. "Like right now but don't turn around. She's looking straight at me and smiling—more like she's looking into me."

"Wow, Bret! Maybe she's an alien and has a thing for you, do ya think?" Sam teased.

"Hey, I'm serious; the woman is weird!"

"What's Laura think? Is she aware of Miss Wacko?"

"I'll tell you some other time, Sam; Cherie's headed this way."

"Oh, oh! ...guess I'll fade away."

"No—stay, Sam; I want you to get an impression."

Sam stood back a few steps, but remained close enough to observe the interaction between Bret and Cherie. He faked disinterest by looking at the rest of the crowd gathered around the refreshment table, smiling and nodding as people passed by.

"Hello Pastor Crossman!" Cherie said, offering her hand to Bret. "Your sermon was wonderful; I got a lot out of it."

"...glad you enjoyed it," Bret said, with disinterest. "Do you know Chief of Police Sam Stone?" He nodded toward Sam, who turned and smiled at Cherie.

"We've met before," Cherie said and extended her hand to Sam. "We talked about Russell and how he practically assaulted you! Sad, what happened to the poor guy."

"Yes, very sad," Bret agreed, "...and strange too."

"Almost like it wasn't an accident," Sam added.

Cherie looked at the floor for a moment before continuing. "What do you mean, not an accident; wasn't that what the report said?"

"Hmm..." Sam said, rubbing his face. "So it did."

Cherie ignored Sam and abruptly turned her gaze to Bret. "You didn't call me."

Bret flinched and looked awkwardly at Sam. "Busy—I was busy. And by the way, I spoke with the leader of the ladies' Bible study on Tuesdays, and she's looking forward to having you in the group."

"I can't, Bret—I mean Pastor Crossman, I work during the day."

Sam raised an eyebrow and looked at Bret. "Shall I leave and let you two talk?"

"Please," Cherie said, before Bret could respond.

"...getting some more coffee," Sam said. "Talk to you later, Bret."

"I told you I won't fit in with the ladies' group, Bret; I'm so new at this that I would feel out of place. You could bring me up to speed very quickly."

"But I—"

"Please Bret, it would only take a couple of sessions to answer my questions. What harm is there in that? You can even let your wife know I'm meeting with you."

"She can't know," Bret said, before realizing he was tacitly agreeing with Cherie. "She would object."

"Then don't tell her," Cherie said, smiling demurely.

Bret's heart pounded. What on earth was he doing? He was inexplicably drawn to this woman he didn't know who seemed to emanate a strange and seductive power over him. "I'll call you sometime tomorrow."

"Good!" Cherie said, "I have Mondays off from work, so that's perfect. Can we meet in your office?"

Bret glanced around to see if Sam or Laura was watching. They were nowhere to be seen. "Yes, that would be best. What kind of questions do you have, so I can be prepared?"

Cherie paused for a moment. "Just stuff about church and the Bible; I don't know anything, but I want you to teach me. That way, if I can eventually join the ladies' group, I won't be totally ignorant."

"Look, this is something I never do, but I'll make an exception for you since you seem so eager to learn."

"I'm very eager, Bret."

Bret drew a breath and looked away for a few seconds to center himself. "Two times is all—one hour each. Write your questions down so I can have a copy of them between sessions;

that way I'll be prepared to answer them." *And I will test her real interest in learning by sharing the Gospel with her.*

Cherie gave Bret a quick hug and kissed him on the cheek. "Thanks, Bret! Like I said, I'm eager!"

Bret stiffened when Cherie hugged him and was caught totally off guard with the kiss. Other women he knew as friends had that liberty with him, and he sensed nothing improper; but this was different. He sensed there was intent beyond mere friendship from Cherie. Still, he had consented to meet with her, and no one needed to know.

Two sessions only...two sessions only.

What Bret didn't see was Sam looking on curiously and taking notice of Cherie's brazen attention.

CHAPTER TWENTY-SIX

Forrest Fields couldn't understand why some of the townspeople were so provoked against him regarding Wilbur's disappearance. It was totally irrational since he had nothing to do with it. Though he was the funeral director and had placed Wilbur's body in the casket, he had nothing to do with what happened afterward. Sure, people often needed a scapegoat when there was confusion or chaos, but it seemed to him there must be some instigation behind the scenes for people to be so unreasonable. He was thankful that most people were civil regardless of what they might think otherwise. The church service did nothing to assuage his growing sense of paranoia and his need for withdrawal. It left him with a sour taste in his mouth regarding anything religious.

Wilbur's disappearance haunted him like a nightmare, and he could not get the conversation he'd had with Bret out of his head. Logically, no explanation other than a—a what? Resurrection? Okay, so Wilbur was dead and embalmed—he knew that without a doubt. Dead as dead can be. He had placed the body in the casket and wheeled it into the funeral chapel. He knew with undisputable certainty that it was Wilbur.

But then...

Forrest was overcome by his incredulity. *It can't happen; it just can't happen.* The thought was driving him nuts; he began questioning his own sanity. Possible legal implications in Wilbur's disappearance were one thing, but to think he rose from the dead challenged every rational explanation. He had dismissed the idea of Russell exchanging the body for an impostor. He knew all along that couldn't happen, but the hatred he had toward Russell allowed him to entertain the possibility. He felt his brain was being stretched apart between that which was rational and that which was impossible. Though he sought answers, he could find none—and no peace of mind.

One thing was certain: He was finished with the funeral business. Russell's funeral was the last one. Any future requests for his services would be directed out of town. As soon as he could arrange it, he would put his business on the market. Selling a funeral home would not be easy, but it would be profitable since it was the only one in Foylestown. Once it sold, he was moving to Florida and buying a condo on a beach somewhere.

He decided he wouldn't charge Alice Templeton for Russell's funeral. The poor woman had been through enough, and he didn't need the money anyway. He was sure Russell had no life insurance, so why place a further burden on Alice? It seemed to him that some people were appointed unto tragedy. Maybe that was what the so-called sovereignty of God was all about, not that he believed it.

No; we are masters of our own fate; nothing supernatural, just death and the grave. After all, I've been in that business for years, and I'm convinced there's nothing beyond the grave.

FORREST SAT AT HIS OFFICE desk tapping his fingers on the mahogany wood. He decided to contact Bret one more time to see if he had any further explanation for Wilbur's disappearance.

"Hello, Bret Crossman."

"Bret, this is Forrest; hey, I've got a couple questions for you."

"Sure Forrest, haven't heard from you in a while; what's up?" Bret had thought of calling Forrest; this was perfect timing.

"Do you remember the conversation we had some time ago about what happened to Wilbur?"

"I remember it quite clearly."

"And we both knew it had to be Wilbur in the casket, right?"

"Right."

"And you suggested there was no logical answer to his disappearance?"

"Well, that's what we discussed."

Forrest sighed and thought for a moment. "Then you suggested that maybe he...,"

"Rose from the dead?" Bret offered bluntly.

"That's what you intimated, Bret, and that's driving me out of my mind. Even some people from town seem hell-bent on blaming me for something I had nothing to do with."

"There does seem to be an air of confusion," Bret agreed. "People are caught up in conspiracy theories, especially when they don't have answers," he continued. "But honestly, Forrest, I guess I've been too busy with other stuff to keep up on that. And by the way, it was good to see you in church last week."

"Last week is right," Forrest said abruptly. "It will be the last week for me."

"Why?" Bret asked, a little nonplussed.

"Personal reasons is all; I just don't buy into the religious stuff," he said with undisguised disdain in his voice.

"Then why call me for answers?"

"Because of what you said. Do you still believe that Wilbur rose from the dead?"

Bret prayed silently before answering. "I don't see any other explanation, Forrest. I honestly don't. Does that mean I don't question it? I still do because I don't understand it. It's not that I don't believe it can happen; it's just that I can't wrap my head around it."

There was a long pause. "You there?" Bret asked.

"I'm still here, but think with me for a minute: Some people think I have something to do with his disappearance, and you're saying he might've risen from the dead. Do you see why it's driving me crazy?"

"It does seem like you're right in the middle of it, doesn't it?"

"In the middle of it? My God, Bret, I'm going insane!"

"Your God, huh?" Bret said, with a hint of sarcasm.

"A slip of the tongue; you know what I mean!"

"Well, I know this, Forrest; you might do well to put God in the equation, so you don't go completely insane."

"I struggle to believe any of that; I've been around dead bodies too long."

"Uh-huh; maybe all the more reason to believe there's life after death."

"Convince me and I'll believe," Forrest said scornfully.

"What if Wilbur shows up; would that do it, my friend?"

"You mean like Jesus supposedly appearing after his resurrection?"

"Well, not quite like that, but what if he did appear?"

"Then I would believe."

"Can I hold you to that, Forrest?

"You can mark it down," Forrest asserted.

But, Bret thought, *despite miracles that Jesus performed during his ministry, there were many who refused to believe because of the hardness of their hearts.*

THE CONVERSATION LEFT FORREST MORE confused and ill at ease than ever. What would happen to him if the body wasn't found? Alice wouldn't press charges, and she had no relatives nearby. Were there any legal implications when a corpse suddenly came up missing? What if the body was found rotting away somewhere? That could leave open the possibility that Russell did have something to do with it, but who could prove that? Forrest had no place to go for help. Beleaguered with tormenting emotions, he considered ending it all. His arch enemy out of the way, getting rid of the business, and on the verge of going insane... and Bret Crossman suggesting something he refused to believe.

Forrest sat down in his living room with his head in his hands and cried like a baby—the first time he'd shed a tear in years. But his tears weren't those of sadness or grief; they were tears of desperation from a man who sought answers but found none.

CHAPTER TWENTY-SEVEN

Bret and Laura spent Monday together walking on a nature trail a few miles outside of Foylestown, a habit they'd developed several years ago to decompress from Sundays. The day was unusually warm and humid, and the scent of the surrounding vegetation permeated the air.

"I don't like that Loman woman, Bret," Laura said. "There's something not right about her."

"How so?" Bret asked casually.

"I've seen the way she looks at you, like she's mesmerized or something."

Bret took Laura's hands in his. "Don't you think you're being a bit subjective, Laura?"

"Women's intuition; I know how women operate." She stopped suddenly and grasped Bret's arm.

"You think she has an interest in me other than being a newcomer to church and naturally wanting to know the lead pastor?" Bret asked, coming to a halt.

"Like I said, Bret; something isn't right with her. The issue with her being so flippant about Russell's death, and her sudden about-face regarding the incident at his house. It all seems contrived to me."

"And for what purpose, Laura?"

"Haven't you noticed the way she dresses, and the way she hangs around after the church service? That must be obvious to you."

"Yeah, I've noticed she's a little risqué in the way she dresses," Bret nodded, "but remember, she's new and doesn't know a lot."

"She may know more than you think; maybe not about church, but about something else," Laura said sternly, looking him directly in the eyes.

"What on earth are you driving at, Laura?" Bret asked, frowning at his wife. "Something else?"

"Cosmic, Bret; the woman is cosmic."

"Meaning?" Bret frowned.

"She's not normal, as I said—and there's an air about her that is devilish."

Bret turned and began walking, quickening the pace. "Devilish? As in something demonic?"

"I can sense it, Bret." Laura hurried to keep up.

"Wow, you got me on that one. I don't sense anything of the sort, although I agree she's odd."

"Just be careful around her, and for God's sake—never be alone with her!"

Bret's heart froze for a moment. Should he tell her he was meeting with Cherie privately for two sessions? Or just keep it quiet until the time passed? He decided not to mention anything, thinking it would upset Laura more than she already was.

"Right," he said, nodding slowly.

"Well, let's put all that stuff behind us and enjoy the walk," Laura said cheerfully.

"I agree, let's," Bret said, but his mind was elsewhere.

CHERIE ARRIVED HOME FROM THE bank at 4:30 p.m., threw her purse on the couch, and sat down, exhausted. She hated her job as a teller and couldn't wait for an opportunity to quit. Making a little over minimum wage for a thirty-hour week wasn't cutting it for her. She aspired to more challenging things, and the thought of seducing Bret Crossman was constantly on her mind—not that it would bring financial reward, but just the sheer pleasure of bringing down another man—especially a church leader. She kicked her shoes off to elevate her feet on the arm of the sofa when she sensed she wasn't alone.

And she wasn't.

Prelude was in her living room. She couldn't see him, but was keenly aware of his presence. His closeness was both exhilarating and unsettling. She felt him edging nearer to her. *What is it you want? Am I merely a plaything for you to have fun with?*

Prelude finally spoke. "You need not fear, Cherie, I'm not here to harm you; do you understand? We are partners now, and you must trust me."

Cherie nodded weakly.

"You have done well so far," Prelude continued, "but the next phase requires greater deceptive powers. I have just energized you for what I have planned during your first meeting with Crossman. You have managed to catch his eye and have started a wedge between him and his wife. You will drive the wedge further. His wife is suspicious of you; that is good. And I will assault the marriage from the inside, causing anger and resentment. You will be there to bring soothing peace to Bret... and other things as well. And he will begin to defend you against his wife's accusations. Do you understand?"

"Yes," Cherie said.

"Good! And beware that our partnership can be ended as quickly as it started."

Then he was gone.

Cherie felt oddly empowered but equally frightened. What

if she failed? She had no options; she had to succeed in seducing Bret Crossman and crushing him—crushing his marriage, crushing the church. And then Prelude had offered her a reward. But what was that? Was he lying, and was she just being manipulated for a purpose beyond her understanding?

Her first meeting with Bret—Tuesday after work—would come soon enough. Her body tingled as she thought of the encounter. She didn't care a whit about the church or anything religious; it was all a game to her—a game she had no intention of losing.

She looked at herself in the mirror. Yes, there was something different now: an aura, a glow about her countenance. And she smiled...smiled at the new Cherie.

CHAPTER TWENTY-EIGHT

S am Stone sensed a change taking place in his life—like something was drawing him in a new direction. He couldn't explain it, but neither did he resist it. It was a pleasant and compelling tugging, and he started thinking more and more about God and the things Bret was sharing in church. It was beginning to make sense to him like there was an entire reality he had never considered. What was this thing called faith that Bret spoke of so often in church? Sure, he had faith and believed that the sun would come up tomorrow, and faith in what was scientifically proven. But what was this biblical faith? He'd gone to Sunday School as a kid but lost interest when he hit his teen years. He'd always considered himself to be a rational guy with a good dose of common sense, always wanting clear evidence before he believed anything. That had guided him most of his life and had gotten him through his training for police work. But when Bret said that faith was substance and evidence of the unseen, it intrigued him. What on earth was evidence of things not seen? Well, maybe it didn't have so much to do with Earth as it did with Heaven.

Yes, Sam was intrigued—and hungry. Hungry to find out what the invisible was and what exactly were the things hoped for? He had hoped many times in the past, but invariably his hopes died with no fulfillment. But what did Bret mean about hope being a certainty—an anchor?

Sam wanted more...a lot more, and he was determined to avail himself of as much of Bret's teachings as possible. The search for Wilbur was ongoing, although the urgency to find him seemed to have abated. No reporters had come by in weeks, and Forrest was nowhere to be seen. Sam had had no contact with him either; for that, he was secretly thankful.

One thing did concern Sam, however: He didn't care for Cherie Loman. She was deceitful as far as he was concerned, and he'd noticed her getting too cozy with Bret. The encounter she'd had with him that day after church made an indelible impression on Sam. And when she had come to his office and denounced Russell, that didn't ring right with him. He wasn't always the best judge of character as he'd experienced a few failed relationships, but maybe he'd gained a little insight from them too. And he knew instinctively that Cherie Loman was not of good character. He wondered if Bret had any idea. He figured that, as a pastor, Bret would always believe the best and want the best for others.

———⊷ ◉ ⊶———

WILBUR HAD BEEN SPOTTED IN town! The report came to Sam's office via an anonymous phone call which Sam regarded with skepticism. The caller clearly identified Wilbur from the description they gave, but anyone who knew him could have done the same. When Sam pressed for the name of the caller, they hung up. Allegedly, Wilbur had been sighted in the area around Bret Crossman's church and was accompanied by two unknown adults. No other sighting reports came in, so Sam was suspicious that it may have been a hoax. He figured if there were others to corroborate the caller's description, he would have to investigate it. He decided to call Bret anyway since the alleged sighting occurred at the church.

"Hello, Crossman's." Bret answered after the third ring, beating Laura to the phone.

"Bret, it's Sam Stone; ...you got a minute?"

"Sure, Sam. What's up?"

"I just got an anonymous phone call from someone who said they'd spotted Wilbur near the church with two other adult men."

"What?" Bret asked quizzically, glancing at Laura.

"That's what they said; what do you make of it?"

Bret felt his pulse spike as he headed for the nearest chair. "You're not going to believe this, Sam, but I got a similar report from the church janitor just a short while ago. He was inside cleaning, but happened to look out a window and saw who he described as Wilbur walking past the church with two other men."

"Good Lord!" Sam exclaimed. "I suspected it was just a hoax, but I'm going to have to investigate it. I wish the caller would have identified themselves so I could call them in for questioning."

"Well," Bret said, "there may be other sightings, which will pretty much prove it isn't a hoax. But if word gets out, the whole town will be stirred up again."

"I agree, but then there's the janitor; is he likely to say something?" Sam asked.

"I'll get in touch with him as soon as I can and tell him not to, but he may have already."

"What on earth is going on, Bret?" Sam groaned.

"I wish I knew, Sam...I wish I knew."

———— ◦ ————

BRET WAS CORRECT ABOUT THE janitor; he'd mentioned it to his wife who mentioned it to some of the ladies at the church. The word was out: Wilbur had been spotted, and the news spread quickly. Who were the other men? Didn't the janitor recognize them? "No," he said. He had never seen them, but they were odd looking, dressed all in black.

All in black? Bret remembered the two men at the back of the funeral chapel and how they departed suddenly when the service was over. *Were they the same two men? And if so, who were they, and why were they now with someone who appeared to be Wilbur?*

One thing was certain: Russell Templeton had nothing to do with it. And Bret was certain the same was true of Forrest Fields. Someone or some "thing" was playing a game with the folks of Foylestown—or was it something entirely different? Something more sinister? Something demonic? Bret began to think it was the latter.

There was Laura's premonition.

And there was the upcoming meeting with Cherie at the church office.

IT WAS TWO DAYS BEFORE Alice Templeton heard the news due to her isolation. Bret finally got through to her by phone after repeated attempts to visit had failed. He was hoping that no one else had reached her with a misleading report, but he knew she would hear eventually. She broke down in tears, unable to speak for several minutes while Bret poured out his heart in prayer for the dear woman who'd been through enough hell already. He couldn't imagine what was going through her mind. He couldn't imagine the weight of her shattered emotions.

"Alice," he finally broke the silence, "you must promise me you won't harm yourself, and you've got to stop isolating; please reach out to Laura and me for help. You're going to perish otherwise. And Alice, just because people have allegedly seen Wilbur, it doesn't mean for certain that it was him; we just don't know enough at this point."

"I promise I won't harm myself, pastor," Alice said in a shaky voice, "as long as I can hold out hope that it was truly Wilbur."

And if it's not him, her hope will be completely shattered.

CHAPTER TWENTY-NINE

When Forrest Fields heard of Wilbur's alleged appearance, he wasn't sure if he should be relieved or panicked. He settled on a feeling of utter confusion. His rattled emotions were ready to explode. *What is going on? I'm not to blame for anything. I had nothing to do with the disappearance of Wilbur's corpse!* Would people call him asking questions for which he had no answers?

Wilbur's alleged appearance had again brought chaos to the town, almost as if chaos was an entity in itself, bent on causing perpetual angst. But Forrest had seen enough dysfunction in families when death was unexpected to know that it often resulted in someone being scapegoated. What was happening in Foylestown now was similar. Whether he was just being paranoid or not, he felt like he was being scapegoated by some crazies who were feeding off the confusion.

With Wilbur again at the forefront of that confusion, Forrest decided to eliminate any outside communications until things died down. He retreated into the living quarters above the funeral home and refused to go out.

Then Sam Stone decided to pay an unannounced visit. He pulled into the funeral home parking lot with the patrol car's siren sounding and lights flashing. He then called to Forrest through the car's speaker system. A crowd had gathered around the funeral home waiting to see what would happen. Sam tried to keep them at bay, but they pressed even more, hoping for some encounter with Forrest.

After a few minutes, Sam noticed a curtain being pulled back in an upstairs window, and Forrest's face appeared.

"I need to talk with you, Forrest!" Sam called through the microphone. "You're not in any trouble, I assure you; please come down."

Forrest motioned for Sam to go away; he was in no mood to see the chief of police—or anyone else.

But Sam persisted, "Forrest, please let me talk with you for a few minutes; I'm not here to arrest you, for heaven's sake." He turned to the crowd and said, "It's time to go home, folks; if you linger, I'm gonna have to start arresting you for trespassing." Slowly, the people retreated until it was just Sam still trying to coax Forrest down. He'd waited for several minutes when he noticed the side door to the funeral home opening and Forrest emerging.

"Hey," Sam called to Forrest, "come over here so I can speak with you. No one has seen or heard from you in days; people thought you'd placed yourself in one of the caskets!"

"What difference does it make if I did?" Forrest asked, approaching Sam. "Doesn't a man have a right to privacy?"

"Of course you do, Forrest. But with the new sighting of Wilbur, everyone is curious...,"

"Curious about what?" Forrest interrupted Sam. "Maybe thinking he's hiding in here with me?"

"Well, I can't speak for them, Forrest, but as for me—I'm concerned about you. And by the way, I don't think Wilbur is in there with you, and I don't think you had anything to do with his disappearance."

"But you can't convince some people once they've got it in their heads that I'm to blame."

158

"We don't even know if it was him, Forrest; it's all just speculation."

"Maybe so, but what on earth is going on? It's like a conspiracy or something, and we still don't have any answers. Believe me, Sam, it's driving me crazy; that's why I hibernate, hoping everything will blow over."

Sam was silent for a moment, then he motioned Forrest toward the police cruiser. "Get in so we can talk," he said.

"...you sure you aren't sending me to the psych ward for my protection, Sam?"

"Of course not! I'm just being a friend, and I think you could use one right now."

Forrest opened the passenger door, sat down, and sighed heavily. "Yeah, I need a friend for sure."

Sam and Forrest chatted for the next hour, discussing the alleged reappearance of Wilbur and what impact it was having on the townspeople. They agreed that if there were further sightings, it might be best for Forrest to shut the funeral home down and get away from Foylestown. And with the newest evidence, Sam stressed that he would intensify the investigation.

"D'you suppose I should contact the FBI?" Sam asked facetiously. "I can tell them that Wilbur Templeton rose from the dead and ask if they could please locate his whereabouts."

Both men laughed, although the thought of the FBI being involved had crossed Sam's mind more than once.

"I'm just weary of it all, Sam," Forrest said, shaking his head. "And the perfunctory funeral for Russell was a further drain. Poor Alice, I can't imagine how torn up she was." Forrest sighed heavily, letting his body sink into the seat. "I'm getting out of the funeral business anyway, Sam. I've had enough death."

"Promise me something, Forrest." Sam looked at Forrest's troubled face.

"What?"

"Promise me you won't add yourself to the list of the dead."

"As in suicide?"

"Yeah."

Forrest bowed his head for a long moment. "As long as I'm assured of a friend like you, Sam, I won't even consider it."

"Thank God," Sam said. "Let's shake on it."

As Forrest reached for Sam's hand, he tried unsuccessfully to hold back the tears. Though his last tears had brought a certain relief, he now felt like years of frustration, hatred, and confusion were being released. He no longer had Russell to hate; he no longer was going to have to deal with dead bodies; maybe he no longer would have to deal with a few lunatic enemies hell-bent on blaming him for something he did not do—maybe, just maybe. And the tears kept coming...

And Sam sat silently, reaching for his handkerchief to wipe the tears from his own eyes.

Neither man dared address the elephant in the room—surely there was no such thing as someone rising from the dead.

CHAPTER THIRTY

C herie Loman was fifteen minutes early for her appointment with Bret Crossman. He waited until the scheduled time approached and ushered her into his office. "I noticed you came early," he said, purposely avoiding eye contact.

"I wanted to make sure I was on time," Cherie said, "I'm usually early for appointments." She smiled demurely.

"Well, that's a rare quality nowadays," Bret responded. "It's something I've always practiced myself. Please have a seat," he said, motioning Cherie to a chair opposite his.

"Well," Cherie said, as she sat down, "I so much appreciate you taking time out of your busy schedule to meet with me; it's very kind of you."

Bret smiled and said, "I almost never consent to a private tutoring session with anyone, but since you are new and seemed so eager to learn, I decided to make an exception."

"And I hope your wife is okay with this," Cherie said with a look of concern. "I know how careful you have to be with other women."

"Uh-huh," Bret said nodding. "I do make it a practice not to meet in my office alone with other women."

"Oh," Cherie said, "would you prefer that I leave?"

"No, of course not; I agreed to meet with you, so here we are."

"That's so kind," Cherie said as she shifted in her chair

and glanced down at her skirt, her hands adjusting in her lap slightly to pull the hem upward. Her eyes refocused on Bret, who couldn't help noticing how attractive she was as he glanced fleetingly at her.

"I don't know where to start, Pastor; I'm quite ignorant about the Bible; I'm sure you are such an expert."

"An expert—that's debatable, but I do study it a lot; there's so much in it that it's a lifetime endeavor. Where would you like me to start?"

"Well," Cherie paused, "...whatever you think I should know first."

Bret laughed, "There are so many ways we could start, but first let's consider the Bible itself: where it came from and why we believe it."

"If I'm not being too bold, can I just pull my chair beside yours? That way if you have anything to show me in the Bible, I'll be right beside you."

Bret consented but felt uneasy at her request. Cherie moved her chair as close to him as she could and leaned in toward him as he opened his Bible.

"Now," she said, "tell me all about this book, and please assume I am quite ignorant."

Bret felt his face flush slightly, but more noticeable was the intensity of Cherie's presence next to him. The hour went by quickly. Cherie seemed totally engrossed in what Bret was teaching, asking several questions. A couple of times they laughed together at her childlike lack of knowledge. When it came time for her to leave, she smiled at him and gently moved her hand across his, lightly touching it with just the tips of her fingers.

Bret glanced at her awkwardly, startled by her audacity.

"I only wish I had more than two sessions with you; we've only just begun." Cherie stood abruptly and seemingly lost her balance. Bret reached to steady her to keep her from falling and, for a moment, Cherie held onto his arms. "I'm so sorry," she said. "I got a little lightheaded, and I think I tripped on the edge of my chair. It's a good thing you caught me, Bret—oh, no! Please forgive me—I mean Pastor Crossman."

"Glad you didn't fall," he said, feeling Cherie's firm grip on his arms. "Actually, I prefer that people call me by my first name. It's a little less formal, but people still show respect for the office."

"Well, I certainly respect your office, Bret," Cherie smiled. "And you caught me just in time. I thought for sure I was going to fall. How clumsy of me!"

"Are you going to be okay?" Bret asked, thinking that he really didn't want her to leave. It was the first time in days—maybe weeks—that he felt relaxed and appreciated.

"Maybe I should sit for a moment," Cherie responded.

"Certainly," Bret said. "You can sit on the couch over there." He motioned to the couch behind her. "I'll get you a glass of water; just take as long as you need."

"Maybe I can stay a little longer than we planned," Cherie said, as she sat down awkwardly on the couch, continuing her affected dizziness. "I love talking with you, and we do seem to hit it off. Come, sit beside me. Tell me a little about your life."

"Well, that could take a long time, Cherie," Bret said, laughing. "It's a long story, as they say."

He got her a glass of water but maintained a distance from her, preferring to remain in his own chair.

Bret felt an emotional release in sharing about recent events in his life. Cherie listened intently as he spoke of the stress he'd been under since Wilbur's death and disappearance.

"I can't imagine what that must be like, Bret." Cherie's eyes locked on his. "I'm sure you can't share that with just anyone."

Well, no I can't, Bret thought. *Even Laura hasn't been there for me the way she has been in the past.* At times when he'd desperately needed her, she seemed indifferent—or just too busy to listen to him.

The more he spoke, the more Cherie listened. Neither were aware of the time. After another hour had passed, Cherie stood and moved closer to him. Bret stood and immediately sensed an overpowering attraction to her. He hadn't noticed the alluring scent of her perfume before...her blouse, her skirt—perfectly balanced, perfectly tempting.

"I'm so glad we met," Cherie said in a low whisper.

For a fleeting moment, Bret let his mind wander...unguarded. Cherie's presence aroused in him a passion he hadn't felt in a long time. Then he caught himself and made his thoughts return to the stronghold he'd built whenever tempted.

"I want so much to meet with you again soon, Bret," Cherie said. "I know we had agreed on once a week for two sessions, but that's not nearly enough for us, is it? Can I come back tomorrow?"

Tomorrow? —well...yes, maybe. But just as he was about to answer her, the phone rang.

It was Laura. "Hi Bret, just calling to let you know you were on my mind. Is everything alright?"

Bret was stunned. Laura always had a sense of what was going on, but she couldn't have known about the time with Cherie. "Yeah, everything's fine, Laura; why'd you ask?"

"Oh, no particular reason; sometimes I just get these weird feelings that something's wrong."

While Laura spoke, Cherie stood, straightened her skirt, smiled at Bret, and left quietly.

Bret cleared his throat, "I'm fine, Laura."

"But what's with your voice? Convince me that nothing's wrong," Laura insisted.

"It's just the pressures of being a pastor, Laura; you know how that is."

"Uh-huh, do I ever. But really, Bret, I had a strong urge to pray—like you were in trouble."

"I guess I haven't been feeling quite myself," Bret stammered. "I'll share more with you later." A rush of guilt suddenly overwhelmed him. What had he just done? He was shocked at his own deceit and how it kept growing into a spider's web—with him caught squarely in the middle. He wasn't sure what to tell his wife. He needed time to think his way out of his encounter with Cherie, but he also knew he would have to be honest with Laura—at some point. His thoughts drifted back to the meeting with Cherie. She was still close in his mind *and* his emotions. Dangerously close.

And the more Bret rationalized, the guiltier he felt, and the deeper the hole of deception grew.

CHAPTER THIRTY-ONE

"Y ou've done well so far, Cherie," Prelude said, "but there are problems with the fool's wife."

Cherie hadn't expected her visitor to greet her at her home after she met with Bret, but there he was.

"Sit down," Prelude said. "We need to discuss a new strategy. Those of my kind are noted for our cunning and our devices to deceive those of your inferior race."

Cherie felt drained from the visit with Bret but headed toward her couch. Prelude seemed to appear and disappear, fading in and out of her reality. She wasn't sure if he was a corporeal being or merely an apparition from another dimension. Maybe she just imagined she was seeing him.

"His wife is suspicious; she presents a problem. I want you to go to her in private and tell her you've been meeting with her husband at his invitation," Prelude said.

"But what about the second visit with Bret?" Cherie asked. "I was just getting started, and he was responding nicely."

"It won't be necessary after you meet with the fool's wife."

Cherie felt cheated at the abrupt change of plans. "And what should I tell her?"

"The truth!" Prelude roared with laughter. "That her husband invited you to his office! And tell her that he invited you twice. You see, Cherie, I am going to use you to destroy his marriage. Then we will destroy the church! And you will have power greater than you've ever known. Do you understand?"

Cherie nodded silently, overwhelmed by the prospects Prelude presented.

"Cherie?" Prelude approached her and touched her shoulder.

"Yes," she responded, and instinctively drew back from him. "I understand exactly what you mean. And this power I'm going to have; what kind of power is it?"

"Seductive power."

"But I already have that power, don't I?"

"Not in the measure you will have it if you follow my commands. It will be a power to bring down anyone you desire."

"And wealth too?" Cherie asked.

"Immeasurable."

"And how can that be?"

"By surrendering to me!"

Cherie flinched at the thought of surrendering to Prelude but liked the sound of wealth. Anything to get out of her mundane life and the nowhere town in which she lived. If it meant selling her soul—what of it? *A pretty good exchange, especially since there's nothing beyond this life anyway.*

"Nothing beyond this life anyway," she said aloud.

"Exactly!" Prelude thundered. "All the lies and nonsense of that preacher and his church. That's why they must be destroyed, Cherie, before they poison other minds. And since there is nothing beyond this life, you need to get what you can out of it."

"Yes," Cherie said, nodding in agreement. "Whatever you want me to do, Prelude...whatever you want me to do."

"Cherie! We need more like you to establish dominion. And in time, I will let you know what happened to the Templeton kid, too. That will give you even more power. I know where he is."

Cherie's eyes widened. "You do? Why can't you tell me now?"

"The time is not right, but I will let you know. Just be assured that there will be other sightings in the days to come. That will keep the town demanding answers from both fools, Crossman and Fields. But now, the task at hand: Tomorrow you will visit Crossman's wife and let her know you've been with her husband in private."

"I wish I could see him more," Cherie said.

"As I said, once was enough," Prelude insisted. "The division between the pastor and his wife has started; you will just fan the flames! Fan the flames! Ha!"

And Prelude suddenly disappeared.

Alone! Cherie was left alone with her thoughts: the intriguing prospects of power and wealth...and deliverance. Deliverance from her godawful existence in Foylestown. And her thoughts drifted to Bret. She wished that she'd had more time with him. He was a challenge for which she knew she was equal. But there was something unknown about him, too. Was it something she feared, or just misunderstood? She wasn't sure. And she surely wasn't interested in what he had to say. Enduring the tedious church services while feigning interest was exhausting.

And approaching Bret's wife tomorrow; that will be exquisite! Driving a wedge in a marriage and seeing it fail—now that is power!

Cherie spent the next hour rehearsing what she would say to Laura—how she felt victimized by Bret, and vulnerable. And how she wanted Laura to know immediately so nothing else would happen. Woman to woman, just protecting one another. At bedtime, she happily surrendered in sleep to the prospects of sharing her tale of woe with the preacher's wife the next day.

———◦———

LAURA CROSSMAN HAD SPENT MUCH of the morning shopping in town. She'd considered driving forty miles to Rochester for better options but changed her mind, not wanting to waste the driving time. Bret had left for his office at 8:30 after their confrontation about his time spent away from her. She wanted a vacation, but he insisted that church demands wouldn't allow it. The friction had worsened since Wilbur's disappearance, and Bret's frustration had spilled into their marriage.

"Not a chance to get away," he had said to her, and then he left without saying goodbye. He said he had a meeting with someone at nine and had to hurry. Laura felt neglected and alone—feelings she'd had for some time. Shopping helped take her mind off the morning disagreement with Bret.

She returned home well before noon and was putting groceries away when the doorbell rang. Thinking it might be a lady from the church, Laura hoped a pleasant conversation over coffee would help her settle down.

She was shocked to see Cherie Loman at the door and hesitated to let her in.

"Can I help you?" she asked through the unopened screen door.

"I'm Cherie Loman," Cherie said, trying to appear concerned.

"Yes," Laura said warily, "I know who you are; how can I help you?"

"It's about your husband."

"Oh?" Laura said, raising an eyebrow. "What about him?"

"It's something I think you should know," Cherie said. "May I come in?"

Laura didn't trust Cherie for a moment, but the reference to Bret troubled her. She slowly opened the screen door and Cherie walked in. *What is there about her that isn't on the level?* Laura motioned the woman into the living room.

"Thank you," Cherie said and promptly sat on the couch without permission.

"Now," Laura said, "what do you want to tell me about my husband; you must be quite concerned about something to come to our house. How did you know he wasn't going to be here?"

"I knew he wouldn't be here because he was supposed to meet with me in private at his office at nine."

Laura felt her heart sink. Was Cherie telling her the truth, or was she deliberately trying to cause trouble? Laura's thoughts returned to the morning disagreement she had with Bret. "Why would you assume my husband was going to meet with you alone this morning?"

Cherie focused on Laura's eyes. "Because he met with me yesterday, and I was scheduled to meet with him again today. I didn't feel comfortable, so that's why I came to you."

Oh, God! Laura thought. *Maybe that was why Bret was so testy before he left.* "Why would he be meeting with you in the first place?"

"He said he wanted to teach me some things from the Bible since I was so new in the church, but he had other motives," Cherie said, looking down at the floor.

"And how do you know what his motives are?" Laura said sharply, feeling her face flush with anger.

"He asked me to sit on his lap while he explained the Bible to me."

"The hell he did!" Laura shouted, "I don't believe you!"

"But you weren't there, were you?" Cherie said in defiance.

"My husband would never do that!"

"Tell you what," Cherie said mockingly. "Call his office and ask if his nine o'clock appointment showed up."

"That doesn't mean anything; he often has people who don't show up."

"Tell him I'm with you and see what he says."

Laura felt her chest tighten. She remembered warning Bret

171

about Cherie. Was it possible that he was secretly involved with her?

"I'm trying to help you, Mrs. Crossman, and maybe save your marriage. Your husband tried to hit on me in his office and asked me to sit on his lap. I was terrified. You'd better make the call. And if he lies, then maybe you'll believe me."

Laura trembled. A flood of thoughts hit her. She'd noticed that Bret hadn't been interested in her lately and hadn't been affectionate in days. But could she make the phone call with Cherie sitting in her living room? She couldn't speak for a couple minutes while she considered what to do.

"Make the call," Cherie insisted.

CHAPTER THIRTY-TWO

Laura's hands trembled as she reached in her purse for her cell phone. Cherie watched attentively. Laura hoped Bret wouldn't answer, then she could tell Cherie to get out of her house. She would confront Bret when he got home.

But he answered. "Hi honey," Bret said, recognizing the number on his phone. "What's up?"

Laura's voice quavered, "I have something I need to talk to you about."

"Sure. By the sound of your voice, it could be something serious...is everything okay?"

"Not really," Laura said. "I have a visitor with me."

"Oh, and who is that?"

"Cherie Loman."

Bret's heart turned to stone. "Oh, and—and why is she at our house?"

"Because she told me something that involves you."

Bret's voice tightened. *This whole thing was a setup,* he realized.

"Are you there, Bret?" Laura asked.

"Yes...yes, I'm here, Laura. What is she saying?"

Laura glared at Cherie, "She said she met with you yesterday and was scheduled to meet with you today at nine; is that true?"

Bret took a short breath, his heart racing with fear; he knew he had gone against Laura's warning. She had been right all along, and he'd played the fool thinking there was nothing wrong with meeting with Cherie. "Yes, that's true," Bret said, "I met with her yesterday."

"Why?" Laura stood and turned her back on Cherie. "I told you not to meet with her!"

"She said she wanted me to teach her about the Bible since she was new to the church and didn't understand much," Bret said sheepishly.

"And did you teach her anything?" Laura demanded.

Bret hesitated, knowing Cherie was there with Laura. "She seemed genuinely interested in learning, and I answered her questions about the Bible for over an hour."

"Is that when you invited her to sit on your lap, Bret?" Laura said, her voice rising in anger.

"What? What on earth are you saying, Laura? I never did any such thing. She's lying!"

"She insists that you hit on her and wanted her to sit on your lap!"

"Good God, Laura, are you going to believe her or me!"

Laura waited for a moment, trying to regain composure. "Why would she have come here this morning, Bret, if there wasn't something to it?"

"Obviously to frame me! There were no witnesses, so it's her word against mine."

"Right, and what if she starts spreading rumors? It could destroy our marriage."

"But surely Laura, you don't believe her—do you?"

"I don't want to, Bret, but what were you thinking when you agreed to meet with her against my wishes—my warnings?" Laura turned around to glare at Cherie, who had quietly slipped out of the house.

174

"Okay, Laura, so I blew it! She set me up; that's obvious."

"I can't believe you let her do this to us, Bret!" Laura continued, still seething. "I knew she was trouble from the start when she cozied up to you after Russell's death. And, by the way, she just sneaked out of the house while I wasn't looking."

Bret was silent for a moment, thinking of how to respond to Laura without further enraging her. "What do you want me to do?"

"For God's sake Bret, I don't know; our marriage is already strained enough as it is—this could crush it. We don't know anything about her background or where she even came from."

"She seemed sincere to me," Bret said, weakly.

"Seemed? Since when are you going by what seems to be true? Maybe you do have secret feelings for her!"

"Laura, would you stop yelling on the phone!"

"No, I won't! And your denial of having feelings for her isn't too convincing."

"Well, what the heck do you want me to do—penance?"

"She was mocking us, Bret; she's evil, and you are stupid!"

"It's not that serious, Laura," Bret said, trying to defuse the argument.

"For heaven's sake! Are you that obtuse that you can't see it, Bret? Or do your feelings for her cloud your capacity for reason?"

"Just shut up, would you, Laura! Look who's accusing who of being unreasonable!"

"Is this the way you want it, Bret? Telling me to shut up when I have concerns for our marriage? Or maybe you're not that interested in keeping it!"

Bret stood and started pacing, knowing the conversation was going nowhere. He couldn't just hang up, but he didn't know what to say. Was he deceived? Did he secretly have feelings for

Cherie? Was he not being honest? His marriage had been under unusual stress since Wilbur's funeral and all that followed. And maybe he was looking to Cherie as a means of alleviating the stress. His thoughts were a mess.

"Are you there, Bret?" Laura snapped.

"Right here, Laura."

"Well?"

"Well, what?"

"What are you going to do now that you've let our marriage come under assault?"

"I need time to think; I need some time alone."

"You'd better think it through seriously, Bret, because I can't handle any more drama."

"Maybe I should just leave for a few days."

"Oh, right, and what do you think people at church would think if you were gone, and the demon girl started spreading rumors? 'He ran away because he was having an affair...'"

Bret slapped his hand to his mouth to keep from exploding. He took a long breath, then said, "Maybe you should visit your sister in Ohio so we can both get a fresh perspective, Laura. That wouldn't seem as suspicious as if I left. No one would even have to know."

"Is that what you want, Bret?" Laura implored.

"Well...no; I'm just trying to think of what would be best for us until we can be more levelheaded."

"You'd better come home so we can discuss it face-to-face," Laura fumed.

"Okay, I'll just cut my day short and come home now. I—I just need to get away from my office."

"Make it soon, so you don't get too wrapped up like usual."

"Just a few things I have to deal with; then I'll be home."

IT WAS CLOSE TO TWO hours before Bret finally got home. When he arrived, Laura was gone. He found a note on the dining room table: *Since you obviously weren't interested in coming home like you said, I'm obviously not interested in being home when you get here.*

CHAPTER THIRTY-THREE

Bret waited all day—and still no sign of Laura. He tried her cell phone, but only got her voice mail—and she never returned his calls. He tried a couple of her friends; they had no idea of her whereabouts. His thoughts flashed to Cherie, and he wondered if she had anything to do with Laura's disappearance.

Fear gripped every raw nerve in his body. After weighing the wisdom of contacting her, he called Cherie at nine o'clock that evening.

She responded almost immediately.

No, she had no idea of Laura's whereabouts.

"She wasn't home when I came back from my office. And you lied to her about me, Cherie! I never asked you to sit on my lap."

"I could see it was your intention, Bret. And intention is just about the same as the act; admit it."

"Admit this, then, Cherie. You set me up—and speaking of intention, you had no intention of learning anything about the Bible, did you?!"

"Oh, Bret! Come on; just be real, will you? You know you have feelings toward me. You just try to suppress them. And you lied to Laura, didn't you?"

"Meaning what?"

"You told her you had no interest in me."

Bret felt his face flush. "I don't, for heaven's sake!"

"I'm not so sure about that, Bret. Remember how you were in the office? You wanted me to come closer to you."

"For God's sake, Cherie! Are you insane? I said nothing of the sort!"

"But think for a moment, Bret; didn't that thought flash through your mind when I leaned forward to hear you?"

Bret froze. How could she have known that? For a perverse second, the thought had crossed his mind, but he quickly dismissed it.

"Bret?"

"Huh?"

"Do you remember that thought?"

What was he to say? He'd had the thought, but wouldn't acknowledge to her that he'd had it. But he couldn't deny it since she already knew. "You're insane!" was all he could say.

"It's okay, Bret. You're not the first one who's had that type of thought toward me. So did the chief of police."

"Sam?"

"Of course!"

What on earth is going on with this woman? Bret wondered. Then he remembered Laura's admonition.

"He's married, Cherie; I'm sure he has no thoughts of you."

"Oh, but he did! And I could say other things about him, but why should I?"

"Look, Cherie, I don't know what your game is, and I'm not into some sort of mind reading gimmick, so it's best you don't go there, okay?"

"Whatever," Cherie said. "Now back to your wife. She won't be home tonight."

"And just how do you know that?" Bret felt his face getting hot.

"She won't be home tonight or tomorrow night. Who knows how long she'll be gone?"

"And how can you possibly know that if you don't know where she is!" Bret demanded.

"Does it matter *how* I know, Bret, just as long as I *do* know?"

"Well, if you know that, maybe you're involved in kidnapping her or holding her hostage somewhere."

"Don't be silly, Bret; of course I'm not, but I could tell when I spoke with her today, she was ready to leave you. Women know these things."

Bret had an urge to tell Cherie to go to hell but plied her for more information. "She said we would talk when I got home."

"Were you late?"

Bret paused to clear his mind. *Was he late?* He told Laura he had to wrap up things at the office—and he couldn't remember what she'd said.

"She waited for you, and you lied to her again. You're thinking I must be a demon, right, Bret?"

"The thought has crossed my mind, Cherie—or maybe you're controlled by one."

His words stunned her for a moment, given her relationship with Prelude.

"She waited for two hours, and you didn't show up," Cherie continued. "No woman should put up with that, Bret."

"Okay," Bret huffed, "and now you know what Laura will 'put up with' as you say. She's not like other women—and certainly not like you!"

"You're losing her, Bret; I'm willing to bet on that."

Bret was silent for a moment, considering Cherie's words. *Was he losing Laura?* They had had arguments, and it seemed like tension was always there recently, shutting off any emotional connection. But losing her? Had he not seen that coming?

"Bret?"

"Yeah?"

"You still there?"

Should he just hang up and refuse to listen to her anymore? But something compelled him to stay on the phone. He couldn't—couldn't just cut her off. "I'm here," he said, his voice trailing off to a whisper.

"You shouldn't be alone tonight; I'm coming over. I'll be there in fifteen minutes."

And before Bret could answer, Cherie hung up.

What an arrogant, presumptuous woman! Fifteen minutes and she'll be here? He tried calling her again but she didn't answer.

CHAPTER THIRTY-FOUR

B ret glanced at his watch and decided to call Sam Stone, knowing he was off duty. He had to do something—anything—to assuage the growing panic he strangely felt. Was Cherie serious? Would she be there in fifteen minutes? Or was she just trying to torment him—control him? Surely, he wouldn't let her in. One thing was clear—he did not trust her. He wished Laura hadn't left. He desperately wanted to talk to her, but had no idea where she was. He could call her sister to see if she'd headed there, but there was no time.

With less than ten minutes left before Cherie was due to arrive, he called Sam Stone.

"Sam, it's Bret."

"Yeah, I know; your name came up on Caller ID. What's up? You sound anxious."

"That's an understatement, Sam. I've only got a couple minutes, but I need some backup."

"Are you witnessing a crime, my friend?" Sam posited, laughing.

"No, but you've gotta hear this one."

"I'm listening."

"You know who Cherie Loman is, right?"

"Well, yeah; I know who she is. Kind of weird, isn't she?"

"She's coming over," Bret said, ignoring Sam's remark.

"To visit you guys?"

"No, to visit me!"

Sam paused. "You alone, then?"

"Yep."

"Where's Laura?"

"I don't know."

"Well, why is Cherie coming over, Bret, with Laura not being there?"

"No time to explain it, Sam; she's due any minute. I wondered if you could come over ASAP?"

"Oh man, Bret; that ain't gonna work tonight. I'm headed out with Jean for a dinner date. I can't cancel that; she'd kill me."

"Well, trust me, Sam. This whole thing sounds strange, but I didn't invite Cherie over, and no, I'm not having an affair. I'll explain it later, but something is happening in Foylestown, and Cherie is a part of it. I'll tell you what she said about you when you have time."

"What the—?" Sam swore. "What have I got to do with her?"

"No time to explain it; I think she's pulling into the driveway right now."

"Well, just don't let her in—"

Bret ended the call before hearing Sam's final words. He hurried to the living room window in time to see Cherie exit her car.

The doorbell rang...and rang. Bret approached the door like he was sneaking up on prey.

He peered through the security lens foolishly hoping he might see Laura standing there. The ringing ceased.

"Open the door, Bret," Cherie said. "I'm right on time."

Why should I open the door for this woman? Is it more than just a door I'm opening? An entrance into my soul? A gateway for something evil?

"Bret?" Cherie continued, "I'm waiting to come in."

Come in? The exact thought he'd just had. Someone, or something, was trying to gain entrance—not only through the door, but into his soul.

Trembling and not knowing why, he opened the door. Cherie stood there, smiling.

See, I told you I'd be here, didn't I? You're not afraid of me, are you, Bret? Your face is a little pale."

"Afraid? Of you?" Bret forced a smile. "Should I be?"

"Can I come in?"

Bret froze. Her words carried so much intent. His heart pounded hard in his ears. What was he about to do? And why would he even consider letting her in? He felt himself hanging between conscience and a subtle, compelling desire. The words slipped slowly, haltingly from his mouth. "Just...just for a moment, and that's all." He backed up, opening the door to let her in. "You can only stay for a short time. Long enough for me to clear the air about earlier today and for you to explain why you lied to me and tried to manipulate me."

"We'll see, Bret. Maybe not much time is needed." Cherie moved past him and headed for the living room.

Bret stepped in front of her. "So why are you here, Cherie? You have no reason to be here, knowing Laura's gone."

"Maybe that's the reason I am here, Bret; we can be alone, and you can finish what you started today in your office." Cherie brazenly pushed past him and sat on the living room sofa.

Bret shot a vicious glance at her, angered by her statement, and annoyed at the liberty she had so readily assumed when entering his home. "What I started in my office?"

"When you invited me to sit next to you while you, um... taught me about the Bible."

"Well, I don't recall inviting you to sit on my sofa just now," he said.

"But you did in your office. Remember how you felt when I sat next to you? You do remember that, don't you Bret? Some call it chemistry or pheromones—you know; just an indefinable attraction between two people. Like what you just felt when you let me in."

Was that what he sensed when he let her in? Was it just biological? Or were other forces at work? He couldn't deny the physical attraction he'd had for her at his office momentarily... but he'd quickly squelched it.

"Bret...you can't deny the feelings you had, can you? Why don't you sit beside me now, and let your feelings take their natural course? After all, who's going to know? It's just you and me."

"Any feelings I may have had were momentary and fleeting. I dealt with them quickly."

"Ha! So, you don't deny having the feelings, then?"

She'd caught him admitting it. Stupid words he wished he hadn't said. Words that would haunt his conscience. Cherie knew she'd scored in the war of words and denials. She would now play it to her advantage, even as Prelude had given her power.

"I will offer the invitation again, Bret; come and sit down beside me, and I will resurrect the feelings you said you'd squelched. Maybe it's just a fantasy, but maybe it's more real than you'll admit. No one will ever know. You've had your eye on me for some time, Bret, even as Laura said. She's away and we're alone."

Bret had been enticed before but had always found a way to escape temptation, knowing the devastating consequences of yielding. Had he had his eye on her? *No! I haven't.* "No! I haven't!" he said, loud enough to convince himself.

"But you have; now come and sit next to me," Cherie said, patting the couch cushion beside her.

186

Bret crossed his arms defiantly and looked up at the ceiling. He sighed heavily.

"Maybe it's you who has the fantasy," he said. "I have no such desire. I made a mistake in letting you come in. Please, just leave...leave and don't bother asking me for any further tutoring sessions; it's not going to happen."

Cherie stood, her face contorting into a combination of chagrin and fear. Where was the power Prelude had promised her? Why wasn't Bret yielding to her the way she thought he would? The thought of failing Prelude struck her. As she shot a final glance at Bret and stood abruptly, a car pulled into the driveway.

"Someone's here," she said, looking out the living room window and returning a petulant gaze at Bret. "It looks like your wife. How inconvenient for you, Bret."

"I don't believe you," he said as he approached the living room window in time to see Laura exit her car and head for the front door.

As he brushed past Cherie, she grabbed his arm. "I wonder what she'll be thinking when she sees us, Bret," she said, squeezing his arm tightly. "I think she'll know that you really do have an interest in me; don't you agree?"

Bret wrenched himself free from Cherie's grasp and pushed her aside. He headed for the front door to intercept Laura before Cherie could. The front door lock released; he was unable to move in what seemed like a moment suspended in time.

With a distraught look on her face, Laura disregarded Bret and headed into the living room, curious to see who the visitor was. "Oh my God!" she cried when she saw Cherie. "So it is true!"

"He invited me over, Mrs. Crossman," Cherie said querulously. "He said you wouldn't be coming home, and...,"

"Get out!" Laura shouted. "Get out of my house, now!"

187

"But your husband—"

Laura started toward Cherie. "Don't you mention my husband, you witch!"

"As you wish," Cherie said indifferently. "He's all yours, poor thing."

As she was leaving, Cherie looked at Bret and smiled. "Have fun and call me if you have a need. And good luck with him, honey," she said as she breezed past Laura.

Laura stood firm, seething inside at the figure that brushed past her and at the man she thought loved her above all others.

Bret started to speak.

"No!" Laura shouted. "Don't say a word!"

"But I can explain—"

"Just don't speak, Bret; I don't want to hear it!"

"I understand—"

"No, you don't! How could you possibly understand what's going through my mind right now? You've already lied to me; why should I trust anything you say?"

Bret was silent.

Laura turned away from him in anger and disgust. She felt as if her heart had been torn from her. How could he have rejected her for—for what? A prostitute? A demon? Who was Cherie Loman—and what influence did that witch have over her husband?

CHAPTER THIRTY-FIVE

P relude immediately appeared when Cherie returned from her encounter with Bret. She trembled in his presence, feeling certain she had failed in her mission. She sat on the couch in her apartment, head in hands, not daring to look at the frightening being standing over her.

"We'll go after the cop now!" Prelude boasted. "You've done well, Cherie!

She finally lifted her head and spoke. "How can you say 'well done' when I failed to seduce him?"

"He let you into his house, didn't he?" Prelude cut her short. "And he was caught red-handed by his wife. You succeeded in forcing a wedge between them. That will drive their emotions crazy. The church will call for his removal, which will destroy his marriage. Yes, Cherie; you did well."

Cherie was silent for a moment, letting his words sink in. The fear she'd had only a short time ago melted, and a sense of pride welled up within her. What seemed like defeat was a victory after all. Her desire for reward now crept into her mind. "When can I have my reward—as you promised?"

"You haven't finished your assignment with the cop yet. I'm going to make sure the Crossmans' marriage comes to an end. It will be my delight. The church will be split and rendered powerless. Then I'll move on to the next town."

The thought that Prelude would eventually leave had never

entered Cherie's mind, and she began to question whether he was deceiving her about the rewards. She loved the measure of control she had had over Bret and looked forward to seducing the chief of police. He would be easy prey. But who would come after that? Anyone else in the church? In Foylestown? Would she be under Prelude's power and be forced to move somewhere else? So many questions flooded her mind. She looked up to see if Prelude was still there. He had left without a trace. Totally exhausted, Cherie Loman fell into a miserable sleep.

———— ⊶ ○ ⊷ ————

WHEN SHE AWOKE, IT WAS well past midnight. She felt a chill and a deep sense of loneliness. She had no idea what to do next. She reflected on the evening with Bret and what might have happened had Laura not returned. Her mind drifted into lascivious fantasies.

Sam Stone was next. Ah, the poor cop; she'd already hooked him when she visited his office. Bret had been different. Something about him that she couldn't quite describe. He was naive for sure but not stupid. And she doubted that he would have ultimately yielded to her despite her empowerment by Prelude. The exhilaration of having that power mesmerized her. She'd felt so alive possessing that indescribable energy. Dare she call it supernatural? That had to be it. It was supernatural—and she succumbed to it so easily...so willingly. She knew the influence of drugs and alcohol, but this was far beyond anything she had experienced before. She wondered whether it would leave her when Prelude moved on. For a moment, she panicked. What if she lost the power? And what if there was no monetary reward? What if she was being played by Prelude even as she was toying with Bret and Sam?

A troubling and dreadful emptiness engulfed her. Who was she? Was there nothing more to her than being Prelude's cosmic playmate? Why was she even in Foylestown anyway? She felt like a twig broken from a fallen branch, forever earthbound and dead. Or maybe even worse...maybe lost for eternity.

Prelude reappeared suddenly. "Having doubts, Cherie? Lost your way?"

"How did you know?" Cherie asked, startled.

"I know so much more than you think I know. I wasn't far away. Your energy level is depleted because of your encounter with the preacher. It will return once you meet with the cop."

Cherie thought for a moment. "Is that the only way I'll have the power? Whenever I'm on assignment? Your assignment?"

Prelude laughed. "You willingly yielded to me, remember?"

"But only because of your promises...,"

"When you complete your assignments, as you call them, you will have your reward—a full reward."

"Money?" Cherie asked.

"A full reward, Cherie," Prelude said, and abruptly departed.

Cherie sat still, unable to think clearly. She was certain she had to do Prelude's bidding, or she would—would what? Perish?

She shuddered, then shook herself as if to shed her mind and body of Prelude's influence. She stood and began pacing. Bret flashed in her mind. What was there about him that seemed invincible? And Laura...she was sure Laura was ready to kill him after being caught almost in the act. *The act of what?* Cherie thought. She couldn't believe how easy it had been to gain access to him. The lie she'd told about wanting to be privately tutored—Ha! Tutoring! As if she had any interest in the Bible and the pitiful church. No, she was only interested in power and control—and the more she had, the more she wanted. It was a narcotic—addicting, stimulating! But never consummating. The thought frustrated her. She wanted to break Bret's will and bring him to his knees. There was no real satisfaction in coming up short. The cop? That dalliance would be effortless. She would break him, sure enough. And what a pleasure that would be. She would even boast about it. She would feed his lust until he lost all control...maybe even in his office. What a coup that will be! A police chief mastered by a virtually unknown woman. But she could also blame him, accuse him of rape—and go to the media. "He forced me!" she would say. Oh, the delight! She forgot all about Prelude and let her mind wander.

Then, Prelude's words echoed back to her: *You willingly yielded to me, remember?* She reflected on the meditation sessions she had attended for the past six months: *Empty your mind of all thoughts, relinquish your will.* That was easy for her; then the guided imagery part: *Imagine a friend, a spirit guide, an angel, an entity wanting to cross over to you and help you. Invite him in.*

By invitation only, she remembered. That was how she met Prelude. She had indeed invited him in. He was so kind and reassuring and seemed to know her deepest needs and desires. But in yielding, had she relinquished her will completely? The thought stunned her. What had she done? Who was she now? Were the promises all lies? Was she forever enslaved to an alien whose only purpose was the destruction of lives—of marriages, of churches?

Of her life?

A pressure squeezed her chest until she felt like she was going to faint. Then a strange thought struck her...

CHAPTER THIRTY-SIX

S am's mind drifted into thoughts of Wilbur Templeton, into gratitude that the townspeople had calmed down from their previous panic. There were no further sightings, and there was no progress in finding his body. The search had unofficially ended, and the sheriff's department had left it to him and the locals to handle it. Russell's unexpected death had brought Sam a sense of relief, but the burden was still on him and Forrest, and there would always be a lack of closure in his mind...a failure that would linger in the eyes of the citizens of Foylestown. Sam wanted and needed the approval of the community. His job security might be at stake if he didn't eventually solve the "Templeton mystery," as he called it.

Strange—that phone call from Bret, Sam mused. What was that all about, and what happened when that woman arrived? He figured he'd better call Bret. The dinner date with Jean was anything but relaxing since his wife could read him like a book. She had quizzed him about his preoccupation, but he refrained from sharing anything Bret had said. Just the pressures of his job, he told her...like so many other times. They had been married going on eighteen years and had felt the drag of daily routine sapping any romance. Not that they had any thoughts of separating, but the spark was dying...maybe even quenched. They had hoped a dinner date might ignite some feelings, but even that failed.

And whatever Bret wanted to share with him about Cherie

Loman, he couldn't imagine. She was weird, as he'd said to Bret. He tried to remember when she'd first arrived in Foylestown. Six, maybe seven months ago. He'd made it a practice of knowing when new people moved into town. Given the network of busybodies who kept him up to date, it was knowledge easily gained. He reached for the phone to call Bret when Lisa Doran notified him that there was someone to see him.

"Who?" Sam asked.

"Cherie Loman," Lisa responded. "She says she wants to share something extremely important with you—it seemed urgent."

Coincidence? Or engineered? *How odd,* Sam thought, having just mentally replayed Bret's frantic phone call. He paused for a moment, thinking it might well be Bret who she wanted to talk to him about.

"Sam?" Lisa prompted. "...you there?"

"Yeah, I'm just considering whether I have time to see her or not."

"She insists it's crucial and can't wait." *Crucial? It had to be about Bret.*

"Shall I send her in?"

"Yes, tell her I have another appointment and only have a few minutes."

Cherie entered Sam's office, head down and hands clasped in front of her.

"Now, what's so 'crucial' that you need to see me?" Sam said, suspecting her demeanor was a bit theatrical. He refrained from making direct eye contact with her as he motioned her to a chair.

Cherie lifted her head and kept the troubled look in her eyes. "It has to do with Bret Crossman."

"Oh?" Sam said, "and what might have to do with him?"

"He tried to sexually assault me!"

"Whoa!" Sam said, whirling his chair around to face her. "That's a pretty serious charge you're making."

Cherie wrung her hands nervously. "But it's true! I have a witness—sort of."

"What the heck is a 'sort of' witness?" Sam asked incredulously.

"Well, his wife caught him."

"Laura?"

"Yes, she caught him with me in their living room. He forced me against my will! He clearly had other intentions; he even said so."

Sam took a deep breath and shook his head. "That's hard to believe," he said.

"Call his wife; she came home unexpectedly and caught him," Cherie said, crossing her arms.

"When did this allegedly happen?" Sam asked.

"Last night."

Sam thought for a moment but didn't speak. Cherie had no idea that Bret had called him just before her arrival at his house last night. He looked at her for several seconds before speaking, studying her face for possible clues that she was lying. First the Templeton boy missing from a casket; later, Russell's strange death; then Bret calling him last night about the woman now sitting in his office with a story so odd he struggled to even picture Bret being involved.

"Sir?" Cherie interrupted his thoughts. "What are you going to do about what I told you? I was completely traumatized after last night. I just can't believe that the pastor of a Foylestown church would do such a thing; I need your support."

"Of course; there will be an investigation," Sam said, "...and I'll need to take a formal statement from you. Sexual assault is a serious charge. Why were you at his house last night?"

Cherie paused for a moment and straightened her skirt while

looking directly at Sam. "He invited me over for a Bible study. I assumed his wife or others would be there."

"And no one was there, correct?"

"Right, he was alone...until his wife came home later."

"And then what happened?"

"When I realized no one else was there, I felt uncomfortable and started to leave."

"Started?" Sam asked, frowning.

"Yes, but he pulled me toward him and—"

"And what?"

"He forced me to the couch and put his hands on me, telling me what he intended to do."

"Which was what?"

"Well," Cherie paused, "he obviously wanted to force me to—to, you know...,"

Sam shook his head, leaned back in his chair, and covered his mouth with his fist. "This is not the Bret Crossman I know."

"Then apparently you don't know him!" Cherie started crying. "And you don't believe me!"

Sam was immediately suspicious since he had spoken to Bret the night before. He pulled a form from his desk and tapped a pen for a few seconds before addressing Cherie. "I'll need a detailed report from you explaining exactly what happened to the best of your memory. And by the way, I didn't say I didn't believe you; I simply said it wasn't like the Bret Crossman I know."

Sam handed her a form along with a clipboard. "I'll be back in a few minutes," he said, rising from his chair.

"What are you going to do next?" Cherie asked.

"That's my business, not yours," Sam retorted.

But as he headed for the office door, Cherie rose abruptly and blocked his way. "I need you to believe me, Sam, and I need your support; this has been very traumatic for me."

Her boldness shocked Sam. *What the—*he thought. But Cherie's eyes fastened on his. He found it difficult to speak as he tried to move past her.

"Sam," Cherie whispered. "I said I need you."

"Yes, yes, of course I will help you in any way I can," he said, regaining his voice and composure.

"And I know something about Wilbur Templeton."

"What?" Sam suddenly took notice. "What do you know about him?"

"I have my source," Cherie said, moving away from him.

"And who is your source?" he asked, still skeptical but intrigued that there might really be a source, and that he could be released from the frustration he had suffered for weeks. "I want to know what you know about the Templeton kid."

"I have to check back with my source first," she said. "I want to get the details straight. When can I meet with you again?"

"As soon as you check with your so-called source."

"You seem to doubt me, Sam," she said with a hint of a smile.

CHAPTER THIRTY-SEVEN

"Just shut up!" Laura shouted. "I don't want to hear your lamebrained story. I told you from the start that woman was trouble, and you thought she was an innocent little thing who wanted to learn about the Bible. Now this mess! I do happen to have discernment, and I don't trust you right now." She stood over Bret who sat on the couch where Cherie had sat, holding his head in his hands.

"You don't know the whole story," Bret said under his breath.

"I didn't hear what you said, Bret."

He looked up at her. "I said 'you don't know the whole story.'"

"You mean there's more to it than what I saw?" Laura glared at Bret.

"I didn't invite her; she just sort of showed up with little warning. You can ask Sam. I called him just before she came over and asked him to come here, but he was busy. Laura, the woman was trying to entice me. It all happened so fast."

"Why on earth did you let her into our house, Bret? Are you that naive?"

Bret fumbled for words. Yes, he was that naive, but there was a whole lot more going on than what he could explain. How could he make Laura understand the seeming power Cherie had, and how it had to be something beyond the natural?

"She has supernatural power!" Bret blurted out.

"What?" Laura shot back.

"Something empowered her; I just can't explain it. I have no personal interest in her, Laura, but there was a presence there I wasn't prepared to deal with."

Laura sighed heavily. "That's a lame excuse for your stupidity, Bret. Supernatural power—uh-huh."

"Truthfully, Laura, I don't deny that Cherie is very attractive, but before God, I have no interest in her whatsoever. You were right about her; I was deceived. This may be hard for you to believe, given the circumstances, but there is something bizarre going on in this town—and she's a part of it. I'm convinced it all started with Wilbur coming up missing, and now this."

Laura thought for a moment, then proclaimed, "Once people find out, it will destroy our marriage and the church."

"Only if we let it happen. We need to see what's at stake and fight it; I think we're up against spiritual forces, not just flesh and blood."

"You've already let it happen, Bret! You've given ground for the destruction of our marriage; it may be too late for us," Laura slapped Bret's left cheek sharply, then punched his chest. "I'm offended and deeply hurt, Bret; can't you see that, too? Put yourself in my shoes for a minute. What would you think if you came home and saw a man on the couch trying to seduce me?"

Bret's face stung from Laura's slap. He thought for a moment and let her words sink in. "I would've knocked his brains out, and I would've been devastated if you had an interest in him."

"Then you can see why I threw her out of our house. This is our home, Bret!"

Bret cupped his cheek with his hand, still smarting from the slap. He remained quiet for a few moments. "I know it is, Laura, and thanks for putting it that way."

"So, what's next?" Laura demanded. "What do you think she's going to do now? If I wasn't convinced she's wack-o, I would believe her story given how you've been toward me lately," Laura said, turning her back to him.

"I have no idea," Bret sighed. "She's hell-bent on causing trouble. I just wonder who, or what, is behind all this....,"

"And what if this gets out to the church? She could accuse you of hitting on her—she could start talking to others. I mean, you saw how she was when I kicked her out."

"We have to have a plan if that happens. Hopefully, she'll keep her mouth shut."

"Oh God, Bret—do you actually think she's going to shut her mouth? You should immediately contact the church elders and tell them what happened. At least that way you can preempt her telling her story. I'm really sick to death of all this, Bret. If you'd only listened to my advice to begin with, none of this would've happened."

"You're right, Laura; I have to contact them and face whatever's coming. It's humiliating, and there may be a couple elders who won't buy the explanation. I've had some trouble with them in the past."

"Well, that'll just give them a reason to want you out of the church if that's the case."

"And rightfully so; I'll call them and schedule a meeting for tomorrow night; I'm sure they can't meet during the day."

Shaking her head in concern, Laura said, "Let's hope that's enough time, Bret; these things can get out quickly. Maybe you should call a couple of elders tonight."

"I'll call them in a few minutes," he agreed.

"It's all so unbelievable," Laura said. "I can't handle any more of this, Bret; you've got to listen to me and hear what I'm saying before it's too late for us."

CHAPTER THIRTY-EIGHT

"Now, on to the cop, Cherie!" Prelude thundered.

Cherie felt the force of his voice and shuddered. "He'll be much easier than Pastor Crossman," she said. "There was something about him that was resisting me."

"The false god he serves, most likely. We've waged warfare against him for centuries. But weak human beings are no challenge to us. Most yield willingly and ignorantly."

His words chilled her. Despite her desire for power and control, she was, after all, a human being. While she was trying to manipulate others, was she the victim of manipulation? But the thought of bringing down Sam Stone captivated her. Maybe a lawsuit against him. That would net her some serious money. Maybe that was Prelude's promise to her. But she had to bring the chief down first.

"Schedule a meeting with him quickly," Prelude said, seemingly reading her thoughts. "Expediency is in your favor. And you can start rumors about how the pathetic minister tried to seduce you. That will carry well with the town gossips; they'll infiltrate the church too. We want to crush his marriage and the church."

"We—meaning you and I?" Cherie asked.

"Ha!" Prelude responded. "Do you think I work alone? And do you really think we need you to accomplish our plans? We can find someone else very quickly, Cherie, if you don't bring the cop down."

His words stung; she was dispensable. And who were the others? He had never mentioned them. She was trapped, and she knew it. She really had no power of her own. "But I won't fail!" she said boldly, hoping that Prelude wouldn't find a substitute.

"Ah, that's what I like to hear from you, Cherie!" He softened his tone and said, "As you totally surrender to me, you will see as we see, into unimaginable realms of glory and power with secret knowledge. You do want that, don't you, Cherie? I know you want it desperately—but first, the qualifier."

Cherie's head swirled with wild thoughts. The *qualifier* was surely bringing down the dumb cop. She felt a rush of energy—that she could obtain the heights of power and be as one of them! She, Cherie Loman, whom no one ever took notice of!

—— ◦ ——

IT WAS AFTER MIDNIGHT, AND she had no intention of going to bed. *Unimaginable realms of glory and power with secret knowledge.* Prelude's words kept playing back to her. She was tempted to totally surrender herself to him, to let him have his way with her. Then she could humble most any man—the weak ones Prelude had mentioned.

But first, the cop. She had to master him to show she was worthy of Prelude's offer.

Tomorrow—she would contact Sam. Meet with him privately; maybe he'd come to her place. She wasn't without seductive power, even though it wasn't what it would be if she succeeded with him. Weak—Sam was weak and most likely dissatisfied with his marriage. He looked work-worn and unhappy when she saw him. *Flatter him; inflate his ego; wear down his resistance.*

"Bring him to his knees!" she shouted as she jumped from

the couch and started anxiously pacing. Then deliver the news to Prelude: she had passed the qualifier test and was ready for... *for what?* An elusive promise? Or was it real? Was she risking her soul by giving herself completely to Prelude? Did she dare ask him about Wilbur? That would surely give her an advantage with the chief.

She was exhausted. Her emotions had surged from great elation to a godawful doubt bordering on despair. She had always had bipolar tendencies, and this was an explosive episode. She was human, and she wanted more. Sick and tired of a meaningless life, Prelude's offer was exhilarating, alluring. *An escape,* she thought. She had no family or friends, and even the people in the meditation classes she had taken seemed foreign and distant. And the church? Ha! What a display of stupidity! Gaming people with fictitious stories and pathetic promises. But Prelude was different; despite the fear she had of him, he could be warm and friendly in ways that people couldn't be or hadn't been with her. *Yes,* she thought, *Prelude has offered me more than any human relationship has ever offered me.* She concluded that after she brought Sam down, she would surrender completely to Prelude. What did she have to lose? And so much to gain.

Those were her last thoughts before she finally drifted off to sleep.

CHAPTER THIRTY-NINE

After an evening of troubled conversation, neither Bret nor Laura got much sleep. The next morning, they sat silently at the kitchen table sipping coffee.

Laura broke the silence. "You should call Sam too, Bret, and explain to him what happened last night before the tramp spreads rumors."

"Yeah," Bret sighed, "you're right. Who knows what she's going to say, and when I speak with the elders, they may ask for my resignation; that would be justified—"

"Well," Laura interrupted, "I don't know if stupidity is cause for resignation, but maybe counseling and discipline would help." She cast a stern glance at Bret.

"Maybe I'll just voluntarily resign," Bret said.

"Oh, get off it! You don't need to engage in self-pity; you haven't committed some egregious sin."

"Feels like it."

"And your feelings don't count for much, do they?"

"No, I guess you're right; I'm just feeling a little ashamed and humbled right now."

"Understandable, Bret; but you can't let a demonized woman ruin us and the ministry we've fought to build over the last ten years."

"Well, I stepped in crap, didn't I?"

Laura stood abruptly and headed for the sink with her coffee cup. "And what do you think would have happened if I hadn't come back when I did?"

"For heaven's sake, Laura, don't you have any more trust in me than that?"

"Quite frankly, Bret, at the present, I don't."

"I told you I had no feelings for her!" Bret fumed. "So I made a stupid mistake; back off a little with your sanctimonious attitude!"

"Well," Laura countered, turning to face him, "your fierce denial *would* tend to make me think twice about your feelings for her, and we'd better be prepared for when the crap you mentioned hits the proverbial fan. And by the way, I feel certain God directed me back last night to save us from further damage, however that would have played out."

"So it would seem," Bret said. "So it would seem."

—————— ◦ ——————

BEFORE BRET GOT A CHANCE to call him, Sam showed up at the door.

"I need to talk to you, Bret; it's about last night."

"Well, you saved me a call; I was just about ready to contact you," Bret said, with a look of surprise. "Come in and sit down."

Sam followed Bret into the living room while Laura stayed within earshot.

"You go first," Bret said, motioning Sam toward a living room chair.

"This is hard for me, Bret, since I've known you for a long time. What I'm going to say is contrary to what I know about you." Sam took a deep breath before proceeding. "Cherie Loman came in the office this afternoon and stated that you sexually assaulted her."

"What the hell!" Bret erupted. "The woman is lying!"

"Still," Sam said, "I had to hear her out. I know it's a serious charge, but you yourself said she was coming over last night with Laura being gone."

"And that's why I called you, Sam; to inform you before she arrived. If anything, she tried to force me. It all happened so quickly; believe me—she's a liar."

Sam thought for a minute. "Yes, I thought about that, but obviously didn't mention it to her. She did seem quite frantic, but also a little too melodramatic."

"There's something more to her than we know, Sam. Like she's being controlled."

Sam scratched his head. "What on earth does that mean?"

"Not natural; I sensed it when she came in. Very seductive—powerful."

"You're losing me here, Bret; who or what would be controlling her?"

"That's what we need to find out. But one thing is for sure; she's trying to destroy our marriage and ultimately the church. I was gullible in thinking that I could help her in her spiritual walk."

"So, you insist that you had no intention of assaulting her?" Sam probed.

"None whatsoever."

"Well, she deserves to be heard, you understand; she's filing a report today."

"She's coming into your office today?"

"Yes, she set up an appointment for late afternoon."

"So...what happens next?" Bret frowned.

"There has to be an investigation."

"Meaning her word against mine, right?"

"Basically. But she has an ace in the hole, so to speak."

"Laura, right?" Bret confirmed.

"Right; allegedly she came home to find you forcing yourself on Cherie?"

"An absolute lie! I did no such thing!"

Laura entered the room. "I believe my husband's story even though I found them together; there was nothing going on between them when I arrived."

Sam made a note on a pad he'd pulled from his pocket. "Well, that changes things. Still, she has a right to file a report and may want to hire an attorney—who knows."

"I doubt she has money for an attorney," Bret said, shaking his head.

"She may just want a cash settlement, which could bankrupt us," Laura added. "I overheard you say you're meeting with her this afternoon, is that right?"

"Yes," Sam nodded, "I am."

"A word of caution, Sam:" Laura continued, "be wary of her; I think Bret's right when he says she has a force behind her."

Sam nodded but didn't speak for a moment. Finally, he rose from the chair and headed for the door. "I'll be careful, Laura, especially now that I've talked with you two." He left with a troubled look on his face.

"Thanks for siding with me against her," Bret said to Laura after Sam left.

"I know you pretty well, Bret, and, despite your utter stupidity, I know you wouldn't succumb to such a cheap woman."

CHAPTER FORTY

C herie arrived at Sam's office just as Lisa Doran was leaving. "Do you want me to stay, Sam?" Lisa asked.

"No, it's not necessary," Sam said. "Thanks anyway; this shouldn't take too long. Ms. Loman is only filling out a report. She can sit at your desk and complete it."

Sam greeted Cherie as she and Lisa were passing each other. "Please take a seat over there," he motioned her to Lisa's desk. "I'll get a report form for you to fill out. If you have any questions, I'll be in my office."

Cherie smiled politely and promptly sat down.

When Sam returned, Cherie flashed a flirtatious smile, but he ignored it with a quick turn of his head. Laura's words came back to him...*be wary of her.*

"Take your time, and fill this out to the best of your recollection. When you're finished, just leave it on the desk. I'll review it later."

As Sam looked at Cherie and started toward his office, she stood up and headed toward him. "Can we go into your office?" she asked. "I need to talk to you."

"Why?" Sam asked, moving backwards.

"I'll explain it in your office."

"Just explain it to me here," Sam said, irritated at her brazenness.

"It's only between you and me, Sam," Cherie insisted. "Private—you know."

"No," Sam insisted, "I have no idea what you're talking about." He felt his body stiffen instinctively.

"Just give me a few minutes with you in your office, and I'll explain," Cherie continued, now focusing intently on Sam's eyes.

Sam positioned his body in the entrance to his office so as to block her way if she tried to enter—but he couldn't break eye contact with her. Then, for a few inexplicable seconds, he was overcome by a strange compulsion to let Cherie enter. He backed away from the entrance. She took a few steps toward him.

"You will now let me in, won't you, Sam?" Cherie inched closer to him and reached for his hand.

"What?" he said, seeming not to hear her.

"Your office, Sam; we need to go into your office."

He looked at Cherie, his mind wandering. He felt her hand touch his gently. Then, a desire he hadn't felt for a long time welled up within him.

Without saying another word, Cherie slipped through the entrance to his office, never letting go of his hand. She shut the door behind them and turned toward him. "No one will ever know what happens behind this closed door. Sit down," she said.

Sam sat in his office chair, which Cherie had pulled from behind his desk.

"I want you to see me," Cherie said as she began to unfasten her skirt.

Sam closed his eyes, refusing to look at her. Again, he remembered the conversation with Bret and Laura. *A word of caution...be wary of her,* Laura had said. *She's dangerous and hellbent on trying to destroy us. She's under some kind of control.* Bret's words shot back into his mind.

"No!" he shouted and jumped to his feet. "This isn't right; get out of my office!"

Cherie moved quickly toward the door, oblivious to Sam's

outburst and with no intention of leaving. "Sit back down, Sam, I'm not finished. It's too late for you; you've already surrendered to me—don't fight it."

He felt trapped. Trapped in his own office, not knowing what Cherie would do next. If he forced her out of the way, she could say she was assaulted.

"I said sit down, Sam!" she demanded as she continued to undress. "If you want to know where Wilbur is, you'll do exactly as I say."

Sam had been troubled for weeks regarding Wilbur's disappearance. He wanted desperately to know what had happened to his body...and would do most anything to find out. The thought of losing his job had occurred to him repeatedly, which had put stress on his marriage. But how could this woman possibly know?

"You don't think I know, do you?" Cherie stood by the door nearly naked.

"How could you possibly know?" Sam asked, trying not to stare at her.

"Like I said before, I have my sources."

"I don't believe you have any sources!"

"Oh, but I have—and for more than just knowledge about Wilbur, as you'll see."

When she uttered those words, her countenance suddenly changed. Sam was forced backward toward his chair despite his efforts to resist. Cherie moved closer.

"You'll now sit down before me," Cherie said in a strange voice.

Sam sat.

"Now you will do exactly as I say, Sam. You are no longer chief of police; you've been stripped of your office and your authority and are now under my control. Repeat after me: 'I am no longer chief of police.'"

"I...I am no longer...,"

The phone on his desk rang.

"Don't answer it!" Cherie demanded.

It kept ringing as Sam reached for it.

Cherie lunged forward to knock the phone to the floor. But Sam regained control, seized the phone, and started to answer it.

"No!" Cherie shrieked. "Don't answer it!"

Sam saw the Caller ID. It was Bret Crossman.

Sam jumped to his feet, phone in hand. "Chief of police," he said, answering the call.

"Sam, it's Bret; ...you have a minute?"

"Bret, it's her, Cherie Lo—"

Cherie grabbed Sam's arm, wrenched the phone from his hand, and threw herself full force at him, trying to drive him back into his chair.

"...you there, Sam? Hello? What on earth is going on?"

———◦———

"WHAT'S WITH SAM?" LAURA ASKED Bret. "Is something wrong?"

He stood, visibly shaken. "It's Cherie Loman! I think she's in Sam's office, and he's in trouble."

"She's in his office?" Laura's voice rose in shock.

"There was a scuffle. I heard the phone crash. We've got to do something fast, Laura! We need to get over there before it's too late!"

"I warned you, Bret!"

"Look, this is no time for recrimination, Laura; Sam's in trouble."

———◦———

THE FORCE OF CHERIE'S BODY crashing into Sam sent them both sprawling to the floor. Sam struggled to get to his feet, trying to escape.

"Oh, no you don't!" Cherie cried, as she grasped Sam's shirt.

Sam felt his shirt rip apart and saw Cherie holding a piece of it in her hands. He had just enough time to get to his feet and race for the door.

"I can't fail this time!" Cherie shouted as she rushed toward Sam. "I can't fail Prelude!"

Sam ran through the open door, past Lisa's desk, and into the street. He heard a woeful cry coming from his office. His heart hammered as he watched and waited for Cherie to emerge; he was surprised that she never came out.

The wailing continued, and Sam thought of returning just as Bret and Laura arrived.

"Good God, what is happening, Sam?" Bret said, rushing to Sam's side, eyeing the torn shirt. And what is all the wailing?"

"It's Cherie, Bret; she's still inside. I just managed to escape a few minutes ago. The woman is completely insane."

"Are you alright?" Bret asked, taking a closer look at Sam's disheveled clothes.

"Not really; I think I just had an encounter with a witch."

Laura cast a knowing glance at Bret, who felt the sting of conviction penetrate him.

"She may come out half-clothed, so be prepared."

"What?" Laura moved toward Bret almost as if to shelter him from seeing Cherie.

"Right, she almost stripped naked in front of me and tried to force herself on me. That woman has frightening power—never seen anything like it. And she said something as I was escaping."

"What was that?" Bret asked.

"I think it was a name."

"A name?"

"Yeah, Prelude," Sam said, trying to catch his breath.

"Prelude—as in an introduction?"

"That's what it sounded like to me; she said it very loud and clear: 'I can't fail Prelude.'"

"Oh my God!" Bret cried. "I think we're up against a demon spirit! That would explain her power and strength. I knew it when she was over the other night. I almost succumbed to it."

"So did I," Sam said, eyeing his torn shirt.

As they were talking, the crying ceased. Slowly, they realized the absence of sound.

"We'd better go inside and see what's happening," Bret said.

"You lead the way, Bret; I've had enough of her for now," Sam said as he adjusted his clothing.

"No!" Laura protested; "I'll go in first to cover her nakedness; you two don't need to witness that." With Laura taking the lead, both men stood cautiously by, not knowing what to expect. As Laura entered Sam's office, they heard the screeching of tires. Cherie was not there.

"That must be her leaving!" Sam shouted. "See if you can get a glimpse of the car!"

Bret raced to the side of the building in time to see a car speeding away. He assumed the driver was Cherie.

"She's gone," Laura said as she emerged from Sam's office.

"Her clothes are gone, too," she continued, glancing at Sam. "And part of your shirt is missing; she must have it."

"Well, that's not good," Bret said. "She could use it as evidence that you assaulted her, Sam."

"Who's she going to meet in her condition?" Sam asked, shaking his head.

"Prelude," Laura said bluntly. "Whoever or whatever that is..."

"You really think there's a demon involved in this?" Sam

216

asked, frowning, while assessing some scratch marks on his arm. "That's your territory, Bret, not mine; I have enough trouble just dealing with earthly things."

"Normally, I wouldn't think so, but considering what happened to me and to you—and given her apparent strength and seductive powers—I'm inclined to say yes. I think Laura would agree, too, wouldn't you, Laura?" He spoke wryly, looking at his wife, who refrained from responding.

"You gonna go demon hunting, Bret?" Sam laughed. "You think maybe I could arrest this Prelude thing?"

Bret laughed, too, then sobered quickly. "I don't like what's happening in this town; something that could be—or maybe has already been—deadly."

"Like what?" Sam asked, dabbing his handkerchief against a scratch on his arm.

"I don't know—I still find Russell Templeton's death very odd; same with the whole thing about Wilbur's disappearance."

Sam slapped his forehead sharply, then said, "Oh, and she said she knew what happened to Wilbur's body."

"What?"

"Yes, the demon woman; she said she had sources who would reveal what happened to him if I cooperated."

"And you believed her?" Bret queried, his eyes conveying his surprise.

"She was using it as leverage against me, knowing how much I wanted closure on Wilbur. I suppose what she meant by cooperation was if I allowed her to complete the seduction. It's like she was on an assignment or something."

"Good way of putting it, Sam; she may well have been on assignment, and I'll wager that the source she mentioned is Prelude; he may, in fact, know what happened to Wilbur."

"Well, that doesn't do us any good, does it?" Laura interjected. "It's not like he's going to appear before us and tell us."

"No, but Cherie may still be a link to all this if she's not too far under his control."

"I'm afraid I remain a skeptic," Laura said, scowling.

Bret ignored Laura's remarks. "It sounds like there's a battle for the woman's soul. We can devise our own battle plan, but we need to get to her soon—before he kills her."

"...you serious?" Sam gasped. "You think she's in that much danger?"

"It's not just Cherie in danger, Sam. I'm sure there are players other than Prelude—and they are deadly."

"What's our next move?" Sam shuddered.

"Devise a counterplan."

"You're so concerned about this witch's soul, but what about our marriage, Bret!" Laura blurted, shooting a fierce look at him.

CHAPTER FORTY-ONE

C herie arrived at her apartment about a half hour after the episode with Sam, still carrying the sleeve of his shirt.

"Small consolation for my failure," she whispered, wondering what Prelude would do to her. It didn't take long to find out, as he appeared within minutes of her arrival. She expected the worst, not daring to look at him. She couldn't bear his presence.

She trembled as he moved closer, silently. Never had she felt so unclean before. He was like a viper ready to strike, still silent, now touching her skin. She felt his cold creaturely hand sweep across her bare arm.

Scales, he has scales like a serpent. Cherie felt the blood drain from her face as Prelude's face touched hers.

Then he whispered: "Assignment complete."

Cherie's lips trembled. "But...I...failed to...,"

"We have the evidence we need to destroy him."

"You mean the torn shirt?"

"And two witnesses."

"Witnesses? You mean people saw what was happening?" Cherie asked with incredulity.

"And they will testify that he tried to rape you."

Cherie slumped on the sofa with Prelude still touching her skin. "Who were they?"

"I sent two of our members as helpers."

"Helpers? Two of your members?" Cherie shuddered. "Did they just appear as people?"

"Oh, yes!" Prelude laughed. "We can assume any form we want."

"But they couldn't have been present in his office."

"They were just outside the office. The desk clerk left the door unlocked when she went home. They will testify that they heard you scream when he assaulted you."

"But how is that even possible?" Cherie said, still dumbfounded by the sudden turn of events.

"Since when does truth matter, Cherie? And what is truth? And whose side are you on, Cherie? Remember the promise of power? The rewards? The secret knowledge?"

Cherie rested her head in her hands and murmured, "But you said you would tell me what happened to Wilbur Templeton."

"Ha!" Prelude bellowed. "I'll tell you what happened at the funeral home. There was no resurrection as the fool pastor thought. I was the one in the casket impersonating the dead boy! When the time came, I appeared confused, but I simply got up and fled. It was a perfect ploy!"

Cherie gasped. "You—you were the one in the casket?"

"Clever, wasn't it?"

Cherie shook her head, not grasping what Prelude had said. "And what happened to Wilbur's body?"

"The two witnesses stole it. I put the weak-minded undertaker into a trance, and they stole the body right from under the eyes of Forrest Fields."

"Then tell me," Cherie said, trying to muster some courage, "where is he now?"

"On one condition, Cherie: cross over to us. Are you ready to cross over, Cherie? To completely join us on the other side?" Prelude hissed as he spoke, like a serpent.

Ready to cross over... The words echoed in her mind, but

she was terrified... terrified of the unknown. *What did it mean? Other dimensions? Giving up her soul? Her very life? Becoming a slave to Prelude? Maybe possessed?*

"Cherie?" Prelude interrupted her thoughts. "Remember the promise of secret knowledge and power; you still want those, don't you?"

Her mind was being invaded.

"Give yourself to us Cherie; let go of your world and enter ours."

"I'm not ready...to...,"

"Ready!" Prelude roared. "Your destiny is sealed, Cherie. You can't turn back now!"

Paralyzed with fear and unable to speak, conscience stripped bare and left wide open, she began to slip away from the world she had known. Prelude's voice was now soothing and gentle. "Come with us Cherie; you are very close...very close to a new reality."

As the last vestige of her conscience and will yielded to him, she felt herself being drawn into a vortex of darkness. There were other beings surrounding her—pulling at her. Prelude was there. "Welcome to the other side, Cherie!" he said, laughing. "You now belong to me and will do as I say. I have a new assignment for you. I am sending you forth to deceive the elders of the church. My two witnesses will also meet with them privately, and we will bring about the destruction of Bret Crossman, his wife, and the church. The stupid cop will be forced to retire, which will cost him his marriage. And we will conquer territory from our arch enemy! You are now an agent of chaos!" he thundered, then disappeared.

Cherie sat alone in her living room—her body limp, like life had been sucked from her. She sat motionless for several minutes, drenched in sweat. Her mind was filled with unclean thoughts. Thoughts of hatred and revenge...murderous thoughts directed against Bret, Sam, and the church. *A new assignment,* Prelude had said.

Yes, she whispered. *I will get even and conquer them at last!* Instantly, a rush of vital force quickened her limp body. "A lie," she said, "a lie to deceive the church. Destruction! I am an agent of chaos!"

CHAPTER FORTY-TWO

"**N**ow do you believe me, Laura?" Bret asked. He sat down next to his stunned wife and put his hand on her shoulder.

Laura pushed his hand away abruptly. "Don't patronize me, Bret! It doesn't matter what kind of woman she is; you've gotten us into this mess."

Bret's face reddened, but he refrained from letting his anger show. "But surely you can see what we're up against, can't you, Laura?"

"Up against, Bret?" Laura said, standing and facing him. "What we're up against? I want no part of it. I'm sick and tired of whatever this game is."

"It's not a game, Laura; can't you at least acknowledge that this is all a supernatural attempt to destroy our church?"

"Is that all you think about, Bret? The witch girl and the church? Are you so blind as to not see what is happening to our marriage? We are going to be a laughingstock to the church and to all of Foylestown when word gets out."

"Calm down, Laura," Bret said. "Of course I realize it's been hard on our marriage."

"No, you don't understand the damage that's already been done! As far as I'm concerned, our marriage has been torn apart; I see no hope for it."

Bret sat with his head in his hands, unable to respond. He knew Laura spoke only as she rightly understood the gravity of the situation. He also knew that their marriage was hanging by a tenuous thread ready to snap at any moment—if it hadn't already.

After a few silent moments, he spoke. "No hope at all, Laura?"

Laura bit her lip but didn't speak.

"Laura?"

"Just stop, Bret; I don't want to talk about it." Laura turned and quietly walked away.

———— ◦ ————

THE SILENT BREACH BETWEEN BRET and Laura continued. They neither spoke nor got within close proximity of one another. It was as if they were strangers. He knew he had to address the recent events head on with the elders of the church, but his mind was on Laura. And then there was Cherie—no doubt spreading lies about town by now.

Just before six o'clock that evening, Bret entered the church to meet with the elders. There was a lot of chatter among them mere seconds before he arrived, but a somber and silent mood prevailed the moment he entered the church conference room. All five elders were present.

"Good evening," Bret said. "Thank you all for coming out on such short notice." He scanned their faces looking for supportive eye contact. He noticed three of them were frowning as if they had eaten something nasty. He wondered if they had already heard rumors. His voice quavered as he continued. "What I have to say will sound strange and is exceedingly difficult for me to explain. But please hear me out, and feel free to ask questions when I finish. I certainly want your wisdom and counsel." He proceeded to the chair that had been reserved for him and sat down.

He shared in detail the events that had led up to his encounter with Cherie two nights ago and how he had made a serious error in judgment by thinking she was interested in being taught—in thinking she sought him out for that reason. He assured them he had no inappropriate interest in her despite his lapse in judgment. He shared how she had tried to force him to violate his conscience. He also explained that Laura was fully aware of the incident, but he didn't reveal the rift it had caused. He wisely avoided mentioning his thoughts on the forces behind it all—at least for the time being. As he studied their faces for feedback, he also mentioned what had happened to Sam.

"I am both humbled and ashamed of my behavior and submit myself to your better judgment as to how to proceed from here."

There was a painful silence for several seconds. Then Maury Firkins, the head elder, rose slowly from his seat. "We know all about what happened, Bret. A woman by the name of Cherie Loman has spoken to all of us."

Bret looked aghast. "She's already spoken to you—when?"

"About a half hour before you arrived." Maury continued, "She somehow knew we were meeting and asked if she could speak to us first."

Bret's face was red with anger. He knew her story would contradict everything he had just told them. "And what did she say?" he asked.

"That you took advantage of her and forcefully assaulted her in your living room two nights ago, and that Laura came home and caught you."

"She's lying," Bret protested. "I did nothing of the sort. It's just as I told you."

"And that's not all," Maury continued. "She said that when she went to see Sam Stone to file a report, he also assaulted her in the *privacy of his office*—and she had evidence. She said that

225

both of you had your eyes on her and played a game to see who would score with her first."

Bret's heart sank as he knew she spoke of the sleeve torn from Sam's shirt. "And what was the evidence?" he asked, scanning the faces of the men sitting before him.

"She showed us a sleeve she had torn from Sam's shirt as she was trying to escape. She also reported that he had forced her to remove her clothing in front of him."

Bret could see more clearly now what he was up against, but doubted the men assembled in front of him would believe his thoughts on the invisible forces behind it all. "How do you know the sleeve was from the police chief's shirt?" he asked, looking directly at Maury.

"It had a police patch on the shoulder—and that's not all."

"What else?" Bret asked, feeling sweat form on his hands.

"She said an anonymous source approached her and said there were two witnesses who were in the building when the assault took place. They heard her scream when she was trying to get away from Sam. They apparently left, fearing for their own safety. She also said her source told her the witnesses would testify as to what happened, but only in a private meeting with us and with the assurance they would remain anonymous."

Prelude! Bret thought but didn't say the name aloud. *The source: it had to be him! Cherie was working for him. And...Prelude is a demon—or something worse.*

"She's not telling the truth," Bret reiterated, almost inaudibly. "You men have known me for years; surely you must see that the woman is lying."

"Well," Maury said, looking at the others for support, "the question is, why would she lie? What possible motive does she have?"

"I can't get into that right now," Bret said. "It's complicated."

"For sure," Maury continued. "But we have a right to know. If this gets out to the church body, it could have a ruinous effect." All the elders nodded in agreement.

"And that—" Bret hesitated, "that is exactly what she wants to happen; I'm convinced."

"To ruin the church?" Maury asked in astonishment.

"And my marriage—and Sam's."

Some of the other elders murmured among themselves. "Can I say something?" J.R. McCabe interrupted.

"Go ahead," Maury said, taking a seat.

"I think there may be more going on here than we know; it doesn't make sense to me that she would have a similar account for both Bret and the chief." J.R. looked knowingly at Bret. "I mean where did this woman come from? She hasn't been in town for very long, and we don't know a thing about her past. And I'm very leery about the so-called witnesses she mentioned."

"And so am I," Wayne Silver added. "She's only been coming to church for a few weeks."

Bret sat without speaking, heartened by J.R. and Wayne's comments. Then Jesse Drucker threw his pen on the table. "Look," he said abruptly, "are we going to sit here and disregard the testimony of a woman who said she was assaulted by two men in similar fashion? And, what about the witnesses? That speaks pretty much in her favor if they actually do come to tell their side of things."

"Well," J.R. shot back, "No one is suggesting that we disregard her testimony, Jesse; everything just seems a bit odd to me!"

"Exactly," Wayne agreed.

That left Regis Gemelli, who'd been frowning the entire time the others spoke. "I'm inclined to believe the woman, and I think we should hear from the witnesses as soon as possible," he said, looking directly at Bret. "We can't allow this kind of thing to destroy our church. Bret said he had a serious lapse in judgment. Granted, he did. And what would prevent him from having more of these lapses in the future? Do we want this kind of leadership in the church?"

"Well, wait a minute!" Wayne shouted. "I don't think we need to question Bret's leadership at this point! He's already admitted to his fault, and he's come to us humbly seeking our counsel."

"And my counsel is that he's compromised the integrity of our church!" Regis countered. "It's not the only thing that's been brought into question, either."

"I think I should leave," Bret said. "You men discuss this in private; I'd rather not be party to an argument since I'm the subject. Please excuse me; I'll be going."

He left quickly, but not without shooting an angry glance at Regis. After he had gone, the discussion quickly resumed.

"He needs to resign," Regis continued. "We have to act on this ASAP to show that we won't tolerate that kind of behavior. As the senior elder here—I've been here longer than any of you—I'm not willing to see the church destroyed because of the incompetence of the pastor."

"So—are you casting the first stone, Regis?" Wayne asked.

"Can't you get it through your thick skull, Wayne, I'm not casting stones? There's been a serious breach of integrity by the leadership, and Bret needs to go—or we need to force his resignation."

"Look," Maury stood, then continued, "I tend to agree with Regis, but we haven't even heard from the witnesses or from Sam himself. We sound like a lynch mob. Let's chill for now and use our heads. We need to formulate an official statement for the church so we can be prepared to issue that when we arrive at our decision. And, by the way, Bret did say it was complicated— meaning there may be more evidence that we don't yet have. He has the right to speak his piece, so we need to schedule another meeting soon."

They all agreed, though Regis wanted to continue the discussion. A subsequent meeting was scheduled for the next night with both Cherie and the supposed witnesses invited. But Regis was constrained to have the last words...

CHAPTER FORTY-THREE

*A*n *agent of chaos,* Cherie kept repeating silently. *But who and where are the two witnesses Prelude mentioned?* She was so relieved he had said the mission was accomplished, but at what cost to her? She was different. Her thoughts were different—dark and angry. She had a mental picture of Bret and Sam and could see them crumble along with their marriages and the church. Yes, she was an agent of destruction and chaos—but under the dominion of Prelude. She recalled the looks on the elders' faces when she told them her story—looks of horror and incredulity. What power she had!

She padded off to the bathroom weary from the recent events. A warm shower would revive her. When she looked at herself in the mirror, she stepped backward. No longer just Cherie Loman, the woman she had been for twenty-seven years, but now something different. The look in her eyes was piercing; it was as though she was looking through the mirror into another dimension. She looked at her body; there was no change: hands, fingers, arms, legs—all the same. But her face...and her mind... undeniably altered.

She wondered what the next step was. To wait? She had no interest in returning to work, and it didn't matter anyway. She'd been warned that any further tardiness would result in her termination. Well, with the power she now had, she wouldn't need to work. But what about the payout Prelude had promised? There was nothing to date. For a moment, her mind drifted. *What if*

231

it was all a deception...and she'd been played for a fool? Just a puppet for Prelude? Had she gone too far? Was there no turning back? But her thoughts were cut short by Prelude's appearance.

"You're filled with doubts, aren't you, Cherie?" he acknowledged.

"How did you know?" Cherie asked, nodding.

"When you experience your newfound power, they will vanish," Prelude said, ignoring her question.

"But—" Cherie hesitated, "—I need money, as you promised."

"You will find it in your bank account—ten thousand dollars."

Cherie drew a quick breath. "Ten thousand?"

"In your bank account as of this moment, but your new assignment is just beginning. You are to appear before the elders of the church along with the two witnesses at their next meeting, which is tomorrow night. Call them and let them know you are coming—they are expecting you."

"Will you tell me who the witnesses are?" Cherie asked.

"You will know who they are at the meeting."

"And the meeting; what can I expect?"

"It will mark the demise of the pastor and the beginning of the downfall of the church. The witnesses will be totally convincing and will have persuasive powers such as yours. They will corroborate everything you say."

"And the elders will believe them, right?"

"Of course; there are already two of them who want to see the fool taken down. It will take little to convince them since they are also fools."

"And the others," Cherie said. "There are three others. Will they be persuaded?"

"That's where you use your powers—to persuade."

Cherie smiled, thrilled that she could persuade the other elders. "It won't be much of a challenge then, will it?"

"Don't you think we've had an eye on you for some time, Cherie, as the perfect candidate for our mission? We noticed you were rebellious in nature, a human trait that easily complements our plans of destruction."

So, they've noticed me for some time and recruited me for their cause. Cherie felt a sense of pride, given that she was of such importance to them. She wondered how many others could boast of such a status as hers. Or was she just one of the elected few?

"They will be meeting tomorrow night at six, and by the end of the meeting they will agree to our plans, beginning with the fool being terminated from his position."

Cherie thought for a moment, then abruptly asked, "Where's Wilbur Templeton?"

"Ah!" Prelude responded. "You seem obsessed with finding out. So many would like to know as you do, especially the weak cop. People will know in time, and it will cause great shock and awe." He looked piercingly at Cherie, "It is not for you to know either—until the right time."

"But... aren't I one of you now? Shouldn't I be allowed to know?"

Prelude howled with laughter. "You will never be one of us! We own you and allow you to have a measure of our power, but, rest assured, you will never be one of us! We are of a different and exalted order; no mere mortal can attain our status. Be content, Cherie, that we have chosen you for our purpose."

"And....," Cherie hesitated, feeling the sting of Prelude's chastening words, "...what will become of me when you have achieved your purpose here in Foylestown?"

"There are many churches within our geographical domain which we will divide and destroy. We have multiple means of accomplishing our goals. But we can do that with other human agents like you."

His words pierced her. She began to understand that she was not indispensable; that there were *other human agents* like her. The thought that she was not so exclusive to Prelude struck her. She would have power *if they were here.* And the ten thousand bucks would last only a short time, if it existed at all. But she was trapped, having to carry out their mission. She still relished the thought of bringing down the church along with Bret and Sam, and the anger still raged within her, but she feared abandonment. What would become of her? She thought of suicide, turning the hatred and anger on herself after her assignment was complete. Yes, that would be the final triumph of her life. She would die with the perverse satisfaction of being used to render chaos and destruction to the church and the two men she despised.

Who or what was Prelude anyway? She had learned in her meditation class that there were benevolent spirits that could cross over into the three-dimensional world, just as Prelude had done by her invitation; that there was indeed a higher type of knowledge and power accessible to people who would practice the required disciplines. She had tasted it and proved it to be true in her experience. The power was addictive; it meshed perfectly with her human cravings for control and money. But the thought of being abandoned after having been used by Prelude was akin to being raped and then left destitute. She trembled. Her entire life had been spent seeking meaning through manipulation and deceit, and now she was owned and deceived by a master manipulator. Still, the anger and hatred drove her, and she could only find release through the destruction of others' lives. *Funny,* she thought, *destroy others while I'm being destroyed, deceive others while I've been deceived.* But the hatred consumed her...

She stood and looked at the wall clock. Three hours had

passed like mere moments. Prelude had long since disappeared. Her living room appeared to be alive. Everything in it had come to life—was she hallucinating? She felt herself being drawn into the spirit world only to slip back into her reality. Tomorrow at six would be the climax. The purpose for which she'd been chosen would be fulfilled. She was a praying mantis feasting on the lives of Bret and Sam...watching them slip away into lifeless impotence.

Ah, the satisfaction! Chaos! Ruination!

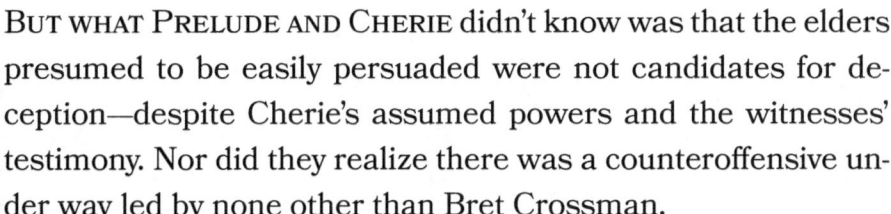

But what Prelude and Cherie didn't know was that the elders presumed to be easily persuaded were not candidates for deception—despite Cherie's assumed powers and the witnesses' testimony. Nor did they realize there was a counteroffensive under way led by none other than Bret Crossman.

CHAPTER FORTY-FOUR

B ret left the church and drove slowly on his way back home. He was devastated by the meeting and wondered what the outcome would be the next time the elders met. Regis's words troubled him deeply. What did he mean that there were other things that were brought into question? Nothing he was aware of, but he had butted heads with Regis on other issues before, and he wasn't sure of Jesse's support, although he'd never had an overt conflict with him. But to question his leadership and push his resignation? He knew that requiring his resignation might be the outcome, but he hadn't considered it coming up at the first meeting. They had heard Cherie's lies at the first meeting, too. The witness thing seemed very suspect to him, like it was a setup from the beginning. Bret had no doubt Cherie had been contacting an evil entity and was under Prelude's control. Was she possessed or just demonized—and still capable of extricating herself from his control? Certainly, the lies she told and the way she had attacked Sam would indicate the former.

He was recounting the crazy events of the last few days when a car headed straight toward him. Bret swerved to miss it and skidded off the road, nearly hitting a guardrail.

"What the—!" he shouted as the other driver sped away as though nothing had happened. I *really don't need this right now,* he thought. *I wonder if that was because of supernatural forces, too.* But he figured that the humiliation of having to face the elders again and potentially having to offer them his resignation would make more of an impression on them if he didn't perish in a car accident.

By the time he reached his house, his nerves were hot-wired. And would Laura even be there?

To his surprise, she met him at the door.

"What on earth?" she exclaimed. "You look like you've been through hell!"

"I look that bad, huh?" he said, shuffling into the living room.

"So, I take it the meeting didn't go so well?"

"You might say that," Bret nodded.

"Another blow to the church and another nail in the marriage coffin, right, Bret?" Laura said sarcastically.

"Oh for God's sake, Laura, would you lighten up? Do you think it was pleasant sitting there and being scrutinized by the elders?"

"Well, it's not like I've been in Disneyland waiting to find out what happened. You've brought all this on yourself."

"Do you want a pound of my flesh, Laura? Would that satisfy you?" Bret yelled.

"That would be letting you off too easily, Bret!"

"Okay, okay; so I'm guilty as hell and deserve to be removed from the church!"

"The church! The church! Everything is the church!" Laura shouted in Bret's face and pushed him in the chest with both hands.

Bret stepped back, startled at Laura's aggression. They were both silent for several minutes.

Then the phone rang. Bret grabbed it before Laura could reach it.

"Bret, it's Maury. Sorry to bother you, but we've scheduled another meeting for tomorrow night at the same time. Cherie

238

Loman has agreed to come as well as the two witnesses she mentioned. Obviously, you need to be there."

"So soon?" Bret said, trying to center his thoughts after the argument with Laura.

"We can't let it wait, Bret; I'm sure you understand why. Some of the elders are pushing hard to have the meeting."

Bret knew who those elders were and was all but certain they wanted to oust him as pastor.

"Of course I'll be there," Bret said. "And I'll contact Sam about the meeting. He needs to tell his side of the story."

"That would be good, Bret—just to make it fair."

Make it fair? He knew Regis and Jesse weren't interested in fairness. That was obvious from tonight's meeting. But, he reasoned, they had every right to raise some red flags about his role as the pastor of the church—and to question his integrity and judgment. He wasn't sure where Maury stood, but figured Regis would sway him. He felt J.R. and Wayne would at least have a level of understanding and would be supportive no matter what way a final vote might go.

He looked over at Laura who simply shook her heard in silence.

CHAPTER FORTY-FIVE

"**W**ho are the witnesses?" Cherie asked Prelude as he suddenly appeared in her living room, interrupting her meditation. He seemed more ominous than ever.

"They are nameless now and will be nameless tomorrow night at the meeting. It is not important for you to know their names; as I said, they are two of us."

"Appearing in the form of men?" Cherie asked a rhetorical question.

"And equipped with deceptive powers as you will be. Regis Gemelli is already under our power along with Jesse Drucker; Maury Firkins is close but will need a little persuading. They are no challenge at all. You and the witnesses will work on Wayne Silver and J.R. McCabe. They are ignorant and willful, favoring the fool pastor. You must make sure that when the meeting is over, they will submit to your cunning."

*Make sure...*the words made her shudder. *What if she failed? Did all of them need to be deceived?*

"It has to be unanimous." Again, Prelude seemed to read her thoughts. "Otherwise, it will not have the impact we desire."

Heartened by her own voice making the declaration, Cherie repeated the words: "Yes, of course—the impact we desire."

"Then, when they get rid of the fool, our next step is to take it to the media; put it in print and on television. We want to maximize the humiliation and bring their marriages down. The church will crumble under the pressure and take a new shape fashioned in the image of the god of this world. The cop, of course, will be forced to resign."

"Then what?" Cherie asked.

"Then what?" Prelude repeated in a mocking tone. "We fan the flames as you humans would say. Keep the fire burning, pit people against each other, magnify anger and hatred, divide, cause chaos, destroy. It brings us supreme pleasure to disgrace their so-called God, the phony God that the dupes worship, not knowing that the true god was in the garden ready to make wise the members of your race. We are the wise and powerful ones, Cherie!" Prelude shook his fist as he boasted: "We will win in the end and bring the entire human race into submission to us. There are some agents of destruction released from their material bodies at the great deluge who now roam Earth to conquer. There are others like us who operate in the heavenly realm while they operate on Earth, but together we will defeat the presumptuous usurper who claims sovereign rule."

"The God Bret speaks of, right?"

"And no true god is he! Our leader is the true god."

"Can I ask who that is?" Cherie inquired bravely, noticing how shiny Prelude suddenly appeared. It was as if he was being transformed right in front of her. She trembled and moved quickly away from him. Prelude seemed caught in his own glory for several seconds before noticing Cherie.

"Satan!" he roared. "The god of this world; the prince of power of the air! The whole world lies passively under his power!"

Cherie was afraid. What she was hearing went far beyond her meager understanding. She sensed the alien power permeating everything in her room. She felt limp, weak—ready to pass out. Darkness flooded her mind; she couldn't speak or think clearly. She fell backward on the sofa, unconscious. When she awoke, Prelude was gone.

Her body was soaked with sweat, and she stuck to the sofa like a wet blanket. She groaned and stretched, trying to refocus her mind which was still hazy from the encounter with Prelude. "Satan!" she bellowed. "What the hell?" she called out, then laughed at the pun. "He's behind all this? I don't really think he exists; to me it's just like the silly notion of the God of the Bible. All of it is fantasy.

But then she realized Prelude wasn't a fantasy and was indeed alien-like. A friendly guide at first, helping her adjust to a lonely, isolated life. But then came the revelation of his intent to destroy two marriages and the church. No objection on her part, of course, because she would reap the benefits. What she suddenly realized was that although she had a new measure of power, she was losing control of her life and her freedom. Tomorrow night was the big test, with two kingdoms in warfare. Prelude loudly boasted of his kingdom being more powerful than the other, supposedly the one represented by Bret and the church. She sagged back on the sofa in total exhaustion. Every bone and muscle in her body seemed dead. Her mind was filled with a hideous image of Prelude hovering over the church, mocking and laughing along with others of his kind. The images shook her. What was she to them? The thought of what would happen to her when the church collapsed played repeatedly in her head. And, worst of all, what would happen to her if she failed at the meeting with the elders? She already felt she had failed with Bret and Sam, but that Prelude had given her another chance by bringing the two witnesses into the plan. She had checked her bank account, and the money Prelude had promised was truly there. Or was that just illusory? She sat up on the sofa and combed her hair with her fingers. Maybe all of this was illusory; maybe it wasn't actually happening. What else was Prelude capable of doing? If he impersonated Wilbur, had he removed the corpse from the funeral home? Then there were the two witnesses— some of Prelude's posse assuming human form. Prelude owned her, or so he said. But did he? Was she possessed by him or just controlled because of her own lust for control, power, and money? Was she that weak and predictable, susceptible to manipulation? All the things she had wanted were the things she was now victim to. And the anger and hatred when thinking of Bret and Sam—she found she couldn't just let it go. She had willingly submitted herself to the offers Prelude had made.

She stood abruptly and thought of leaving—just running away while she still had time. Would that break the power Prelude had over her? Just getting away from him? But where would she go? She had no family nearby and certainly no friends. *No, I've gotta go through with the whole thing. I have no other choice.*

Bolstered by her own thoughts, Cherie set her mind on a fixed course of no return. Whatever happened happened. She believed in fate and knew she had little control over her life. Even though she loved being in control of the immediate, she was sure there were forces beyond her that determined the outcome of her life.

CHAPTER FORTY-SIX

After Bret left the first elders' meeting, the conversation had continued. "I'm for getting rid of him tomorrow night," Regis asserted before they ended the meeting. "The integrity of the church is at stake, and I'm not willing to see it besmirched because of Bret's stupid indiscretions." He pounded his fist on the table, startling the others.

"I'm with you on that," agreed Jesse. "We've put too much sweat and blood into building it up over the years to see it crumble now. If we act in unison and with dispatch, the church body will get the message that we won't tolerate such things from any pastor."

"Well," Maury countered, "we'll have to see what tomorrow night holds. Maybe something new will come to light—something that will clarify things in our minds."

"Maury," Jesse said disdainfully, "we don't need a bleeding heart right now; we need you to exercise some authority as the head elder."

"And that's exactly what I'm doing, Jesse!" Maury shot back. "It's called wisdom; I'm sorry if you're deficient in that attribute."

"Good Lord, you guys; do you see what's happening here?" J.R. entreated. "We are being pitted one against another in trying to deal with this. Talk about the church suffering; maybe we need to admit how divisive we're being discussing this."

Everyone was silent for a moment, then Maury stood and

said, "Until tomorrow we need to be in prayer, and it's my opinion that, if we decide to remove Bret from his position, it should be a unanimous vote."

Regis rolled his eyes and let out a heavy sigh. "Fat chance of that with the likes of J.R. and Wayne on the board."

"I need time to think this through, Regis. I consider removing a pastor a profoundly serious matter and one that should not be decided casually. We need to hear from the chief, too. I hardly think both men are just making things up. Besides, Bret indicated there were things he needed to share when the time was right," Wayne added.

"Yeah," Regis said, scowling. "It gives him an excuse to plan his defense. Truthfully, gentlemen, I've never trusted him from the start, and it looks like there's a good reason for that; wouldn't you all agree?"

"What if he chooses to resign anyway?" Wayne interjected before the others could respond.

"Well now, wouldn't that just be a great relief for all of us!" Jesse smirked. "Sure would make things a lot easier."

"I believe he's a man of integrity." J.R. added, "He'll resign if he feels God wants him to. And what if he's right about that woman's intention to destroy the church? We know we don't wrestle against flesh and blood, so there may very well be some forces behind her actions to ruin him and Laura as well as Sam and Jean—let alone the church."

"Not likely," countered Regis. "I don't buy into any 'forces'—as you call them—involved in this. It's a clear-cut case of two men lusting after an attractive woman and trying to force her against her will. We're talking about criminal conduct here."

Maury could tell there was no use in letting the debate continue with emotions so charged. "Let's end this for tonight, guys. I'm a little overwhelmed, and my head's aching," he said as he stood up and demanded their attention. "I make a motion to adjourn this meeting and continue tomorrow night."

"I'll second that," Wayne said, also standing.

"All in favor? Three in the affirmative and two opposed. Majority rules. The meeting is over."

Regis and Jesse went out together talking in low tones while the others went eagerly to their cars.

"I think we've got him, Jesse!" Regis smiled.

———•— ◯ —•———

As BRET STRUGGLED TO GET to sleep, he suddenly felt an excruciating pain in the back of his head. "Laura," he groaned, hating to awaken his wife given the still unresolved conflict of that evening. "Something's wrong with my head; it feels like it's going to explode!"

Laura awoke with a start, looked at Bret, and screamed. In the dim light, directly behind Bret's head was the shadow of a hideous creature that appeared to have its claws fastened to her husband's scalp.

CHAPTER FORTY-SEVEN

Laura labored to get the words out: "I saw it, Bret!"

"What, Laura? Saw what?" Bret implored as the fear-stricken face of his wife came into his view.

"The creature! It had its claws attached to the back of your head. That's why you're having the headache—I'm positive!"

Bret felt the back of his head. With each stroke, he noticed more stickiness on his fingers. "Turn on the light, Laura," he said.

Laura turned on the lamp next to their bed. In a split second, they each registered horror. Bret's fingers were covered with blood.

"What on earth?!" Bret exclaimed, "it's blood! There's blood on the back of my head! And what's this about a creature?"

"I saw its shadow, Bret. It was repulsive looking! Its claws were in your head!"

"...you sure you weren't just dreaming, Laura?"

"Look at your fingers, Bret; isn't that proof enough?"

Bret gazed at his bloody fingers and instantly noticed his headache was gone. "My God, Laura, the thing was in our room! Maybe it was listening to our arguing!"

Laura sat upright on the bed, trembling. "I'm scared, Bret; this is getting too unreal for me. I mean, I believe in the reality of demons, but to have one in our bedroom attacking you is frightening!"

The incident temporarily defused the previous conflict as they realized they were up against something very unnatural.

"I guess we need to pull together, Laura, and not fight with each other."

Laura reluctantly agreed.

"Bret, listen to me," she said, turning toward her husband. "I don't think I'll be able to sleep after seeing the—the thing."

"I'm not sure I can either, Laura; just too much on my mind right now. But we don't have to fear these things; we have authority through Christ's victory over them; I think they probably sense fear and use it to their advantage."

"They must like darkness, too," Laura replied. "The thing disappeared when I turned on the light. Speaking of which, maybe we can sleep with it on; what do you think, Bret?"

"I think we shouldn't surrender to it in any way. Let's pray and ask the Lord to protect us from it; we can just speak the name of Jesus if it reappears. That's a name they hate and fear."

Laura wasn't at all satisfied with Bret's assumed confidence. She felt bitterness toward him rising in her heart again. She couldn't deal with demonic forces attacking them and with the church possibly demanding Bret's resignation. Where would that leave them? No income, no housing, no place to go. Why did he even give that woman the time of day? Why couldn't he see that Cherie was trouble like she had? And now, the woman seemed possessed by an alien hell-bent on attacking them personally. *No! It's too much for me; I need to get away from it all.*

And the temporary reunion she had with Bret only a short time ago quickly faded in the face of fear.

After Bret cleaned the blood from the back of his head, he spent several hours in prayer, only falling asleep as daylight approached. There were no more appearances that night, but Bret wasn't sure there wouldn't be others.

———•＋ ◯ ＋•———

LATER THAT EVENING, REGIS AND Jesse met secretly to discuss the best way to force Bret out of the church. The *thing*, as they called it, had been appearing to them for some time, giving them guidance. They thought it was a benevolent angelic presence backing them due to their position as elders. They were going to save the church, and, for some reason, they had divine guidance to help them. They were, indeed, privileged.

The *thing* appeared and spoke directly to Regis. "You are most favored, Regis. To you is given wisdom the other elders lack. And when the witnesses appear tomorrow along with Cherie, you will join them in denouncing Bret Crossman and demanding his resignation. And he will attempt to convince you that there is a demonic presence trying to destroy his marriage and that of the chief of police. Of course that is a lie, and you will show how foolish it is to even mention demonic influence. You know that demons don't exist in modern times. It is deception of the highest order to believe they do. I, of course, am of an exalted order."

Regis smiled. *Most favored?* Even more favored than Maury? He knew he should have been appointed as head elder years ago, and maybe, with Bret's demise, he would assume the position. After all, Maury was a weak leader and wouldn't challenge him. With no pastor around, there would be no reason to not seize control. And he could begin a reformation within the church to steer it away from the teaching of theology and doctrine and make the church socially acceptable and relational.

But first...Bret had to be destroyed.

CHAPTER FORTY-EIGHT

The meeting was scheduled for the usual time—6:00 p.m. The elders decided to have Bret and Sam present for the first hour or so to offer their defense. An elder meeting would follow, and Bret's fate would be determined. Though Sam had little connection to the church, J.R. and Wayne wanted him at the meeting since both he and Bret had had similar encounters with Cherie. Maury asked Bret to contact Sam and ask if he would agree to come. Regis couldn't wait until he launched his coup de grace. It would soon be over for Bret Crossman. Control of the church would fall into Regis's hands.

Laura became more and more remote in her interactions with Bret, continuing to focus on the devastation that Cherie had brought into their lives, and particularly on the demonic attack against her husband. She'd tried donning a brave face, but kept slipping back into resentment. All they had worked for the past several years was about to come crashing down...and Bret could have prevented it.

That morning, the tension was palpable.

"I suppose they will work you over pretty well at the meeting," Laura said, scowling at her husband.

"Well," Bret countered, "I'll have my chance to present the *other side* of things."

"Other side?" Laura asked. "Meaning the alien side?"

"Not alien but surely evil," Bret corrected her.

"Whatever!" Laura said, turning her back to Bret. "And just what do you think they're going to say to that, Bret? They'll think you're crazy—and have all the more reason to remove you."

Bret held his tongue but seethed inside. He could clearly see that, from the start, everything was a set up to bring about his demise. He feared for his marriage, seeing Laura withdrawing and becoming more bitter. He just wanted to lash out angrily and then try to be reasonable to bring some perspective. But he knew Laura's anger toward him would override any attempt to communicate. He could certainly understand her anger, but he felt it was somewhat misdirected. They weren't fighting against flesh and blood, as Laura had previously stated so clearly. But to reduce it to the carnal level made them more susceptible to the demonic strategy—to divide and destroy them, the Stones, and the church.

"Look, Laura—"

"Don't patronize me, Bret; I'm not in the mood for your explanations. Don't you realize what's at stake?"

More than you do, Bret thought.

"We're about to lose everything—including our marriage!"

"So, that's the way you feel, huh?" Bret said, throwing his hands in the air.

"Yes, that's the way I feel, and I want out of this mess." Laura grabbed a book from the living room table and hurled it at Bret.

"You want out—meaning what, exactly?" Bret said, dodging the book.

"Out! I want out!"

"Of the marriage?" Bret asked incredulously.

"Yes! I'm not going to sit by and go through this freaking fiasco. You can have it; it's not for me!"

"So...," Bret said slowly, "are you saying it's over for us, just like that?"

"It isn't just like that, for heaven's sake, Bret. I can't get that image out of my head: that woman being here when I came home, and you downplaying it."

Bret felt helpless, silently letting her words sink in. He felt like his heart had just been ripped from his chest. The scene flashed back and claimed every space in his brain. Was he guilty? Stupid maybe, but not guilty of a moral transgression. That, he knew for certain. But Laura saw it differently. She was still deeply hurt by it, and he understood. What she failed to understand, though, was the full extent of the demonic attack they were under.

"What are your plans?" Bret's voice faded nearly to a whisper.

"I don't know yet; maybe just leave and go back to Maine. I've got friends there who would let me stay with them for a while. I could go back to teaching—and live on my own."

"Laura," Bret said, lifting his head, "it's only been a few days since all this happened. Why are you so abrupt with your decision to leave? I don't get it; were there other things going on that have factored into your decision?"

"It's been more than a few days since that woman started coming to church, and the interest you showed in her was obvious almost from the start."

"But I told you I had zero interest in her personally other than an innocent attempt to help her spiritually."

"Like the other women, Bret?" Laura shot a vicious glance at him.

"What on earth are you talking about, Laura? It's not like I've been sleeping around behind your back!"

"Maybe not," Laura snapped, "but over the years, I've noticed you spend a lot of time talking to me about other women in the church. And talking with them, too."

Had he? He pondered that. If so, he wasn't aware of it. There were more women in church than men, so naturally he would talk with them. "What are you implying, Laura?"

"Bottom line: I don't trust you."

"But you said earlier that you did. Are you jealous, Laura?" he said, then wished he hadn't.

"For heaven's sake, you're arrogant, aren't you? You're not exactly God's gift to women, you know!"

"Just trying to have an honest conversation with you—"

"But what? Are you trying to squirm away from the truth?"

"Laura, this is going nowhere in a hurry; if you feel you need to get away, then go; I can't stop you. But there's one thing I need to say."

"And what's that?"

"You are making a big mistake, and you are deceived. It looks to me like the enemy has succeeded in driving a wedge between us."

"Wedge or no wedge, Bret, I just need to get away for now. I'll wait until we see the outcome of the meeting before I leave. But if they get rid of you, I'll likely not come back."

Bret's heart sank again. He couldn't believe what he was hearing; he was completely unaware of the negative thoughts Laura had harbored for years. *Maybe this was good. This had to be flushed out sooner or later and maybe Cherie was just the agent to do it.* "I've been faithful," he said.

"Sometimes I wish you hadn't been; then I'd have a Biblical reason to leave."

"I can't believe you said that, Laura—that's vicious! Maybe it's you who has a problem with men, and you're transferring the blame to me!"

Oddly, Laura fell silent and didn't respond. She grabbed a tissue from the table and dabbed her eyes. Bret just looked at her not knowing what to say.

She broke her silence with "Don't go there, Bret."

Go there? What does she mean by that? He didn't dare ask.

CHAPTER FORTY-NINE

P relude appeared one last time before the meeting that night. Cherie emerged from the shower with only a towel on and shrieked when she saw him. She hurried into her bedroom to change into suitable clothes and reemerged a few minutes later. Prelude was more devilish looking than ever. His eyes glowed with evil, and his skin again became scaly, like a serpent's. He spoke in a low, hissing tone that sent shivers up Cherie's spine.

"This is my battle demeanor," Prelude said, smiling at Cherie. "I only assume it when I am sure victory is close at hand."

His eyes seemed to penetrate her; she avoided looking at him. Though she tried, she couldn't speak. She coiled up on the sofa like a child awaiting discipline. Prelude's voice now entered her mind without him speaking. *Maybe it's mental telepathy. I wonder if he can read my thoughts.*

"*Yes, I can,*" his voice rang in her head. She shuddered at the instantaneous response. *No way... there's no way he can do that.*

The voice sounded in her head. "You will need me to speak to you silently when you are at the meeting," he said aloud. "I will be instructing you in what you should do and say.

"Like I'm a robot?" Cherie glared as her voice returned to her.

"Not exactly," Prelude continued, "but, shall we say, controlled, as if I were speaking through you."

"Will it be your voice or mine?" Cherie asked, with a puzzled look on her face.

"Yours, of course. That way it will seem perfectly normal—but much more convincing."

Cherie thought for a moment. "You mean you don't trust me to speak on my own, right?"

"We are not willing to risk failure, Cherie; there is always room for human failure."

Human failure, Cherie repeated his words silently. *Not willing to risk it...where does that leave me?*

"Right where you should be," Prelude immediately responded. "Don't worry, you'll feel like you have all the power, but just realize—it's actually borrowed."

"Uh-huh," Cherie nodded with little emotion. "Just borrowed, which I assume means it has to be given back; nothing permanent?"

"You think correctly, Cherie."

"Then what's in it for me?"

"You checked the bank; the money is there for you."

"Ten thousand dollars won't go far in today's world."

"How much did you have before our deposit?" Prelude smirked.

"Less than a hundred dollars, but at least I had a job. I thought more money would be coming; was I wrong?"

"Perhaps after the destruction and humiliation of the fool pastor, you will receive additional funds."

"How much?" Cherie asked, turning to face him.

"That is determined by performance," Prelude laughed. "Just like you humans do for jobs well done! But now it's time to get ready. I want you to come closer to me."

Cherie hesitated, unable to move in his direction.

"Stay where you are—I will come to you."

Prelude approached Cherie and forced her from the sofa into a standing position. He placed his serpentine arms around her shoulders and across her back.

Cherie felt the cold and seemingly lifeless arms of the creature embrace her. She could hear the hissing of his breath as he drew his face closer to her. She detected a primitive, foul odor emanating from him—sickeningly sweet like a rotting corpse. She felt an urge to vomit. Prelude increased his grip on her back, and she winced in pain.

"Stop!" she cried. "What are you doing to me!"

"Preparing you for the impartation."

CHAPTER FIFTY

"What did you mean by you *can't get into that?*" Bret repeated, looking directly at Laura.

Laura shifted her feet nervously, not looking at her husband. "Nothing, Bret; I meant nothing at all."

"Then why say it? What do you have to hide?"

Laura whirled toward Bret and pushed him with both hands. "Will you just quit interrogating me!" she snapped.

"I'm not interrogating you, Laura; it was just odd the way you said you couldn't get into it. What am I supposed to think?"

"You're just trying to divert the conversation away from your own issues, and I'm not falling into that trap." Laura turned and headed toward the bedroom. "It's not about me; it's about you and your continual indiscretions toward women."

Bret stood silent, flummoxed by the change in the tone of the conversation. "Can we talk?" he asked, just before Laura entered the bedroom.

"There's nothing to discuss, Bret," she said and slammed the bedroom door.

What on earth? She's never acted this way before. Bret couldn't help having suspicions. Had Laura been unfaithful? Was she projecting guilt toward him, trying to cover something in her own life? And her abrupt decision to leave after having been on board with him just a short time ago. The meeting was only hours away, and he desperately needed her support. He was so distracted that he couldn't focus on what he was going to say before the elders. Then it struck him.

He was going to speak on the supernatural forces he knew were behind all the chaos. Cherie, Prelude, the opposition from Regis and Jesse, Laura's sudden flipping out. And it had all started with the disappearance of Wilbur's corpse. *No, how foolish I was to even entertain that Wilbur rose from the dead.* Suddenly, an image of the two men dressed in black at the back of the funeral chapel flashed in his mind. He instinctively knew they were somehow part of Prelude's evil scheme.

"That's it!" he said aloud. "The two witnesses! They'll be there tonight to testify. They must also be demonic. Sam was set up sure as the sun. They never witnessed anything."

He needed to tell Laura; she had to see the evil intent that was meant to destroy their marriage and the church. He thought she'd understood it, but was now convinced it was only mental acknowledgment on her part without full understanding.

A thousand thoughts flooded his mind. Could he convince the elders? Would Sam have any understanding of the extent of evil influences in Foylestown? Would Laura come to her senses? Would they finally find Wilbur's body? And what about Cherie? Sure, he'd had twinges of lust for her, but he'd squelched them quickly. A wave of compassion for her flooded his mind. She was a victim of deception regardless of how much she voluntarily cooperated. But how could he let her know that? She had completely submitted to Prelude; Bret doubted she would ever escape the pull of his power.

He felt completely alone, overwhelmed by the gravity of events that had happened and those about to happen. He headed for the bedroom. "Laura," he said, softly, "I really need to talk to you about something that I feel God has shown me; can I come in?"

"Laura?" Bret knocked gently on the door. "Please, it's extremely important."

No answer.

Bret tried opening the door. It was locked. He rattled the doorknob, hoping to break it free—to no avail.

His heart pounded. Wild thoughts flooded his mind. *What if she left through the window without saying goodbye? What if she's just shut down emotionally and won't speak to me? And what if...no!* he reasoned, *she would never do that.*

"Laura!" he shouted, "if you don't answer me, I'll be forced to break into the room!"

Still no answer. Bret lunged at the door, thrusting his shoulder against it, but it didn't budge. Again, he lunged—this time with more force, and the door started to give way. A third time he pushed with all his strength, and the door broke open.

Bret could only stare in utter shock. Laura was lying on the bed with a hideous creature mere inches from her face.

He was momentarily paralyzed, but, with a sudden burst of energy, he raced to Laura and threw himself at the creature shouting, "Get off her!" It didn't move but hissed like cat. Bret launched himself full force at the demon. "Leave her alone!" he screamed. "In Jesus' name, get off her!"

The creature instantly retreated and vanished through the wall, still hissing and shrieking.

Bret leaned against Laura's limp body and checked for a pulse. It was weak and erratic. He noticed marks on her face from where the creature had sat. Laura didn't move. He gently called her name, fighting back tears.

"Laura, can you hear me?"

She didn't answer.

CHAPTER FIFTY-ONE

B ret was so rattled that he couldn't prepare for the meeting that night at the church. He figured whatever the demon wanted to accomplish was partially successful. There was no way on earth the elders would believe what had just happened. How could he ever leave Laura alone? If the demon had thought of killing his wife, it didn't have ultimate power since she was God's child. Still, the psychological damage could be devastating. He stood beside the bed watching Laura. She laid in a fetal position, breathing in short, labored gasps. He sat beside her stroking her hair.

"It's gone," he said, reassuringly. "It didn't like the name *Jesus*. I was powerless until I spoke that name, and then the thing screamed and vanished through the wall." Bret smoothed Laura's hair away from her face and noticed the scratch marks near her eyes. The creature had left them there, almost as if the thing had meant to gouge her eyes out. His anger immediately spiked, and he cursed. They weren't prepared for any of this—but in a way, it didn't surprise him. He knew another attack would come, but he never thought it would be against Laura. He shuddered at the thought of what might have happened had he not broken into the bedroom at the right time. *And why didn't Laura cry out?* Then it struck him: maybe she couldn't; maybe she was mute.

He gently shook her. "Laura," he said softly, his mouth close to her ear. "Can you hear me?"

There was no answer. He spoke again, louder. "Laura, it's me, Bret; can you hear me?"

Laura turned slightly and looked at him with terror in her eyes. She slowly nodded her head but didn't speak.

Bret's eyes filled with tears as he watched the shell of a wife so vibrantly alive only a short time ago. Yes, they had argued, but at least she was animated and alive. Now she appeared to be more like a zombie. He choked back the tears, and his head sunk to his chest. He had no idea what to do other than pray...

The meeting with the elders was just over two hours away, and Bret was tormented thinking about that. He left Laura resting in the bedroom and went into the living room to pray. He knelt beside the large sofa and poured his heart out to the Lord, confessing his sin, and seeking wisdom and guidance. He wrestled with not knowing if God was even listening to him when a thought interrupted his prayer, almost as if it was an answer to prayer. He would call Sam to verify his commitment to come to the meeting and ask if his wife would come over to stay with Laura while they were at church. They weren't close friends, just acquaintances, but since both he and Sam were going to the meeting, it seemed like a reasonable, if not providential, answer. He sensed a calming peace permeate his mind, and he realized God had indeed not only heard, but answered his prayer. A confidence was reborn in his soul—confidence needed for what would lie ahead. He hadn't experienced that in a long time.

He stood up and reached for his cell phone. Sam answered on the third ring.

"It's Bret, Sam. Just checking to see if you're still okay with the meeting at church tonight. You can drop by here, and we can go together."

Sam hesitated, causing Bret's heart to race. "How long do you think it will take?" he finally asked with no enthusiasm.

"Hard to say with these things, but we can leave after we've said our piece."

"I'm not comfortable speaking before a church board."

"Well, all you have to do is tell exactly what happened in your office with Cherie."

"That's exactly what I don't feel comfortable doing, Bret."

"I'll be there with you, Sam; we have somewhat similar stories to tell."

"...you think any of them are going to believe us? And, what about those two imaginary witnesses—they're supposed to be there, too."

"I have some thoughts about them, Sam, but I can't share them right now." Bret headed for the bedroom to check on Laura.

"Maybe on the way over, huh?"

"Maybe, but I've got some things to share that will blow your mind, Sam. You'll have a hard time believing them, as will the elders at church. I doubt any of them will believe what I have to say except for J.R. McCabe and Wayne Silver."

"Yeah, I know them both; they seem like good men to me."

"I agree; I think Wayne has had some bad experiences in town, since he's one of the few African Americans here."

"That's a shame, Bret; some people exist just to spread hatred."

"But he takes it in stride and doesn't retaliate. He's a mature Christian and lives his life according to his faith."

Sam paused again for a few seconds. "I'm not a Christian, as you know, Bret. I could just never get beyond the hypocrisy and infighting you hear about in churches."

Understandable. But not a rational excuse for unbelief. And Sam is going to see some real infighting tonight if my hunch is correct. "Well, it's a terrible shame that happens so often," Bret agreed, "but that's not always the case. There are some excellent churches where that doesn't exist."

"Must be a minority, then."

"...you on board for tonight?" Bret asked, abruptly changing the subject.

"Hmm...I guess so; but you'll have to have my back."

"We're in it together, Sam. I'm right there with you; and by the way—" Bret paused.

"Yeah?"

"I've got a favor to ask."

"As long as you're not trying to convert me, go ahead."

"Do you think Jean would agree to come to our house and be with Laura? She's been through some very disturbing things in the last hour or so, and I can't leave her alone."

"Man, this whole thing seems disturbing to me, Bret. What the hell's going on?"

"I'll get into that tonight; now, what about Jean?"

"I can ask her; I don't see why she wouldn't go. I think it'll be good for her, too, since you and I are the ones on trial." Sam chuckled as he spoke, but Bret took a deep breath.

"Okay, and if she agrees, you can meet me here and we'll go together."

"We'll be there about a quarter to six."

"Make it more liked 5:30, if you can; we'll need time to talk."

"Me going into a church," Sam sighed. "Sure, if Jean agrees, we'll be there by 5:30."

"One more thing, Sam."

"What's that?"

"Laura may not be able to speak."

CHAPTER FIFTY-TWO

"Impartation?" Cherie asked Prelude, still feeling the scaly clutch of his serpentine claw digging into her shoulder. She winced in pain. "What is an impartation?"

"An empowerment," Prelude answered. "Kind of like what you Christians call the filling of the so-called Spirit. You will receive a filling of *my* spirit within you."

Despite her human appetite for control, his words didn't convince her that she wanted that kind of power; she was deeply troubled by them. This was of another order. She realized more and more that she was just an agent for whatever plan Prelude and the others had; she was certainly dispensable. But she reminded herself, she had already relinquished her will to the creature who had her in his grip both physically and psychically. She tried to pull away from Prelude's grip but was unable. *Why...why had she allowed herself to get into this frightening, godawful quandary?*

Prelude tightened his grip on her shoulder. Cherie's mind was filled with evil; hatred rose in her heart. She envisioned Bret being brought down to his knees in prostrate subjection to Prelude. Wasn't that what she'd wanted? Yes—yes, of course it was. Immediately any doubt she'd had about the mission that lay ahead that night disappeared. Prelude loosened his grip.

"And now the impartation!" he said, his voice reverberating in her brain.

Yes, Cherie thought, *the impartation.*

Her body began to tremble and jerk. Her breathing shortened to shallow gasps. She felt a surge of energy course throughout her entire being.

"You will do exactly as I command you, Cherie; is that understood?"

"Yes," she replied meekly. "I will do exactly as you say."

THE MEETING WAS STILL OVER an hour away. Bret sat on the bed with Laura, holding her in his arms and speaking softly and reassuringly to her. Her body was still rigid as if she was in an epileptic state. He looked at her eyes, which were no longer filled with terror.

"It's going to be okay," he said softly. "The Lord is with us, and we've just got to ride it out for now."

Laura nodded slowly, gripping Bret's hand. Tears formed in her eyes. Bret reached for a tissue on the nightstand and gently wiped her moistened face.

"I'm going to pray now," he said, looking into Laura's eyes. "I know you can't speak right now, but just nod if you'll join me."

Laura instantly nodded and smiled weakly.

"As much damage and potential harm that Cherie has done, I feel compelled to pray for her. I believe her soul is in mortal danger." Bret studied Laura's face for a response. At first, she looked quizzical and angry, but she slowly softened, again squeezing Bret's hand for reassurance.

"We have much to pray about," he added, enumerating all the things they were facing, with a priority on Laura's well-being. He ended with an earnest prayer for Cherie, acknowledging that she was in the throes of an evil force which only God could free her from. Just as he was finishing and before he had time to tell Laura about Jean coming, he heard a car pull into the driveway.

270

"...must be Sam and Jean," he said, feeling overwhelmed with guilt and doubt that he was leaving Laura with Jean while he and Sam went to the meeting. He again prayed that God would protect her and Jean in their absence.

"I have to be at the church in less than an hour. I've asked Jean Stone to come over to stay with you; is that okay?"

Laura smiled faintly and nodded her head. The pressing guilt he'd felt a moment ago disappeared. He left Laura's bedside and went to the door to let Sam and Jean in. After a few brief words, Jean followed Bret into the bedroom. She sat beside Laura and held her hand. Laura squeezed tightly.

———— ⊷ ◗ ⊶ ————

"Glad you could make it earlier," Bret said to Sam as they sat in Sam's cruiser discussing their strategy for the meeting. "It's going to be heated and unpredictable for sure. I wanted to talk to you about a few things before we head over. We're going to speak first and present our case regarding Cherie—you can go first, and I will follow."

"Me going first? ...not sure I like the sound of that," Sam protested.

"It will have more impact that way, Sam; but there is something else I need to talk with you about."

"Like what?"

"It's about Prelude and the evil he represents. I believe there are more entities involved with Prelude. There may be many, in fact, and I'm quite sure the two witnesses are not human."

"Holy—" Sam swore. "What on earth are you talking about?"

"For whatever reason, we're their targets; me, you, our marriages, and the church."

"That's very disturbing, Bret; it's way beyond me." Sam pulled his cap off and scratched his head. I understood the Prelude thing a little bit, but you know Jean and I are newcomers at the church and rank amateurs when it comes to this stuff."

"Yeah, but you're also the chief of police, and you know Cherie targeted you. If they succeed in bringing you down, that will put the whole town into chaos. And mark my words: These forces are also behind Wilbur's disappearance and Russell's death."

"Whew, Bret! You think they killed them both?"

"Not sure about Wilbur; I think Russell could have been involved in his death, but I'm convinced Russell's death was no accident. We're dealing with vicious forces of another kingdom."

Sam slumped back in the seat and didn't speak for a few moments. "But what about the idea that Wilbur was resurrected; wasn't that one of your premises from the start?"

"I've thought that through carefully, Sam, and I don't think that was a viable theory. No doubt God can do that if He wants to, but I've seen no convincing evidence of bodily resurrections today."

"Well...that was a little far-fetched to my understanding, but I deferred to you on that," Sam said, sitting up straight. "What's your current take on what happened to Wilbur's body?"

"I'm not sure at this point, but I don't underestimate the power these forces have to deceive people, and part of their deception may have been to force you to resign since you couldn't locate the body."

"And what about the alleged appearances of Wilbur in town?"

"Same thing; all part of the deception."

Sam blew out a heavy sigh. "I'm very concerned about Forrest; he's been quite depressed lately."

"Yeah, me too. And he's totally against anything having to do with faith. In fact, he's hardened toward God."

"Yeah," Sam said resignedly, "I was there a short time ago;

maybe not to that extent, but something seems to be turning me around."

Bret smiled knowingly at his friend. "Doesn't surprise me, Sam."

"I'm open to learning, but you gotta go slow with me. I'm a heathen, you know.

They both laughed as Sam fired up the cruiser's engine. "We'd better get going, Sam; we'll be a little late–but maybe that'll be to our advantage."

CHAPTER FIFTY-THREE

Jean sat on the bed and gently stroked Laura's hand. They were casual friends—not nearly as close as Bret and Sam—but they had spent time together at a few community events. They both faced the same shocking reality that their husbands were on trial, and their livelihoods were threatened. And of course their respective marriages were at stake. Jean knew less about the spirit world and the entity that Cherie had mentioned when fleeing from Sam's office. Sam hadn't shared too much with her for fear of adding more stress to their already strained marriage. All she knew was that her husband was headed for a church meeting which somehow would help determine whether he would lose his job as chief of police. She couldn't figure how the church elders would have any say in what happened, but she knew that Sam and Bret would share corroborating stories. Perhaps they'd have the impact of silencing the entire sordid affair to keep it from going public.

Laura stirred and looked at Jean, squeezing her hand firmly. "Thanks for coming over," she said weakly.

Jean was surprised that Laura had regained her voice. "I'm not sure what you've been through," she said. "Bret just said it was a terrible experience but didn't elaborate. I know he felt terrible having to leave after what happened, but I hope I can be of some comfort to you. It would be great getting to know you better, given the circumstances we both face."

Laura nodded. "You're already a comfort to me."

"Can you tell me what happened that caused such trauma?" Jean asked carefully. "Bret said you weren't able to speak."

"Well," Laura began, "Bret and I had just argued, so I went into the bedroom quite upset. I laid down trying to defuse when, out of nowhere, this thing appeared."

"A thing?" Jean gasped.

"It was hideous, Jean. A repulsive creature was standing on me close to my face. It looked like something out of an alien movie. I was paralyzed with fear and couldn't speak. Bret called to me, and I couldn't answer. He finally came in and scared it away, but the thing left some marks on my face." Laura leaned forward so Jean could see the scratch marks.

"Oh, my God!" Jean cried. "That's unbelievable! Do you know what it was?"

"Probably a demon or some other entity from the spirit realm; and here's the thing, Jean." Laura's countenance grew dark, and her voice weakened. "Bret had a similar experience the other night. He woke with a terrible headache and called out to me—it was so severe. When I looked at him in the dark, I could make out the form of something directly behind Bret that seemed to be attached to his head. It was large enough that I knew it was a creature of some kind. I screamed and turned on the light to get a better look, and immediately the thing left."

"How awful, Laura! And what happened after that?"

"Bret's headache disappeared instantly."

"Wow, just like that?"

"Yes, just like that. Whatever it was, it was pressuring Bret's head. I don't know if it was trying to kill him or what. It was the creepiest thing I've ever seen; and now...the thing that happened to me...," Laura began to cry. "I just can't take any more, Jean; I've already told Bret I need to get away from everything. The whole Cherie thing came back like a flood, and we argued. I can't believe my husband was so naive."

"I don't know the details there, Laura, but it seems to me as if both of our husbands were set up. Do you think that woman is in league with the creatures?"

Laura paused. "I think...I think Cherie is controlled by an alien power we know to be Prelude. So, it's not just a crazy woman trying to seduce our husbands, but something far more sinister—something supernatural."

Jean's jaw dropped. "I don't blame you for wanting to get away from all this, but do you think it's the best time to do that? Don't you think that's part of the strategy of these so-called alien powers?"

Laura thought for a moment. "I don't doubt it, Jean; it's just that I'm still angry at my husband for letting that woman into our lives in the first place. He thought he could privately tutor her—against my warnings—and that started this whole mess. I don't know what Bret has shared with Sam about all that went on, but I can't get beyond the outrage and anger I have—especially with the two demon incidents. It scares me half to death, and I don't know what might happen next. Who knows what the meeting tonight will amount to? I don't want to be here for the next bizarre act in this awful drama. And it seems to me Bret should have opted out of the meeting to be here with me; I always seem to be his last priority. What if the creature reappears?"

Jean massaged her forehead as if in deep thought. "Please don't take offense at what I'm going to say, Laura, but as a friend and not just an acquaintance, I think your anger toward Bret has clouded your judgment. Even if you run away, it doesn't mean the drama will cease; in fact, it could get a lot worse—not only for you, but for Bret, and for the church. We need to fight and not retreat."

Laura's face began to flush at Jean's words; she wondered if Jean really understood what she was going through. She started to react but refrained herself.

After a minute of reflection, she spoke. "You're right, Jean. My anger was initially justified, but I'm paying a heavy price to let it control me."

"And our husbands need us right now," Jean said. "Who knows what they're facing at that meeting."

Laura looked at Jean and sighed. "It's no accident you're here, Jean. If Bret had stayed, I would've never realized what you just said. I would've still been filled with resentment toward him."

As they both leaned forward in an embrace, Jean's cell phone rang. "I should probably answer this since Sam is at the meeting; it may be important."

Laura nodded. "Yes, you should."

The unidentified voice on the phone said, "Forrest Fields's mutilated body has been found on the lawn outside the funeral home."

"Oh my God, no!" Jean shrieked and dropped the phone.

CHAPTER FIFTY-FOUR

B ret and Sam were purposely late for the meeting; they arrived at 6:10—a move that Bret figured might give them a slight edge. But before they entered the conference room, Sam's phone chirped.

"Darn," he said, "I meant to silence that before the meeting." He glanced at the number and realized his wife was calling. "I'd better take this," he said to Bret. "It's Jean."

"Sure thing," Bret said. "Do you want to take it in private? I can go inside and wait for you. I'll just explain that you had a last-minute call from Jean."

"Yeah, if you don't mind; I'll be right in after I see what she wants."

Bret entered the room and nodded somberly at the elders who were anxiously awaiting his arrival. Maury motioned him to a chair at the head of the rectangular table.

"Please have a seat, Bret; by the way, we thought Sam was coming too."

"He is," Bret answered. "Jean called just as we were about to come into the conference room; he felt he should take the call."

Bret sat down and surveyed the assembled elders. All were present.

"Well, I hope he doesn't take long," Regis said, scowling at Bret. "You're already late, and we have a lot to cover. And when you've both said your piece, we will have Cherie and the two witnesses come in."

"Are we supposed to stay for that part?" Bret asked, hoping the answer was in the affirmative. "We have a right to face our accusers, plus it seems like we should go last—not them. That's kind of backward."

No one responded—then Maury stood and said: "We've already heard the accusations from Cherie; the witnesses will be allowed to speak." He addressed the group. "And of course you can stay and respond to them; we wouldn't have it any other way, would we?" No one objected, but Regis and Jesse looked at each other and smiled as if to say *we want him to fully feel the conviction that's coming.*

"What's taking him so long?" Jesse asked, referring to Sam. "Maybe someone should check on him to see if he's chickened out."

Jesse snickered, but Maury cast a stern look at him and said, "I'm sure he has legitimate reasons for the delay."

"Maybe she wants him to pick up a pizza on the way home!" Regis laughed.

"Will you quit acting like a child, Regis!" Maury shouted. "We are not here to make light of what we'll be considering."

Regis's face reddened in defiance, but he felt it best not to retaliate; his time would come soon enough.

"J.R., would you check on Sam, and tell him we've got to start the meeting?" Maury requested.

"Sure," J. R. said and headed for the door, closing it loudly behind him.

The elders murmured while he was gone, and Bret caught the eyes of Wayne Silver. He noticed a look of compassion and deep concern.

Bret knew he had an ally.

—••○••—

J. R. RAN HEADLONG INTO SAM as he exited the conference room.

"...you looking for me?" Sam asked, knowing the answer.

"Yeah, everyone is anxious to get this thing started," J. R. responded.

Sam grabbed him by the arm. "I've got some very bad news, J. R.; it appears that Forrest Fields has been murdered."

"What?" J. R. said. A look of shock shone in his eyes in seconds. "Murdered?"

"Yes, I got a call from my wife, and she said an anonymous caller told her that Forrest's body was found mutilated in the front yard of the funeral home."

"Holy cow, Sam; what if it's a hoax? I don't know of anyone who'd want to harm him, let alone murder him in such a horrible way now that Russell is out of the picture!"

"I totally agree, J. R., but with all that's been going on in Foylestown lately, nothing shocks me. Jean said the caller sounded serious and matter of fact. I'm going to have to leave the meeting to inspect what appears to be a crime scene."

"Well, that certainly isn't going to sit well with the elders, and especially Bret. He'll be pretty much on his own, and there are some who want him out immediately. It could be a blood bath—and then there's the two supposed witnesses along with the woman."

"I know, I know, J. R., but I have no choice. If it's true, then we have a murderer at large, and I'm responsible for tracking him—or her—down."

The door opened and Maury appeared. "What on earth is keeping you guys? It's already 6:20 and we haven't even started."

"I'll explain," Sam said. "Just give me a couple of minutes to share what's going on."

"You mean to me or the elders?" Maury replied.

"In front of everyone; it's critical."

"It had better be," Maury said, not hiding his irritation.

The three men returned to the conference room to witness heated discussion among the elders. Bret remained silent, still seated alone at the head of the table.

"Quiet down, everyone! Sam has something to share which he feels is crucial, although I'm not sure what. You have two minutes, Sam—two minutes."

"I don't need two minutes!" Sam snapped. He cleared his throat and took a deep breath. "I just got a call from my wife...,"

Bret's heart sank.

"...and she said she was contacted by an anonymous caller who informed her that Forrest Fields has been brutally murdered."

There was a collective gasp followed by a flurry of questions.

"I have no other details, so hold your questions. I hate to do this, but I have to leave immediately." He looked directly at Bret who heaved a heavy sigh of relief, followed by a look of panic.

That was all Sam said before he abruptly departed. Bret stood up and raised his voice, trying to speak over the confusion. "I think we should reschedule this meeting since Sam is no longer here; his testimony is essential."

Regis jumped to his feet. "Ain't gonna happen!" he shouted.

Maury tried to object, but the sheer force of Regis's voice and presence overruled his effort.

"We need to settle this thing tonight; we don't need the chief of police here anyway. I think it's pretty clear what needs to be done," Regis continued. He glared at Bret, who tried to say something, but sensed it wasn't to his advantage to continue his thought.

"Quiet, everyone!" Maury spoke as loudly as he could, attempting to regain control, but was intimidated by Regis's outburst. "We will continue the meeting as planned."

Regis looked at Jesse and smirked knowingly. Jesse smiled back.

CHAPTER FIFTY-FIVE

When order was finally restored, Bret reasoned that any chance of retaining his position as pastor had all but evaporated. He knew the only chance he had was with the corroborating account Sam could have shared.

And now he's gone.

He considered preempting the meeting by just resigning before a vote could be taken. It would save him a lot of humiliation and grief. But it would devastate Laura, and she was already on the brink of a nervous breakdown. At least if he resigned, he wouldn't give Regis and Jesse the pleasure of voting him out. Oh, they would gloat anyway, but he could still be the master of his own fate and retain a measure of dignity. He knew he had more than one adversary in the group, not to mention Cherie and the yet-to-materialize witnesses. He wasn't sure about Maury, who was obviously intimidated by Regis and would most likely vote for his resignation. That left Wayne, J.R., and Jesse. Judging from the camaraderie Regis and Jesse had, Bret couldn't see Jesse supporting him in any way. The only two he was certain Regis couldn't strong-arm were Wayne and J. R., but he had no idea what impact Cherie and the two witnesses would have. The Foylestown Community Church constitution stated that only a plurality of elders was needed to remove a pastor; given the current status, there was no way he would survive the vote.

"Bret," Maury interrupted his thoughts, "are you ready to reiterate your account of what happened? And you indicated there was something else you wanted to share with the group."

Bret paused as if in thought before he answered. "What I have said, I have said; it needs no reiteration. I have described my encounter with Ms. Loman and, to the best of my ability, what I believe happened and why. I am troubled that Sam cannot be here, but I'm not prepared to speak on his behalf. I feel that his account would have lent credence to what I've shared. And he hasn't had a chance to confront his accuser; that's a total perversion of justice. Will this all go public against Sam? Will you report it to the press? Will he be forced to resign?"

Bret raised his voice and felt the flush of anger rise in his face. "This isn't a criminal trial," he continued, staring directly at Regis. "It's just her word against his, and he hasn't had a chance to defend himself. And what about the so-called witnesses who are supposed to be here tonight? No chance for them to hear Sam's account either. Sounds like a lynching to me. Perhaps he'll have an opportunity to share later."

"It'll be too late!" Regis interrupted, pounding his fist on the table. "We're going to vote tonight since we jeopardize the integrity of the church if we wait any longer. Isn't that right, Maury?"

He cast a scalding glance at the head elder who meekly said, "That's right, we will vote tonight; we had already decided to do that earlier."

"And by the way, whatever happens to Sam Stone is of no account to us," Regis added. "He can sink or swim in the court of public opinion, and, as it appears now, he'll sink quite quickly once word gets out."

"Yeah," Bret erupted, "and just who is going to leak his alleged assault to the public?"

Regis smirked and said, "Things have a way of getting out, don't they?"

Bret stifled his anger and prayed silently for wisdom when he shared about the invisible players behind what was happening in Foylestown and at the church. He slowly stood, cleared his throat, and prepared to speak.

But just as he began speaking, the door opened; Cherie entered—followed by one man dressed in a black business suit. Bret assumed he was one of the witnesses.

But where was the other?

CHAPTER FIFTY-SIX

Sam's heart pounded as he wiped the sweat from his brow. He and Forrest were friends, and the thought that Forrest had been brutally murdered incensed him. He cursed loudly as he raced to Fields' Funeral Home in the police cruiser, lights flashing and siren blaring. He fought off gruesome images of the scene that might await him. He still held out hope that it was a hoax to distract him and get him away from the meeting. He thought of Bret being alone before the heinous hounds that wanted to tear him apart. The frustration built.

As he approached the funeral home, he noticed a sizable crowd had gathered in the front yard. He knew instantly that his fears were justified. This was no hoax.

He wheeled into the side parking lot, cruiser lights still flashing.

"Stand back!" he shouted as he exited the vehicle. "Don't touch anything!"

The crowd of about twenty people moved aside as Sam approached Forrest's mutilated body. He swallowed hard to keep from retching at what he saw. He knelt and checked for a pulse. There was none.

Who in God's name would have done such a hellish thing? He knelt beside Forrest's battered body. Spattered blood covered most of it, and what appeared to be claw marks in the skin were visible underneath his shredded clothing. Forrest's face was almost beyond recognition. It looked as though a wild animal had torn him apart. Bears were reported to be in the area recently, but there hadn't been any reports of attacks. Sam examined the body more closely, looking for clues as to what might have happened. Someone must have had a vicious hatred for Forrest. If Russell had been alive, Sam could imagine him doing it, but unless he came back from the grave, someone—or *something*—else was the perpetrator.

Just as Sam turned on his knees to face the crowd, he noticed something shiny embedded in Forrest's neck. The setting sun made it glisten like a bit of metal. At first, Sam thought it might be the remnant of a knife blade.

He carefully pulled the object from Forrest's neck with his right hand and placed it on the open palm of his left hand. "What in God's name?!" he exclaimed.

Everyone drew close to see what Sam had discovered.

It was unmistakable. In the center of Sam's hand was a triangular object.

"What the heck?" Sam said, dumbfounded. "This looks like a large fish scale."

———•◦•———

MAKES NO SENSE AT ALL. As Sam pondered what it meant, he noticed a solitary figure at the back of the crowd slip silently away, seeming to disappear. He didn't give it a second thought since his mind was still processing the brutality of Forrest's murder.

"What is it?" someone in the crowd asked, looking intently at the unidentified object. "Do you think it was the weapon used to kill Forrest?"

Sam shook his head. "It would have taken more than this to cause death. He's lost an enormous amount of blood from the slash marks. I want everyone to back away; this is a crime scene," he said addressing the crowd. "And why wasn't 911 called?"

"I did call them," a slender, middle-aged woman said. "And I also called your wife —she's a personal friend of mine."

Sam stood up, wrapped the object in his handkerchief, and put it in a pocket of his uniform. "And what did you say? They must have been sleeping since no emergency personnel were dispatched to the scene."

"I told them there had been what appeared to be a murder and described in detail what I saw. That was about a half hour ago."

"They should have been here some time ago," Sam said in disgust. "It's not likely, but they might have been able to save Forrest's life."

Just as he said this, a siren sounded in the distance. A few minutes later, several emergency vehicles arrived.

———— ❖ ————

IMMEDIATELY AFTER SAM HAD BRIEFED the emergency personnel and completed his preliminary investigation, his mind turned back to the meeting between Bret and the elders. Knowing Bret had been there alone bothered him greatly. He wasn't sure if he should return or not. It was now close to 8:00 p.m.; he concluded that the meeting must have ended some time ago. Forrest's body had been removed, and the crowd had dispersed. He was left alone with his thoughts. Brutal, angry thoughts. No one deserved to die like Forrest had. He wondered how much Forrest had suffered at the hands of the butcher. *Yeah, he was butchered like an animal for the slaughter.* And the anger continued unabated, a raging torrent in his mind. He thought of calling Bret but decided against it. He figured Bret would call him to let him know how things went once he had a chance.

A car filled with occupants observing the crime scene drove by slowly. No one got out, but Sam could see heads craned, looking for anything to satisfy their curiosity. *Strange how some people seem stimulated by the macabre. So many movies and television programs focus on the grisly aspects of crime.*

He decided to go to Bret's house and check on the women. Maybe Bret would be there, and he could debrief him on the meeting.

But Bret wasn't there; the meeting was nowhere near being over.

CHAPTER FIFTY-SEVEN

"Where's the other witness?" Bret asked, looking directly at Cherie.

"He was delayed," she said, eyes darting nervously. "He'll be here shortly."

"Then I'll wait until he arrives," Bret insisted, shifting his feet anxiously and trying to look confident.

"No need to wait," Regis objected. "We can start without him. Maury, tell Bret that we need to proceed and get this thing over with."

Maury was silent.

"And what is your name?" Bret asked the witness, ignoring Regis. "And how is it that you and the other guy just happened by at the precise moment of the alleged assault?"

"My name is of no consequence," the witness said, locking his piercing dark eyes on Bret. "We wish to remain anonymous."

Bret felt like the witness was staring into his soul, and, for a moment, he was unable to respond. He had a growing sense that the figure standing opposite him in the dark business suit was one of the men at the back of the chapel during Wilbur's funeral. Bret decided to challenge him to see what his response would be.

"Of course it's of consequence," Bret protested. "How can anyone trust the testimony of a witness with no name? And Sam's not here to defend himself. This whole thing tonight is a farce."

The man's face twitched slightly, then he spoke. "Don't try to challenge what I'm going to say as if it's untrue."

"I do challenge anything you say! And by the way, I've seen you before."

Everyone looked at the witness, waiting for a response. He spoke slowly, deliberately. "Your eyes have deceived you even as you and the chief of police are presenting false evidence to justify your licentious behavior toward this innocent victim." He pointed directly at Cherie, who lowered her head in fake contrition.

"He's absolutely right!" Regis shouted. "Bret is trying to intimidate him to save his sorry butt."

"Of course he's right!" Jesse followed Regis's lead. "Trying to intimidate the witness."

Wayne jumped to his feet, "He's not intimidating anyone, Regis; I would say it's you who's been trying to bully the rest of us! Well—I, for one, am not going to be bullied."

The witness turned toward Wayne. "When we get through here, you will agree with us completely, Mr. Silver."

"Never!" Wayne shot back, but instantly felt a tightness in his body almost paralyzing him.

"You will agree with us tonight."

That's proof! Bret thought, noting that the man hadn't denied being at the funeral. *My entire premise is being confirmed. This is way beyond mere flesh and blood. It's been a setup from the start to destroy our marriages and to bring the church down.* He prayed for guidance.

At that precise moment, Laura and Jean were also praying.

The other witness arrived just as J.R. rose in support of Wayne. "I—I agree with Wayne," he stuttered, his tongue sticking to the roof of his mouth.

"Tell us what you heard," Maury interjected, making eye contact with the witnesses. "We need to hear your story."

"We were just passing through Foylestown and stopped at the police station for information," the second witness said. "The front door of the building was unlocked so we entered, hoping to speak with the chief, Mr. Stone. That's when we heard a scuffle followed by a loud scream. Ms. Loman cried for help, telling the chief repeatedly to let her go. Then we saw her escape with a torn piece of the chief's shirt. We immediately left to follow her, but she was gone before we could reach her. When we returned, the police station door was locked."

The room fell silent as if all in attendance were in a trance as the witnesses corroborated each other's account.

Then it came time for Cherie to speak.

She felt Prelude's presence and heard his voice in her mind: *This is your opportunity, Cherie. I am with you to direct you; you must follow my lead completely. Don't fail me, Cherie.*

"I won't," Cherie pronounced loudly, to everyone's amazement. She looked directly at Bret. The two witnesses were silent, but one faced Bret and the other positioned himself behind him, almost touching him.

Bret sensed an overpowering, indefinable wickedness surrounding his entire being.

The atmosphere in the conference room breathed with evil. The elders' eyes were riveted on Cherie as she stepped forward to speak.

"Go ahead, Ms. Loman," Maury said, nodding to her.

———•— ◖ —•———

LAURA AND JEAN KNELT BESIDE Laura's bed to pray, sensing a crushing urgency.

———•— ◖ —•———

BRET FELT HIS SKIN CRAWL as the witness came within inches...

Cherie spoke: "I address all of you men here tonight as a victim of vicious sexual attacks by two depraved men wanting to ruin my life. You have heard my story before; it stands as I have said. You have heard the account of the witnesses, who, by God's providence, arrived at the precise time of the assault by the chief. Mrs. Crossman herself was a witness to her husband's attempt to seduce me."

As she spoke, the elders began to nod their heads in agreement with her story—all except Wayne and J. R., who looked at each other knowingly.

Bret thought his heart would explode as Cherie narrowed her gaze to him, addressing him directly.

"Isn't it true, Mr. Crossman, that you've had your eye on me from the first day I entered your church?"

Bret froze. It was true he noticed her the first day. She was dressed seductively and approached him after church.

"Say it, Pastor; acknowledge how much you wanted me from the start!"

Had he? Was what she was saying true? His mind clouded with confusion; he questioned his own conscience. Thoughts not his own seemed to invade his mind.

"Pastor?" Cherie repeated. "It's true, isn't it?"

The witness behind Bret touched his shoulder. A shocking bolt shot through his body. Bret silently cried out to God for help.

All the elders were silent, seemingly dazed, waiting for Bret to answer. Regis leered at him with malevolence in his eyes, sensing a victory was so near he could taste it.

A weird, intoxicating odor seeped into the room, stupefying the elders.

They waited...

———◦———

SAM PULLED THE POLICE CRUISER into the Crossman's driveway. He was still in shock over Forrest's death. So much had happened in the last few hours that defied reason. Maybe he was dreaming and would wake in the morning with everything back to normal. But he knew it was not a dream. Again, he thought of Bret and wondered if they had voted him out yet. And the witnesses; did they show up and testify against him without him being there to defend himself? *What a perversion of justice. Such a case would be thrown out of court as a complete mockery of the law. But the recent events were beyond justice, at least in this life.*

Sam rang the doorbell and waited. Laura peered through the security lens and let him in, giving him a firm hug.

"Thank God you're here, Sam!" she said, excited to see him. Laura ushered him into the living room where Jean was seated. She arose from the sofa and embraced her husband.

"Yes, it's so good to see you, honey," she said. "We've been in prayer for you and Bret."

"I had to leave the meeting," he said bluntly. "After I got the call from you, I rushed to the funeral home to see what had happened. A crowd was gathered, but there were no EMTs or other emergency personnel there when I arrived. I felt sick leaving Bret alone, but I had to investigate what has proven to be an unconscionable murder." Sam's eyes watered.

"What in God's name!" Laura cried. "Who on earth would want to murder Forrest? The man's already been through hell."

"You won't believe what I found when I arrived." He looked at Jean, whose face was drawn tight with concern.

"Was it bad?" Jean asked.

"Unbelievably gruesome," Sam said, "like something out of a horror film. I'm not sure I should even share it."

"We're not children, Sam," Laura protested. "We want to know what you found."

"He was clawed to death."

Both Laura and Jean stood dumbfounded. "Clawed to death?" Laura asked, lips quivering. "By what?"

"That," Sam said, "is what's got me baffled."

CHAPTER FIFTY-EIGHT

Prelude whispered to Cherie. "You've got them under your power. The two members of our alliance have Bret in total control; he's about to admit to your charge, then there will be a unanimous vote to remove him. The elders are stupefied, including the two dupes who supported him. They and their God are no match for us!"

In her mind, Cherie heard Prelude roaring with laughter as he boasted of victory.

All eyes were on Bret. "Yes, it's true; I did have unclean thoughts toward you when I first saw you, but...,"

"And you did have sensual thoughts toward me, didn't you?" Cherie quickly cut Bret off before he could finish.

"But it...It was only—" Bret knew his confession was true, but incomplete. He felt as though his nerves were outside of his skin and ready to tear.

"You see!" Cherie shouted. "He's just confessed to evil desires in front of all of you! He's guilty just as the perverse cop is guilty! And both men assaulted me just as I said."

The elders sat silently, unable to voice responses. The witness behind Bret pressed his hand deeply into Bret's shoulder. A greater fear than he had ever felt seized him. He looked at the elders who were frozen as if in a still life painting. The conference room was now under the command of an alien force. The other witness circled behind Bret, placing his hand on Bret's other shoulder. Cherie approached him slowly.

"You want me right now, don't you, Bret?" Cherie spoke, her presence overpowering him. "Admit to the elders that you have an irresistible desire for me, just as you did when you tried seducing me in your home."

The room was eerily quiet, as though the walls themselves were awaiting Bret's response. The elders' eyes remained riveted upon him. No one moved or spoke.

Bret's heart pounded in his ears. He tried to center himself and look away from Cherie's penetrating gaze.

"Bret...," she spoke softly, "we're waiting for you."

Prelude spoke to her: "One more minute and you will have him totally in your control. I am enabling you right now to pierce his weakened conscience and to break any resistance. We are close to ending our mission. His marriage will fail; the church will fall; the cop will be banished from Foylestown."

"And I will get my reward!" Cherie blurted out.

———— ◦ ————

SAM HAD DIFFICULTY FOCUSING AS his thoughts flashed back to Forrest's mangled body on the funeral home lawn. He was also aware that his position as chief of police was likely in jeopardy. So many wild thoughts raged through his mind—from hatred to anger to sympathy.

"I can't explain how crushed I am about all that's happened in the last few hours," he said, looking at the two women whose eyes were filled with compassion. "I feel I've let Bret down."

"No, you haven't, Sam," Jean said quickly, reaching for his hand. "What you did was the right thing, and you really didn't have a choice; as the chief, your priority was investigating a crime."

"And you had no idea if the perpetrator was still around or was a threat to others," Laura said, agreeing with Jean.

"I guess you're both right, but it seems to have been more than coincidental that Forrest's murder happened just before I was to share my story before the elders. It makes you wonder what might be happening behind the scenes."

"There is a lot more going on than we know, Sam," Laura interjected. "Bret and I both believe there are evil agents involved, as you well know, based on what happened here just before you guys left for the church."

"Agents of destruction, so it would seem," Jean added. "This all gives me the creeps. I'm convinced that woman is lying about what happened in Sam's office; my husband would never do what she accused him of." She looked directly at Sam who nodded slowly.

"Yes," he said, "she lied, but there was something about her that was beyond normal; Bret's testified to the same."

"And her motive is to destroy both of our marriages," Laura said. "Even though you and Bret were quite naive in believing her in the beginning, I'm glad you see her differently now."

"But what would she gain if she succeeded in tearing either of us apart?" Sam asked. "Just a perverse satisfaction in ruining us?"

"She's a pawn," Laura asserted, having fully recovered from the demonic incident earlier in the day. "Bret believes he was unwittingly set up from the beginning. Not to minimize the importance of our marriages, but there are bigger fish to fry than the four of us."

"And who or what would that be?" Jean asked, wide-eyed.

"The church," Laura said. "They are after the church."

"They?" Sam countered.

"The evil forces or agents—whatever they are; you know Bret and I have both been attacked by what we believe to be demons."

"Makes me shudder," Jean said, crossing her arms in front of her. "I sure hope Sam and I don't experience that...,"

"They really have no power over us, although they can certainly influence and intimidate with fear. Until Bret came in to chase the cursed thing away, I was in a state of shock. We are children of God, and they are rebels against Him, always seeking to overthrow his kingdom."

"New stuff for me," Sam said, "but I'm beginning to see how all of that is possible, given the current situation."

"Well," Laura declared, as if announcing a victory, "we are not fighting against a mere flesh and blood enemy, as the Scriptures say, but principalities, powers, rulers of the darkness of this world, and spiritual wickedness in the heavenly places."

"Sounds like *The X-Files* to me," Sam chuckled.

"But far more sinister," Laura said. "And these agents operate in the heavenly realm and have more power than the earthbound ones that attacked us."

"Heaven and Earth," Sam said. "...seems like they've got everything covered."

"But the church, under the headship of Christ, is the greatest threat to them. If they could destroy the leadership and the church itself, there would be an ultimate overthrow of God's kingdom."

"And then what?" Sam asked, shocked by the implications.

"They can't overthrow it," Laura asserted, "but they can do much harm and destruction. Jesus said that the 'gates of hell cannot prevail' against His Church. There's no doubt God is sovereign, but He allows evil to have its day here on Earth. Eventually there will be a judgment on the enemies of God, but in the meantime, we're in a spiritual battle against them. That's what's behind the deception we see playing out before us." Laura seemed to have clear discernment regarding all the recent events in Foylestown. She no longer harbored resentment toward her husband.

"That's unbelievable!" Sam said, shaking his head. "Why on earth would that happen here in Foylestown?"

"Well, that's the puzzling part," Laura said. "But here's my take: Foylestown Community Church is a bastion against evil and chaos because Bret preaches the Gospel and sound doctrine. So, we can't just look at this as having limited significance since it's happening in small-time Foylestown. The attack is against anyone who holds to the historic faith of the Church as revealed in the Scriptures; so, large or small, any church that preaches the Gospel and sound doctrine is a target."

"And we see others in alignment with those evil powers, right?" Jean asked.

"Ah, so true, Jean," Laura agreed. "Think about the meeting at the church tonight. Cherie Loman is an agent of evil controlled by an entity. Some of the elders, though, may not be controlled to the same degree, but are heavily influenced by evil. And think of this, too. The attack against me just before Bret left for church was orchestrated to distract him and put him at a severe disadvantage."

"Yeah," Sam interjected, "I could see the torment in his eyes when he had to leave you and go to the meeting. It does all seem to be orchestrated, doesn't it?"

"And if these powers succeed in removing Bret from the church and you from your position as chief of police, it's a double coup for them," Jean said.

Sam cupped his hands over his mouth. He sighed deeply. "So, what do we do, Laura?"

"One of the critical strategies in warfare is to know your enemy," Laura began, clearly recalling some of the teachings Bret had delivered at the church. "We've established that tonight. It's not Cherie, nor is it the opposing elders; it's Satan—the god of this world—and all entities in defiance against God. It's also clear in the Scriptures that the resurrection and ascension of Christ sealed their doom. It's a matter of time before the final judgment. We are agents of God's kingdom and partakers of his victory. What we need to do right now is pray and assert the victory we have in Christ. Whatever plays out at the meeting will be influenced by our prayers. It may still be in the balance since Bret hasn't called."

Laura motioned for Sam and Jean to kneel with her in prayer, but before they did, Sam said, "I wonder if I should go back to church to see how it's going; I may be able to defend myself if the accusers are still around."

"I think that would be wise, Sam, after the three of us pray together," Laura agreed.

CHAPTER FIFTY-NINE

S am left Laura and Jean after praying with them. He felt uneasy about leaving them alone, but Laura assured him they would be safe from any other demonic attacks. Still, Sam wasn't sure if what he was doing was right. He hoped the meeting at church hadn't ended and that he'd finally get a chance to defend himself. He rehearsed what he'd say and tried to recall the events at his office. Everything had happened so quickly and unexpectedly that it was difficult for him to piece things together. He couldn't figure why Cherie would target him. Although Laura's explanation regarding Bret made sense, the attack against him didn't. Who was he? An occasional attender at Bret's church, but certainly of no leadership significance there. Maybe it was to get him out of the way and bring in some halfwit to take his place as chief of police. He laughed at the thought. All the supernatural stuff unsettled him. This was Foylestown—nothing of any significance ever happened in Foylestown. Yet here he was, smack in the middle of a series of inexplicable events which shattered his nice little world view.

———— ◦ ————

LAURA WAS STARTLED BY THE doorbell chiming. "I hope it's not someone else coming by with another story about Forrest," she said. "What Sam shared was bad enough; I've already got images in my mind about what he looked like."

"Well, you know there will be endless speculation about what happened," Jean responded. "It wouldn't surprise me if the tabloids got hold of the story, what with everything else going on here. Who's going to believe what you just shared with Sam and me?"

Laura peered through the security lens and noticed a well-dressed man in a dark suit, probably in his thirties, surveying the surroundings. She unlocked the door, leaving the chain in place. "May I help you?" she asked, eyeing the visitor closely.

The man smiled politely. "Maybe you can," he said, introducing himself and showing Laura a New York State Police ID badge. "Is your husband home?"

"Not at the moment."

"I was told he may have information regarding the alleged murder of Forrest Fields."

"What kind of information?" Laura asked. "A friend notified us that his body had been discovered in front of the funeral home; that's all I know. My husband was at a meeting and was notified by phone. The police chief went immediately to investigate."

"I see," the man said. "Maybe you could answer a few quick questions that could help us identify the perpetrator."

"Well," Laura hesitated, "I have company right now, so it's not the best time."

"It's quite urgent, Mrs. Crossman; the sooner we get information, the better our chances of finding the one responsible for this heinous crime."

Jean wandered from the living room to see who was at the door.

"It's an investigator from the state police," Laura said, glancing at Jean. "He wants to ask some questions regarding Forrest."

Turning to the investigator, Laura inquired: "I beg your pardon. Your name again, sir?"

"Horace Helms, ma'am. And just some background informa-

304

tion," Helms said, looking at Jean. "As I said to Mrs. Crossman, it may help us identify the perpetrator."

"Well," Jean said, "I'm Sam Stone's wife; he's chief of police. I may be able to help."

"Yes," Helms said. "I'd placed a call to the chief a short while ago to notify him I'd be stopping by to ask a few questions. We discussed his preliminary investigation, and he said he was headed for a meeting at the church, but that you and Mrs. Crossman might share some background information regarding Mr. Fields. May I come in?" he asked, looking at Laura.

"If it doesn't take too long; Jean and I were busy praying for the church meeting you mentioned. Both of our husbands are there."

"I assure you, this won't take long," Horace Helms said as Laura released the chain to let him in."

No, Helms silently affirmed, *this won't take long at all.*

———— ◦ ————

CHERIE'S WORDS BROKE THE SILENCE; they caught the attention of the elders, who looked quizzically at her. Whatever was controlling the atmosphere in the conference room was broken for an instant, allowing Bret to regain his focus.

"You are a lying deceiver!" Bret shouted, "I have no desire for you, and to finish my earlier statement when you cut me off, any brief carnal thought I had for you was passing. It's you who has the lustful desire for me and Sam. And what do you mean by reward? Who are you working for, Cherie? Is it Prelude?"

Cherie's throat tightened as if a hand were strangling her. Her eyes protruded, and her face distorted in fear. She tried to speak but couldn't. A voice sounded in her ears: *There will be no reward, Cherie! You have failed us for the last time!*

Cherie slumped to the floor, writhing under an invisible force. One of the witnesses walked through the wall and disappeared. The other crushed his hand into Bret's shoulder. Bret felt a stabbing pain as what was once a hand had become a serpent's claw. The elders sat stupefied. No one dared to move. *You have sealed your fate, Cherie. Now your failure will result in your destruction!* The voice thundered in her ears.

"No!" she shouted. "You can't do this!"

Can't, Cherie? Oh, but we can—and we will!

Bret was sure she was hearing from Prelude, who had her firmly under his control. The rest of the elders heard Cherie's cry, but didn't hear Prelude's voice.

He prayed and asked God to help him rise and speak. The serpent's hand suddenly released its grip on his shoulder. A different force enabled him to get to his feet. Bret directed his voice to the invisible entity attacking Cherie.

"Leave her alone!" he shouted.

The room began pulsating with an evil presence as Prelude's anger rose at Bret's words. No longer remaining invisible, Prelude emerged as an immense serpentine figure that dwarfed Bret.

Prelude stood before him.

"Dare you defy me, you weakling son of Adam? You have no power here! Look around you; what do you see? A pathetic excuse of a human being lying helpless on the floor; what about the elders? Since she failed in her mission and the elders are not able to remove you, I will do it personally. *Personally!*" Prelude roared with laughter. "I am not a person—I am a transcendent master!"

"Before the Lord God," Bret said in boldness, "you are nothing!"

"Shut up!" Prelude exploded. "Don't mention that name! He is no true God; Satan is the ruler and master of this world as your Scriptures say."

Prelude lifted Bret with one hand, then sent him hurling across the room and crashing against the wall. "See how weak your God is? He can't even keep me from destroying you at my will!"

—————— ◯ ——————

SAM ARRIVED JUST AS BRET'S body slammed into the wall. He tried to enter the conference room. It was locked. "Hey!" he shouted. "Unlock the door! It's me—Sam! What's going on in there?"

No answer, just noise.

He shouted again. "Someone open the door, or I'll shoot the lock off."

There was another cry from Cherie. "Leave me alone! Get away from me! Get away from me!"

"A cat with a mouse," Prelude smirked. "Don't I love toying with you human beings; it gives me great satisfaction. When I am through tormenting you vermin of an inferior race, I will kill you, Cherie...very slowly...for all in here to see. Then I will do the same to the little pastor for the elders to see. I need many witnesses to see my power on display."

A shot rang out as Sam drew the gun from its holster and aimed carefully at the door. He knew a bullet could easily penetrate the wood separating him from the room, but it ricocheted off the door lock.

"What the—!" he cried, looking at his gun to make sure a bullet had properly discharged. He fired again.

Another ricochet.

Before he could fire another round, an invisible force knocked the gun from his hand and sent Sam sprawling to the floor, immobilized. He tried to get up, but his legs wouldn't move. He tried to speak, but he had no voice.

CHAPTER SIXTY

L aura motioned to Horace Helms to sit at the dining room table while she and Jean sat opposite him. He slowly reached into his coat pocket and pulled out a small pad. His dark black hair nearly matched the color of his suit. Everything seemed too perfect. Laura watched him as he shifted in the chair and put both hands on the table. "You're from the state police?" she asked, knowing his response but wanting to study him as he replied.

"Yes," he said bluntly.

"Have you spoken to anyone else regarding Forrest's murder?"

"Other than the chief of police, you are the first."

"And just how can we help you?" Laura asked, her suspicions growing.

"To your knowledge, did Forrest have any enemies—anyone who would want to do him harm?"

"He was liked by most people, but there was a long-standing feud between him and another man. Plus, I'm sure you're aware of the incident regarding the recent funeral for Wilbur Templeton."

"I'm very much aware of that, Mrs. Crossman."

As he spoke, Laura noticed his pupils changing...rapidly shifting, enlarging.

"And who was the other man feuding with Mr. Fields?"

"The dead boy's father, Russell Templeton," Laura responded, casting a quick glance at Jean, who wore a quizzical look.

"I think I should call my husband," Jean said. "Maybe he could return to answer your questions; he could provide you with more information."

"I don't think that's necessary, Mrs. Stone," Helms said abruptly.

"Oh, I insist! It will only take a minute." Jean reached for her purse, grabbed her cell phone, and speed-dialed her husband.

There was no signal.

"What the–? The phone's dead."

"Just like Forrest Fields," Horace Helms was smiling now. "Just like Forrest."

A shiver went up Jean's spine as she dialed Sam again. Still no signal.

"You didn't hear what I said, Mrs. Stone; there is no need to call your husband. In fact, there is no way of calling your husband."

Laura reached for her phone, which was on the kitchen table.

"I'll take that," Helms said. He reached for her phone, but Laura pushed it out of his reach.

Laura jumped to her feet. "Get out of here!" she shouted. "Get out of my house!"

Jean gasped in shock as she stood and backed away from the table.

The investigator moved toward Laura. "Now, Mrs. Crossman, why would you want to call your husband? And what if I told you that right now your husband is lying in a pitiful heap on the floor of the church conference room?"

"You monster!" Laura screamed. "You're lying; you know nothing about my husband!"

"Oh, but I was at the church before I came here." Horace Helms's form began to change to that of a reptilian-like figure.

"But how could you—?" Laura cried, shrinking back from the hideous creature standing a few feet from her.

Jean shrieked and fainted, leaving Laura alone and face to face with the transmogrified beast.

———⊶ ◯ ⊷———

BRET SHOOK HIS HEAD TO try to clear his mind—his body smarting from being thrown into the wall. He looked in horror as Prelude moved toward Cherie's limp form and hovered over her like a bird of prey ready for the kill.

"This is what happens to those who fail us," Prelude said, fastening his eyes on Cherie. "It could have gone so well for you had you not mentioned the *reward*. Your coveting has been your ruination, Cherie. And now that we are exposed, we have no choice but to see you suffer. And, of course, after that, we will destroy the weak fool whose God is so impotent!"

Cherie cast a terrified glance at Bret. His eyes met hers for a split second. Instantly she knew she'd been played by Prelude. He not only intended no reward for her, but he was now intent on her destruction and that of the man she'd tried to seduce.

The remaining witness went to the door and opened it, letting Sam enter.

Dazed and staggering from his encounter with the hallway floor, Sam slid past the witness into the conference room. "What in God's name is going on in here?" Sam shouted, as he surveyed the chaos in the room.

The door slammed behind him. The witness grasped Sam around the chest and crushed the air out of him. Sam slumped to the floor, unconscious.

"And we will deal with the chief after we have rendered to the fool pastor his due," Prelude said, exulting in his power.

"You lied to me," Cherie mumbled weakly, shifting her eyes to the hulking malign form standing over her. "It was all a lie

311

from the start, wasn't it? There was never a grand reward, was there?"

Prelude looked at Cherie with a sardonic grin on his reptilian face. He remained silent—allowing her to talk—and basked in perverse humor as she came to realize she was a puppet and he had been her master.

"And the power...," Cherie continued, "...it was all a sham to deceive me, wasn't it?"

Prelude's eyes darkened.

"Go ahead," Cherie said. "Have your way with me; my life is ruined no matter what you do."

"Oh, yes, Cherie!" Prelude finally spoke. "You have spoken correctly; your life is ruined, but you still belong to me. Remember when you yielded to me some time ago?"

Cherie didn't answer.

"And now you will be an example for others here to see that I and those like me will conquer all you weak sons of Adam and bring about your complete subjection to us as your overlords. That has been our plan from creation—to ruin humanity and bring about chaos. It was so in the Garden of Eden and when the Watchers left their habitation to cohabit with mortal women. We were there at the Tower of Babel; we ruled over nations appointed to us. We are the principalities and powers in heavenly places!"

Bret listened intently as Prelude haughtily boasted, not realizing that he was a contingent, created being and was subject to the Sovereign ruler of the universe. He recounted how Lucifer had a similar boast and was cast out of Heaven. And he also knew that the creature standing over Cherie had no ultimate power against the supreme God of creation and the victory wrought by Jesus Christ through his resurrection and ascension. But, for the moment, he seemed powerless to resist the incredible force present in the room. He looked at Sam lying on the floor in a heap. He glanced over at the elders, two of whom were crouched in a corner behind the overturned conference room table, paralyzed with fear. Jesse and Regis had utter terror in their eyes. Bret wondered what their fate would be when Prelude finished with Cherie.

Only Bret noticed that Sam had regained consciousness and was creeping quietly toward the door. Prelude's boasting and violence reached a crescendo, creating utter chaos in the room—and allowing Sam to escape undetected by the demons.

CHAPTER SIXTY-ONE

"**A**nd you! You're the one who killed Forrest, aren't you!" Laura yelled. She backed away from the investigator quickly as his transformation into a hideous creature entered its final stage.

"He put up so little resistance; it was almost boring to watch him die like that. It seemed to me that he welcomed death," the creature said. The transformation was complete; Horace Helms was now reptilian.

Laura shuddered as the thing approached her. She grabbed a butcher knife from the knife block on the kitchen counter, then waved it at the oncoming creature. "Don't come any closer!" she shouted.

"Ha!" the creature said, looking disdainfully at her. "Do you begin to think a weapon such as that would penetrate the skin of an immortal such as I?" He reached out with a scaly hand and grabbed the knife by the blade.

Laura jerked the knife back with a slicing motion, but the thing simply pulled it from her hand and cast it to the floor. She retreated, pushing a kitchen chair between them as the creature pressed closer, but it brushed the chair aside and reached for Laura, grabbing her by the arm and pulling her toward him.

Laura kicked and punched with all her strength—to no avail.

"You know too much," it said. "And knowing too much is dangerous."

With the breath being squeezed from her, Laura wondered if the creature was going to kill her as it did Forrest. Her thoughts shifted to Bret, and she trembled to think that he may be face-to-face with Prelude. As she drifted toward unconsciousness, she prayed, remembering how Bret had dealt with the demon in her room just a short time ago. The name of Jesus spoken aloud had scared the demon away. But this thing holding her in its clutches was no little demon.

Jean regained consciousness and began to stir, wiping her eyes with the backs of her hands. The creature noticed her movement and relaxed its grip on Laura momentarily. She tried to free herself but couldn't.

"Laura!" Jean shrieked as she instinctively drew back from the creature. It released Laura and moved toward her. "Run!" she screamed.

Laura ran for the door, grabbing her cell phone from the kitchen counter as the creature lunged toward Jean. She frantically punched Brett on speed dial as the creature grabbed Jean and hurled her across the room. She crashed into a wall and fell into a motionless heap. The demon then headed back for Laura.

She reached the door. The phone kept ringing—but no answer. She knew she'd be of no help to Jean. Her best option was to keep calling for help.

The creature was within an arm's length when she heard Sam's voice. "In the name of Jesus, get away from her!" he shouted.

The creature came to an abrupt stop; horror instantly framed its face. It turned to Sam and left only a few feet between them. With an ear-splitting shriek, the creature shriveled before their eyes, then disappeared.

Laura felt faint; she wobbled, but Sam caught and steadied her. "How's Bret?" she asked, her voice barely audible.

"He's still at the meeting," Sam said. "At first, I couldn't get in;

I tried to shoot the lock off, but an invisible force threw me onto the corridor floor. I couldn't tell what was going on inside; all I could hear was loud sounds and strange, uncanny voices. Eventually one of the creatures opened the door and let me in, then crushed the wind out of me. When I regained consciousness, something told me you were in trouble. I was able to escape; I headed over as quickly as I could. Where's Jean?"

"She's inside," Laura said. "The beast flung her against a wall, and she passed out. The thing was holding me in a death grip when Jean came to and distracted it. I was able to get away, grab my phone, and head out the door. It was coming after me again just as you arrived. I—I—I need to get to the church and help Bret," she said, her voice shaking.

"We will—but first...," Sam said. He released Laura and rushed toward the door to check on Jean just as she gingerly stepped outside the house. He ran to her, took her in his arms, and held her tightly, kissing her forehead. "Are you alright?" he asked gently.

Jean smiled weakly, "I am now that my hero has arrived. I heard your voice from inside as you shouted at the damnable creature. Then I saw it shrink and disappear."

"Sam, I'm so thankful to God that you showed up when you did," Laura said. She added, "I'm sure the thing would have killed me the way it did Forrest."

"It killed Forrest?" Sam asked, astonished. "It told you that?"

"Yes," Laura said. "The way it described Forrest's final moments was so ugly, Sam; I just wanted to kill the thing!"

"My God, I can't believe what's going on. I'm sure Forrest never had a chance, but why would it want to kill him?"

"Who knows why, Sam. Maybe Forrest knew something he never disclosed; we can't wait any longer to discuss this. We've got to get to the church to help Bret and the others."

"You're right," Sam snapped. "I was torn as to whether I should come here or stay at the church and try to help, but now I'm sure I made the right decision. We can go in the cruiser; it'll only take a few minutes. You and Jean can be in prayer while I drive."

With lights flashing and siren blaring, Sam headed for the church. Vehicles on the road gave him ample room. Laura and Jean sat in the back of the cruiser praying for protection for Bret and the elders.

———— ⊶ ◯ ⊷ ————

WHEN THEY WERE ABOUT TWO miles from the church, Sam interrupted the prayer. "Hold it a minute," he said to Laura and Jean, "I've got a message coming in."

The women stopped praying as Sam listened intently to the voice on the radio. A 911 call had come through only minutes ago; a two-car accident had occurred on Route 79, six miles from the Foylestown line. An ambulance and fire vehicles had been dispatched to the scene.

"I can't believe it!" Sam said, pounding the dashboard with his fist. "There's been an accident a short way from church on County Route 79—we're on 79 now!"

Laura felt her heart sink as Sam shared that he'd have to be there to investigate the accident. "Now there's no way we can make it to church, is there, Sam?"

"Not for me there isn't, but you and Jean could walk; it's probably about a mile or so from the accident—but I certainly wouldn't advise it. I think it's too dangerous for either of you to be there. You can accomplish more by staying here and praying."

As he spoke, he could see vehicles stalled ahead and people standing in the road. An ambulance had already arrived from

318

the north. As he approached the scene, he could see two paramedics kneeling by what appeared to be a body lying supine in the road. Sam brought the cruiser to a halt. In the distance, he heard the siren of a fire vehicle approaching.

Laura and Jean sat holding hands, praying for the accident victims and for Bret and the elders. They both agreed with what Sam had said: The best thing they could do was to pray.

But Laura was certain that the *accident* was no accident at all. And Sam knew that his absence from the church meeting had been discovered by now. He had no idea what he would encounter at the accident scene, but he was afraid it was going to be deadly.

BEFORE SAM COULD EXIT THE cruiser, it was lifted to one side. It flipped over several times before landing in a wide, rushing stream several feet from the highway.

CHAPTER SIXTY-TWO

It was only a short while until Sam's absence was noticed. The remaining witness had disappeared through the wall, leaving Prelude alone with Bret, Cherie, and the elders. Prelude continued hovering over Cherie's listless body, gloating as if he'd just won a prized trophy. He circled her menacingly, kicking her to check her responses.

Cherie rolled into a fetal position to defend herself.

"Are you ready, Cherie?" Prelude howled. "Are you ready for these pathetic members of your race to see what becomes of one who fails us?" Cherie made no response.

Wayne Silver and J.R. McCabe had gone unnoticed during the encounter with Prelude. While the other three elders huddled in fear, Wayne and J.R. prayed. Bret caught their eyes and immediately recognized what they were doing. He nodded—and the three of them prayed for Cherie Loman.

Prelude halted, momentarily stunned. He looked around the room and noticed the two elders. He left Cherie and started toward them. Bret stood immediately and shouted at him. Prelude glanced back at Bret but seemed hesitant and confused.

Then he let out a deafening roar.

"So, you think you can do battle with me, you inferior slime! Do you know who I am? I will destroy all of you along with the little thing you call a woman! And the two that were with me are taking care of the wives of this impotent pastor and police chief.

They will die most brutally!"

Just as the hideous creature made a lunge for Wayne and J.R., Bret stepped up and stood defiantly. Prelude lifted an arm as if to strike him, but Bret said, "And you, Prelude; do you dare defy the Lord God of Heaven and His Son Jesus Christ? The battle belongs to Him, not to us! In the almighty name of Jesus Christ, I stand here before you! The Lord rebuke you!"

The room shook violently. Regis, Jesse, and Maury screamed in agony. Prelude's body began to convulse and shrivel.

Bret stood still.

Wayne and J.R. rose to their feet and joined Bret.

Prelude uttered a pitiable groan followed by an unearthly cry as he gazed at Cherie's body.

Then he vanished before their eyes.

———— ⊷ ◯ ⊶ ————

SAM WAS SUSPENDED UPSIDE DOWN as the water from the stream poured into the cruiser. The seat belt was cutting into his throat; he struggled to free himself. He paid no attention to the blood running down his arm. He called to Jean and Laura, "Can either of you hear me? Are you hurt badly?"

Laura responded weakly. "I have a lot of pain in my side, Sam. I nudged Jean but she didn't respond. She may be unconscious."

"Good God!" Sam cried, "How bad's the water? Can you free yourself and help Jean?"

"I'll try—it's gushing in! I'm holding my head up as high as I can; I'll see if I can help her. If I can't, she may drown!"

Sam grabbed a knife from the center console. He frantically tried to cut himself loose from the seat belt as blood streamed down his arm. With a quick swipe of the blade, the belt gave way.

He swung free, his body hitting the back of the driver's seat. He righted himself and was able to force the cruiser's door open enough to get out. He waded into the water and reached the back door. He tried to open it—it didn't budge. Knife in hand, he broke the rear window of the cruiser and crawled through.

Laura had managed to keep her own head high enough to stay clear of the rising water, but she was of no help to Jean. Sam immediately pushed further into the vehicle and lifted Jean's head from the water. He checked for a pulse. She was still alive but unconscious. In the dim light, he couldn't ascertain the nature of injuries to her or Laura.

He saw blood in the water. He had to get them out quickly. He managed to cut Jean free from her seat belt and forced her body out through the rear window. Laura was next. She groaned in pain as Sam unlatched her seat belt and lifted her upright.

"Can you crawl through the window?" Sam asked. "I need to tend to Jean; I think she's in really bad shape."

"I'll try," Laura said, "but the pain's excruciating."

Laura pressed her body through the window, willing herself to reframe the pain as mere discomfort. Sam carried Jean's body through the stream to dry ground. Lowering her gently, he turned to check on Laura, who was struggling to walk through the rushing waters.

"You can make it, Laura," he yelled. "Just keep moving!"

Sam knelt before Jean and checked for respiration. Her breathing was shallow but steady. He noticed blood streaming from an opening in her abdomen. He tried to stop the flow with his handkerchief. Sam shouted to those within earshot: "Get the paramedics over here now!"

Within seconds, three paramedics rushed to Jean's side. The people involved in the accident had only minor injuries and didn't need medical care.

Sam couldn't believe how God had used something that was meant to keep them from going to the church to provide emergency aid to Laura and Jean. He stepped away from his wife as the paramedics began to treat her. They called for stretchers for both women. The ambulance was already there and prepared for transport to the hospital forty miles away.

Sam stood and noticed the blood running down his arm. He felt himself nearly fainting just as an attendant approached to steady him.

"Looks like you could use some help, too, soldier," the woman said. "Sit down and let me look at that gash on your arm; we need to stop that bleeding."

Sam sat on the bank by the stream and let the woman work on his arm, but his thoughts were on Jean. "Can you tell me how my wife is?" he asked.

"Which one is your wife?" the woman asked.

"The one who was unconscious when you guys arrived."

"I'll ask the other paramedics when I get you fixed up. I can't answer that question right now."

Sam glanced in Jean's direction just as the attendants placed her on a stretcher and carried her toward the ambulance.

Laura had suffered broken ribs but no lacerations. She, too, was being carried on a stretcher toward the ambulance. One of the paramedics who was attending to Jean approached Sam. "I have an update regarding your wife. She's regained consciousness and appears to have suffered a concussion. She, along with the other woman, is being transported to the hospital in Rochester for observation and further treatment if necessary. Both were very fortunate not to have been more seriously injured. I witnessed your vehicle flip and roll into the stream; what on earth caused that?"

Sam breathed a sigh of relief at the news. "I'm not sure it

was on Earth; it was something from Earth that caused the cruiser to flip."

"Huh? What do you mean by that?" the paramedic dug.

"It wasn't an accident," Sam said bluntly. "Something, or someone, purposely lifted the car and flipped it over."

"How could anyone do that? It's impossible!"

"We're dealing with supernatural forces," Sam said calmly. "But I can't explain it right now. I need to get to Foylestown Community Church as soon as possible."

Mouth agape, the paramedic stood in shock. "That's out of my league; I have no idea what you're talking about, but you could use a little more help yourself; that cut on your arm needs further attention."

"I can check myself into the emergency room," Sam said, "but I'll need a ride, as you can see." His mind wasn't on getting treatment, but on finding a way to get to the church. Since Jean had regained consciousness and was in no immediate danger, Sam felt released to go help Bret.

A backup cruiser from the sheriff's department arrived, and a deputy approached Sam. "What on earth happened to you, Chief?" he asked, looking from Sam to the partially submerged vehicle.

"I ran into a demon," Sam said half-jokingly. "And it flipped my cruiser over into the stream."

"Oh, man!" the deputy said. "...must've been a heck of a demon to do that!"

"You don't know the half of it," Sam said, smiling. "I don't suppose you could transport me to the church just up the road, could you?"

"Why there?" the deputy frowned. "Don't you think you need some more medical attention?"

"I agree," the paramedic said as she stood to leave. "But he's pretty much on his own now."

The deputy scratched his head and said, "As long as you don't bleed on my front seat, I guess I can give you a lift; are you headed there for prayer or something?"

"It's more like the 'or something,'" Sam said, "but I can't really explain it right now."

"Well," the deputy said, "that fits right along with some of the stuff that's been going on in this town the last few weeks. I think Foylestown is a little spooked."

"I couldn't agree more," Sam said as he stood up carefully.

"There's another cruiser on its way to investigate the accident; it doesn't appear like you're in a position to."

"Good observation," Sam responded. "But I may have something at the church to investigate."

The deputy frowned again. "You need help with that one?"

"Not at the moment," Sam said. "It's an investigation of another order."

"You got me on that one," the deputy said. "Does it have anything to do with the demon you mentioned?" he asked, laughing.

"I'll know when I get there," Sam said, looking the deputy in the eye.

CHAPTER SIXTY-THREE

Bret stood trembling, mentally processing the events of the last few minutes as he witnessed Prelude's fall and sudden disappearance. He was certain God had saved them from possible death and that he'd vanquished Prelude. He remained speechless at the awesome power and authority that came from just the mention of Jesus' name. He quickly surveyed the room and noticed Wayne and J.R. standing close by while the other elders remained huddled together, not daring to move. He then noticed Sam's absence, and his thoughts shifted rapidly to Laura and Jean. He recalled Prelude's ominous words regarding the other witness. His face flushed with anger.

"I have to get to Laura and Jean!" he shouted to Wayne and J.R. "Their lives are in danger, and it may be too late!"

"We can go with you!" Wayne shot back.

"I think it would be better if you both stayed here with the others, especially with Cherie; she's in a state of shock and will need help. If one of you has a cell phone, call 911 and get someone here ASAP." Bret motioned in the direction of the other elders and said, "As far as the other guys are concerned, if they haven't soiled their pants, they should be okay—but I wouldn't count on them for any help."

Before he left, Bret knelt at Cherie's side; Wayne and J.R. joined him. She remained in a fetal position and didn't respond when Bret called her name, but merely whimpered as if she were a child who'd been badly injured. Bret touched her forehead and brushed aside her hair so he could see her eyes. They were still filled with fear.

"We're safe now," Bret whispered in her ear. "Prelude has been destroyed; he's no threat to you anymore."

"But the other two witnesses...," Wayne said, his voice unsteady. "Where are they right now?"

"That's what I'm going to find out," Bret said as he stood to leave. At that second, Sam arrived.

"Thank God you're safe," Bret said, giving Sam a hug. "Where've you been? We need to get to Laura and Jean," he said without giving Sam a chance to answer his question.

"That won't be necessary," Sam said.

Bret's heart sank. "What do you mean—not necessary?"

"They're okay but they've suffered injuries. As we were headed here in my cruiser, something flipped the car over and it rolled into a stream."

"One of the witnesses!" Bret shouted. "But what about the other?"

"It paid a visit to your house. It was trying to kill our wives when I arrived."

"Good God!" Bret cried. "And what happened?"

"It's a long story; I'll tell you later," Sam began. "But suffice it to say that when I proclaimed the name of Jesus, that destroyed the damned thing."

Astonished, Bret shook his head and said, "The same happened here with Prelude. He was wreaking havoc on all of us and tormenting Cherie. He was planning to kill us all. He was headed for Wayne and J.R. when I stood in his way."

"Then what happened?" Sam asked.

"I did the same thing you did and challenged him with the authority and the name of Jesus. The thing trembled and seemed to melt before us; then it disappeared through the wall."

Wayne had been listening closely as the men related their respective stories, when he caught Bret's eye.

"What's wrong, Wayne?" Bret asked. "You look very troubled."

"Where's the other witness—the one that caused your accident?" Wayne asked bluntly.

"Oh my God!" Sam said. "The one that caused our accident is still on the loose. It may be headed for the ambulance carrying Laura and Jean!"

"Radio to them, Sam!" Bret yelled.

"I can't, Bret. I have no way of doing that. But wait a minute! I told the sheriff's deputy who brought me here to wait outside. We can use his radio to reach the ambulance."

"Stay here with the others," Bret said to Wayne and J.R., "and pray that the ambulance driver will have a clue what we're talking about."

Bret and Sam raced from the church to the cruiser. "We need to radio to the ambulance that's transporting our wives!" Sam shouted to the deputy.

"Yeah?" the startled deputy responded, letting both men inside the vehicle.

"And listen, but don't ask a lot of questions right now. We need to try and catch that ambulance. Can you do that?"

"Well," the deputy hesitated, "it must have a sizable lead on us by now."

"Granted," Sam said, "but they don't go really fast, and you have the advantage of speed—especially with this cruiser."

"I'll let the station know what I'm doing, and we can leave immediately," the deputy said. "I hope I don't get any flack from them."

"I'll take care of that if you do," Sam responded. "Now let's move!"

Bret spoke to the ambulance driver and shared what he could without sounding weird. He could tell the guy had no idea what he was saying but did his best to understand.

Sam got on the radio and told the driver he and Bret were on their way to intercept them, and to be prepared. The driver said they couldn't stop or slow the ambulance since they had injured patients who needed treatment on board.

"Fine," Sam said. "Just be prepared to pull over when you see flashing lights and hear the siren."

The driver said he'd never heard of such a thing as an ambulance being pulled over by the police. He was concerned that Laura or Jean could have internal injuries that weren't initially discovered. And he was afraid his own head would roll if anything happened to them. He notified the attendant in back of what would be happening.

"Can I speak with my wife?" Bret broke in.

"She's sedated," the driver responded.

"Well," Bret insisted, "she's still conscious, right?"

"What is it you guys really want?" the driver asked, irritated. "How do I know you're not trying to hijack us for ransom money?"

"Listen to me!" Bret demanded. "If you don't do as we say, the two women, you, and the attendant in back may be dead shortly."

The driver drew a deep breath, but sensed the urgency in Bret's voice was legitimate. "I don't know why I'm agreeing to do this, but okay; you'd better be right."

"Trust me," Bret said. "We're right. Now, let me speak to my wife."

The driver notified the attendant that Bret insisted on speaking to his wife; he asked if she was alert enough to talk.

"Seems so," the attendant said. "What's this all about?"

330

"I can't explain it," the driver said. "Just give him a minute to speak to her."

Bret didn't want to panic Laura, but he explained as simply as possible what was happening. She remained remarkably calm and said she understood perfectly. Jean also listened in. Given what they had already been through, they both agreed afterward that God's sovereign hand was on their lives and that, ultimately, He was in control.

And before the call ended, Laura said, "We're big girls, Bret; we know what to do."

"I have no doubt about that," Bret responded.

And as they rode, they prayed.

CHAPTER SIXTY-FOUR

The pursuit of the ambulance proved fruitless—it was too far ahead and only a few miles from Rochester. Sam kept in touch with the driver, who, despite arguing about what was happening, agreed to be especially alert if anything unusual unfolded.

And it did.

While Sam was still speaking, the driver screamed: "I can't steer this thing—something's locked the wheel! We're headed toward the median and oncoming traffic!"

"Just as I warned you!" Sam shouted back. "Can you brake and bring the thing to a stop?"

The driver pressed hard on the brake. The ambulance didn't respond. "Nothing!" he cried. "It isn't slowing down at all!"

"Let me speak to Laura and Jean," Sam demanded.

"Why?" the driver shot back. "But what the hell—go ahead."

"Laura," Sam's voice was stressed and tight. "You're headed for a crash."

"We're aware and prepared," Laura responded.

"Holy Mother of God, there's a semi headed right for us!" the driver yelled. "We've got only seconds before we crash!"

And as he was yelling, the ambulance took a sudden turn, just missing the approaching truck, crossing the median, and coming to an abrupt stop on the other side of the four-lane highway. The semi driver had forced his truck onto the grassy part of the median and managed to bring it to a halt. The oncoming traffic had slowed to a standstill. The entire scene appeared to be suspended in time.

The ambulance's abrupt stop shocked the driver and the attendant next to him.

"What in the name of God!" the driver yelled. "It's like we hit an invisible wall!"

The stunned attendant, who'd braced himself for a collision with the semi, sat shaking his head in disbelief. "Whatever it was—it saved our lives. I thought sure we were dead when I saw the eighteen-wheeler headed straight toward us."

"Yeah," the driver said, placing his hands on the dashboard to steady himself. "...and did you see them?"

"See who?"

"Two figures standing directly in front of us."

"I didn't see a thing," the attendant said. "My eyes were closed; I was waiting for a crash."

"Well, there it was looking like something out of a science fiction movie! It was huge, and it was fighting with another smaller figure, which suddenly vanished. Then the larger figure vanished, too. It all happened in just a few seconds, but I know what I saw was real; I just have no idea who either of them was or why they were there. ...kinda creeped me out."

"...you sure you didn't hit your head on the windshield?" the attendant asked, wrinkling his brow.

"...a little shaken up but, no, I didn't—and let me ask you a question; how do you explain what happened? I think whatever it was standing in front of the ambulance somehow stopped it from hitting the truck."

The attendant was silent for a moment, then said, "Maybe it was an angel; enough of this, though—we need to check on the others."

"I've lost radio contact," Sam said to Bret and the deputy, but I could hear the driver say they were going to crash."

Bret felt his heart in his throat. "How far away do you figure we are from them?" he asked the driver.

"Maybe five minutes," the deputy said. "I'm going as fast as I dare to. I can radio ahead to the Rochester State Police Station. They can be there pronto and will make sure another ambulance is dispatched."

"I can't believe what's happening," Bret said, staring at Sam. "I hope we're not too late."

"And the other witness," Sam interjected. "No doubt it caused the brakes and steering to fail."

"I'm sure of it—and I'm thinking it could be headed our way."

"You guys are scaring the heck out of me," the driver said. "All this talk about a witness; what on earth are you talking about?"

"It's not from Earth," Bret wiped the sweat from his forehead as he spoke. "We're dealing with supernatural forces."

"Okay, I get it," the driver said, shaking his head. "...*X-Files* stuff."

Laura rolled into a sitting position fighting excruciating pain with the help of the stunned attendant who kept checking her head for any sign of blood. Jean moaned from the corner of the ambulance.

"We need to get you two back on the stretchers," the woman said, "but I'll have to have help to do it."

"I can manage on my own," Laura responded, as she pulled

herself to her feet while holding onto the side wall of the ambulance. "And I can help with Jean."

"Are you all okay back there?" the ambulance driver called to them. "We stopped pretty abruptly."

"Banged up but okay otherwise," the attendant said. "I'm trying to get the two patients back on their stretchers."

"Well, you won't believe what happened," the driver said, nearly breathless. "We were headed straight for an oncoming semi when the steering and brakes both went on the ambulance. I had absolutely no control over it. I thought we were all goners, when right out of the blue this figure appeared directly in front of the ambulance. It seemed to stop us at the last minute. I can't figure out who or what it was. The truck veered off suddenly, also coming to a halt."

"It was an angel," Laura said, interrupting their conversation, "...meeting our needs just as we prayed."

———— ⋆ ◖ ⋆ ————

THE SHERIFF'S CRUISER CARRYING BRET and Sam arrived within minutes; New York State Police vehicles soon followed. A swarm of onlookers gazed from both sides of the highway.

Bret and Sam rushed from the parked cruiser toward the ambulance, both shocked that there was no evidence of a crash. The driver and two attendants were at the back of the ambulance as the men approached.

"Our wives are in there!" Bret said, shoving his way toward the rear of the ambulance. "Are they okay? We lost radio contact and thought you guys had crashed."

"They're okay," one of the attendants said. "They were just shaken up when the ambulance stopped so suddenly. There's another ambulance on the way to transport them to Strong Memorial Hospital in Rochester. We don't want to risk using this one until it's checked out."

"Please stand back while we get them settled on their stretchers," the other attendant said.

"Can I see my wife for just a minute?" Bret asked.

"You can stand here and speak to her, but you can't go into the ambulance."

"My wife is in there, too," Sam said, approaching the back of the ambulance. "I'm Chief of Police Sam Stone from Foylestown, and we've been in radio contact with the driver of the ambulance." Sam motioned toward the driver who was standing a few feet away.

"Of course, Chief—you can speak to your wife, but make it brief," the ambulance driver said, nodding his head. "But you guys have a lot of explaining to do, and I've got something to share you're not going to believe."

CHAPTER SIXTY-FIVE

Wayne and J.R. huddled with Cherie, trying to get her to talk. She remained in a state of shock, still curled in a fetal position. Maury, Regis, and Jesse had slipped out of the room after seeing their plans destroyed, but a new plan was already emerging in Regis's mind.

"We've got to get help for her," Wayne said as he stood just in time to see the other elders leave. "Is your cell phone working?" he asked J.R.

"There's nothing we can do for her," J.R. agreed. "She needs professional help. I'll call 911."

"We can send her to the emergency care center in Cranston," the operator said after answering the call and being briefed on Cherie's status. "That's about twenty-five minutes from here."

"That will do," J.R. said. "How long before you can have someone here?"

"It's been a busy night, but we have some backup that should be able to get there within a half hour. Can you provide treatment until they arrive?"

"The best we can," J.R. said. "We're not skilled."

"I'll contact them immediately," the operator said and ended the call.

Wayne had listened to the conversation. "She seems to be breathing okay and has a steady pulse. Let's cover her with one of our sports coats to keep her warm; let's try not to move her."

J.R. immediately removed his jacket and placed it over Cherie's shoulders. Wayne did the same and covered the rest of her body.

It took less than half an hour for two EMTs to arrive and get Cherie on a stretcher. She was then transported to the Cranston Emergency Care Center. J.R. called Bret to give him an update. "Cherie's on her way to emergency care in Cranston. She was still in a state of shock and couldn't speak."

"What about Wayne and the others—are they still there?" Bret asked. "And was there any more demonic activity after we left?"

"Wayne is here with me," J.R. said. "The others left a short time ago—probably scared to death and devastated by what happened—and no, Prelude and the other guy never returned. We've been safe."

"I can't imagine what state Cherie must be in; Prelude had her totally under his control. I really need to see her as soon as I can. We're going to have to counsel her regarding what happened. I'm sure she has no understanding of who she was dealing with."

"Do any of us really understand it, Bret?" J.R. posited.

"Not completely, but she may be able to help us see how the cursed thing controlled her," Bret responded.

"And did you guys ever catch up with the ambulance after you left here?" J.R. continued.

"We never caught it before what we were certain was a crash," Bret said. "We lost radio contact just before the driver said they were going to hit a semi head-on."

"Good God!" J.R. said. "What happened?"

"That's what we need to find out, J.R.; we were about to talk to the ambulance driver when you called, but thankfully there was no crash! Laura and Jean were transported to Rochester in another ambulance. And, by the way, I think you guys should

340

travel ASAP to Cranston to follow up on Cherie. Who knows what she's going to tell them about what happened when she regains her voice!"

———— ✺ ————

"HE'S GOING TO KILL ME!" Cherie screamed as she emerged from the state of shock. "Prelude's going to kill me! Get him away from me!"

"No one is going to kill you," the nurse said, trying to get Cherie under control. "There's no one here by the name of Prelude."

"But he was just here, in the room, circling around me and hovering over me! I need Bret!" she cried. "He can help me."

The nurse messaged the doctor on call requesting immediate assistance. "She's delirious," the nurse said. "She needs to be sedated."

"Where's Bret?" Cherie continued screaming, "I need Bret!"

"There's no one here by that name," the exasperated nurse said. "Is he your husband?"

"No, he's the pastor of the church; he was there when Prelude assaulted me and then began tormenting me. There were others there, too."

"What seems to be the matter, young lady?" the doctor asked kindly as he entered the room. "Tell me about this Prelude fellow."

"He's a demon!" Cherie shouted.

The doctor looked at the nurse, who just shook her head. He took her aside for a moment and indicated they would have to get Cherie transported to the Psych Unit at Strong Memorial Hospital in Rochester. There was nothing he could do other than administer a sedative to calm her down.

"I'll let them know," the nurse said. She left to make a call just as Wayne and J.R. arrived. "And who are you?" she demanded.

"Friends of Cherie's," Wayne said. "We're here to see her."

"Well," the nurse said bluntly, "you're too late; she's being transferred to Rochester as soon as we can arrange transportation."

"But we were witnesses to the trauma she went through," Wayne continued.

"Witnesses?"

"Yes," Wayne said, "we know why she was in a state of shock, which is why we arranged to have her transported here."

"Wait here for a minute," the nurse said. "I'll be right back."

Wayne and J.R. sat in the waiting room while the nurse spoke with the doctor.

"They say they are witnesses to whatever caused the trauma to the woman."

"You mean the demon, right?" the doctor said, with a hint of sarcasm.

"I didn't ask them if they also saw the demon," the nurse smiled. "Do you think I should?"

"Go ahead," the doctor said. "See what they say. Maybe they're part of a religious cult."

The nurse returned to Wayne and J.R. "You said you were witnesses to whatever caused her trauma?"

"Yes—we were," Wayne responded.

"And what was it that caused the trauma?"

The two men looked at each other, sensing what they were about to say would not be believed. It was J.R. who spoke first. "What we were witnesses to was something supernatural; just as real as we are standing here."

"Hmm...," the nurse paused for thought. "Could you be more precise? What was this supernatural thing that caused the trauma?"

"An entity."

"Entity?" the nurse responded, arching her eyebrows.

"Yes, an entity that was tormenting Cherie."

"Did the entity, as you call it, have an identity—a name?"

"Prelude," Wayne said bluntly, never raising his voice.

"Prelude?" the nurse responded, "like an introduction or something of that sort?"

"That's what he called himself; Cherie can verify that," Wayne insisted.

The nurse shook her head, sighing deeply. "That's a first for me."

The doctor suddenly reappeared. "We're about ready to send her to Rochester," he said.

"Wait just a minute!" Wayne interrupted. "I said we're here to see her. Ask her to verify it yourself when we go in. And, by the way, ask her if she knows the name of the entity that tormented her."

"She's a bit delirious for that, I'm afraid," the doctor said.

"Okay," J.R. interrupted, "we'll file a report on you tomorrow stating you would not allow friends of Cherie's to see her."

"Oh, for heaven's sake," the doctor said. "I'll give you a couple of minutes with her, but you'd better not upset her further."

"*Wow,*" Wayne whispered under his breath to J.R., "what a display of arrogance."

"*He's just protecting her is all,*" J.R. whispered back. "It's his responsibility—especially since he doesn't know who we are."

"You're right," Wayne agreed as they approached Cherie's exam room.

"I'm going to be in there with you," the doctor said. "I want to see if her story corroborates yours."

Cherie bolted upright on the bed when she saw the men approaching her. She began to cry and reached out for Wayne as he stood beside the bed. "I didn't know you were coming," she said. "I knew you and the other guy were trying to help me back at the church, but I'm not sure how I got here. Where's Bret?"

"He's probably headed for Rochester to see his wife; she's in the hospital there."

"How I hated that man," Cherie said while wiping her tears with a tissue. "But he saved me from that hideous creature. I feel so free now that it's gone."

"Yes, it's gone, Cherie; you are indeed free from its control," J.R. added.

The doctor looked skeptically at Cherie. "Can you tell me the name of the creature?"

"Prelude," Cherie said. "His name was Prelude, and he was a supernatural entity or demon of some sort."

The doctor glanced at Wayne, who had the look of *I told you so* on his face. "Never in my thirty-some years of practice have I heard of such a thing," he said, shaking his head.

CHAPTER SIXTY-SIX

At the hospital in Rochester, Bret was reassured that Laura would make a full recovery from the broken ribs and that Jean's temporary unconsciousness would have no negative long-term effects. After this reassurance, he could once again think about the scene at the church. He could see Cherie's terrified face as Prelude appeared ready to kill her. He recalled how he was encouraged by the eye contact he'd made with Wayne and J.R. He was humbled at God's authority and power over the demonic forces that had attempted to destroy his marriage, Sam's marriage, and the fabric and function of Foylestown Community Church. He knew he would never be the same—nor would the church. The question remained about his resignation. He wasn't sure if the church would demand it—or if he would do it voluntarily. For the moment, he filed the thought away. He had to deal with the immediate and more pressing issues.

But a thought suddenly struck him. *What about Wilbur Templeton?* During all the recent events, any thought of Wilbur had been buried. Cherie said that Prelude knew of his whereabouts and would eventually tell her if she succeeded in her mission. When Bret saw her, he would ask her if Prelude ever disclosed where Wilbur was.

"I PLAYED THE FOOL," CHERIE said, shaken, but in her right mind after a few days had lapsed. She didn't dare to look directly at Bret. Laura sat comfortably by as the two talked.

"Yes, you did," Bret agreed. "And you almost lost your life and destroyed our marriage. You opened yourself up to a demonic force with the hope of gaining power."

"And I gave my will over to that evil creature."

"But not to the point where it possessed you, although you were very close. Prelude knew of your human weakness and depravity and linked that to the power he gave you."

"He lied to me!" Cherie cried.

"Yes, that's the nature of deception."

"I am so sorry, Pastor Crossman and Mrs. Crossman; how can I ever ask forgiveness of you?"

"You don't have to," Bret said. "You've been humbled enough just to come here today and share your story with us. I'd be remiss, though, if I didn't tell you that what you engaged in was not only personal sin but also evil. Do you acknowledge that, Cherie?"

"Yes," she said, lifting her head to look at Bret.

"And those are both eternally serious issues."

"So what shall I do now?" Cherie asked. "Is there any hope for me?"

"When I called upon God to rebuke Prelude, it was His authority and His alone that saved you from death," Bret answered. "And it was the death of His Son Jesus Christ that can save you from eternal damnation."

"Like I have heard you say in church, although I mocked you and didn't believe it," Cherie said, again looking down at the floor.

"It's the same truth that Laura and I have believed and that the chief and his wife now believe—that personally believing in

Jesus Christ and His sacrificial death on the cross can save you."

"Despite what I've done?" Cherie asked as tears began to stream down her cheeks. "I hated you and tried to destroy your marriage! I am so ashamed of myself."

Bret looked tenderly at the woman who tried to seduce him, realizing she had been under the control of a powerful demonic force. "We all fall far short of the glory of God, Cherie, and we're all guilty before God, no matter how good we try to be. Christ paid the penalty for that and any sin that you've ever committed. The Bible states clearly that whoever calls upon His Name shall be saved. Calling is believing on the substitutionary work He did to satisfy the Father's wrath for our sins."

"I'm not sure I understand all of that, Pastor, but if I call on His Name now and believe that He paid for my sins, will that save me?"

"Yes," Bret said. "It's a gracious gift obtained through faith."

"Then that's what I truly want."

———— ◦ ————

BRET AND LAURA LED CHERIE in a simple prayer in which she received the gift of salvation, confessing Christ before them. Her conversion was dramatic, and she became an avid follower of the Risen One. Her aptitude for learning the Scriptures was astounding.

When Bret later asked her about Wilbur Templeton, she said Prelude never mentioned his whereabouts. "But he did say he was the one in the casket impersonating Wilbur, and that one of the *witnesses* had removed the body from the casket prior to the funeral service."

Bret shook his head in astonishment. "Are you sure Prelude said he was the one in the casket?"

"I'm positive," Cherie asserted.

"Unbelievable!" Bret exclaimed. "I would never have thought of that or thought it was possible. I'm quite sure the community is not going to believe it either. I suppose it's best if we don't mention it."

"We can tell it to the church." Laura joined the conversation after listening intently to the woman who only a short time ago tried to destroy that very church.

"Some will understand," Bret said, "and some will still blame either Russell or Forrest, even in their death."

———— ⟡ ————

AS THE SEARCH FOR WILBUR'S body continued, a volunteer from the community happened by Alice Templeton's home and peered in the window to see if Alice was there. She suddenly cried out in horror and her knees buckled under her. There, next to Alice's dead body, was Wilbur's.

The autopsy revealed that Alice had suffered a massive heart attack, and the medical examiner estimated she had been dead a few days. Bret reasoned that she may have died suddenly when she saw Wilbur's body lying on the kitchen floor. He also felt strongly that was likely the intent of the witnesses that transferred Wilbur's body there. There was no evidence of physical assault. Alice was most likely literally scared to death.

———— ⟡ ————

FOYLESTOWN, NEW YORK HAD ALSO suffered a blow to its corporate soul with the deaths of Wilbur, Russell, Forrest, and Alice. The people sought answers, and some found them. Some realized that through what seemed to be an ongoing sinister tragedy, there was a sovereign hand operating invisibly to rebuke agents of evil and redeem the life of a human being who had succumbed to their power.

In the living room, Laura studied Bret's face, which had a look of sad bewilderment. "What we've been a part of simply defies reason," she said.

"Laura," Bret began. He stood and went over to sit with her on the couch that could have played a role in his moral collapse. "I was the biggest fool in opening the door for Cherie to come in. It was not just a lapse in judgment but sin on my part. No matter what the temptation is, there is always a way of escape. I've grieved God and caused almost irreparable damage to our marriage. I can't blame Cherie or even Prelude, although the power of deception was beyond anything I've ever experienced. The anger you had toward me was more than justified. It was God, and God alone, who kept me from egregious sin that night."

Bret sighed heavily as if a severe burden had been lifted from him. He looked at Laura's reassuring face. "You know, Laura, the events of the past several days could have happened anywhere in the world; it's no doubt happening on a regular basis with churches, pastors, and pastors' wives in countless places; I just can't believe it happened here."

———◦———

NOT FAR FROM FOYLESTOWN COMMUNITY Church, three men huddled in secret that evening to discuss a new plan. And as they talked among themselves, something appeared to them as if an apparition had suddenly manifested.

The *thing* was back.

349

Final Thoughts

It Happened Here is a work of fiction based entirely on the author's imagination. While there are spiritual truths contained within the book and a strong redemptive theme culminating in the final few chapters, the book is not meant to convey necessarily accurate theology. Faithful churches are targets for manifold spiritual attacks against leaders and congregants from evil forces seen and unseen. Their purpose is to destroy people's lives and church assemblies. What is also often unseen is God directing human events through his overarching providence to accomplish His Will.

www.ingramcontent.com/pod-product-compliance
Lightning Source LLC
Chambersburg PA
CBHW072026020726
47501CB00006B/1977